HUSH

HUSH

LEANNA SAIN

HUSH BY LEANNA SAIN
Lamplighter Mystery and Suspense is an imprint of LPCBooks
a division of Iron Stream Media
100 Missionary Ridge, Birmingham, AL 35242

ISBN: 978-1-64526-250-3
Copyright © 2019 by Leanna Sain
Cover design by Elaina Lee
Interior design by AtriTeX Technologies P Ltd.

Available in print from your local bookstore, online, or from the publisher at:
lpcbooks.com

For more information on this book and the author visit: www.LeannaSain.com

Brought to you by the creative team at Lighthouse Publishing of the Carolinas: Eddie Jones, Shonda Savage, Darla Crass, Elaina Lee and Amberlyn Noelle.

Library of Congress Cataloging-in-Publication Data
Sain, Leanna
Hush / Leanna Sain 1st ed.

Printed in the United States of America

PRAISE FOR *HUSH*

Like Dean Koontz, Leanna Sain's strength lies in her ability to take ordinary people, thrust them into extraordinary situations, and guide their transformation into the people they never dreamed they could be. And she does this without being heavy-handed or using cheap literary tricks. Even the title, *HUSH*, is not what it seems. And the story, which starts out like a slice from any of our lives, soon takes us on a dark, twisted journey that ultimately makes us want even more of Sain's special kind of literary magic.

—Thomas Smith
Author of *MONSTERS, Something Stirs*, and *Unthinkable Choice*

The haunting words of an age-old lullaby weave through this book, binding the elements of suspense, murder, love, drama, mystery and a touch of humor into a gripping, satisfying story.

—Rose Senehi
Award winning author of *Catching Fire*

Leanna Sain crafted a suspenseful romance that also tenderly captures a daughter's love for her mother who suffers from Alzheimer's disease . . . Their relationship brings a unique perspective and generational depth to this fast-paced mystery.

—Margaret A. Noel, MD
Founder, MemoryCare

Leanna Sain weaves a riveting tale of a young woman, Lacey Campbell, whose nightmares foretell the next victim of a serial killer, but not in time to stop him. No one believes her stories, except Ford Jamison, a detective assigned to the case. Will Lacey determine the killer's identity or will he complete his nursery song, *Hush Little Baby,* with her death?

—Carol Heilman
Author of *Agnes Hopper Bets on Murder*

In Leanna Sain's deliciously suspenseful *Hush*, the familiar verses of a childhood lullaby become the calling card of a serial killer terrorizing a small island community off the coast of Florida. A young chef, struggling to keep her job while caring for her aging mother, tries frantically to solve the mystery before the killer strikes again, but who can she trust? Determining the answer will keep you turning pages late into the night!

—Cassandra King
Author of *Moonrise*

Acknowledgments

As always, I owe endless gratitude to the many people who helped through the process of getting words transferred from my heart into print.

Two writers' groups: Weavers of Words (WOW) and the Blue Ridge Writers' Group helped me hone and shape the story, giving constructive criticism where needed, especially with that darn back cover copy. Thank you!

A huge thank you to Darla Crass, for meeting with me at the Asheville Christian Writers' Conference, taking me under her wing, and taking a chance on me. Here's to hoping it was one of the best decisions you ever made.

To my editor, Amberlyn Noelle, for her expertise in fearlessly guiding me through the twists and turns of the publishing process.

For Christina Creasman and her willingness to be a guinea pig to test this thing out on, and for her amazing skill in spotting typos.

To my husband, Randy, my hero, personal editor and best friend, who deserves all the good adjectives in the dictionary, plus those no one has come up with yet. Thank you for your unwavering love and support.

And most of all, I thank God, who has blessed me with the ability to put the twenty-six letters of the alphabet together in such a way that they make stories people actually love to read.

Dedicated to my Mama.

Here's to the day when I see you again, and you know who I am.

Dear Readers,

I chose Amelia Island for the setting of my story this time, or maybe I should say, *it* chose *me*. It's in the northernmost part of Florida, just across the river from Georgia on the Atlantic side of the state, the home of Fernandina Beach. This is the place I spent a week every summer for most of my childhood, a place where happy memories abound. If you've never visited, I highly recommend it. Fernandina Beach is a beautiful, historic town with an abundance of Victorian architecture.

Like my other books, *Hush* features a strong, creative heroine—in this case, it's Lacey—who has to overcome some big problems, coming out stronger and better on the other side. But this book is a little "darker." You see, Lacey's mother has Alzheimer's, something I can relate with, because my mama had it too. This terrible disease took her June 13, 2018. I used this book as a sort of therapy, if you will. It's been cathartic for me; a way to filter out some of the sadness, frustration, even anger as I dealt with this terrible disease. Alzheimer's is a monster that turned my mama into a stranger, someone who looked like her, but wasn't. Even worse, it turned all her loved ones into strangers to *her*. She's a big reason of why I love to read and write so much. Just like Lacey's mom, many, many students knew my mama as the "Reading Lady." She read hundreds of books to thousands of children over the years, but Alzheimer's stole that woman away.

So, similar to the way I donated proceeds from my novel *Red Curtains* to help the homeless, I will donate half of the royalties from *Hush* to Alzheimer's research. Hopefully, in the not-so-distant future, Alzheimer's won't be the unbearable death sentence it is today.

Blessings,
Leanna

Hush Little Baby

Hush, little baby. Don't say a word.
Mama's gonna buy you a mockingbird.
And if that mockingbird don't sing,
Mama's gonna buy you a diamond ring.
And if that diamond ring turns brass,
Mama's gonna buy you a looking glass.
And if that looking glass gets broke,
Mama's gonna buy you a billy goat.
And if that billy goat don't pull,
Mama's gonna buy you a cart and bull.
And if that cart and bull turn over,
Mama's gonna buy you a dog named Rover.
And if that dog named Rover don't bark,
Gonna buy you a horse and cart.
And if that horse and cart break down,
You'll still be the sweetest little baby in town.

– A traditional lullaby

CHAPTER ONE

Lacey

"You're late, Lacey Campbell," Pearl's near-baritone voice barked. "Hurry up! We need to go over tonight's menu."

A glance at my watch told the truth. *Um ... no, actually I'm seven minutes early.*

I squelched a sigh, pasting on a smile instead. "Give me a second to put my stuff away. I'll be right back." I hurried to my locker and flung my purse inside. It was the same thing almost every day. The haranguing started before the door even *swished* shut behind me. It was Pearl's restaurant, yes, but did that make it okay for her to verbally beat up her employees?

"The Black Pearl Bistro would still be 'Pearl's' without me," I muttered, hastily gathering my hair into a high ponytail and securing the mass of curls with a pink plastic clip. "They'd still be deep-frying everything ... frozen seafood, limp green beans, Oreos, even pickles." I shuddered at the thought. "Fat-clogged arteries, chemical-laden food ... I saved the customers from all that. Now we're packed every night. She must see the correlation. So why does she treat me like this?"

But I knew why. She did it because she could.

Pearl had me over a barrel and she knew it. I *couldn't* leave, even though we both knew I'd have no trouble finding a top chef's position at some other high-end establishment. Sure, my roots ran deep in this town, but that wasn't the reason I stayed. No, I'd pack up and move tomorrow if it was only up to me. Jacksonville, Miami, New York City, Los Angeles ... Shoot! I could even go to a different *country* if I wanted to. Unfortunately, it wasn't about what *I* wanted. I had Mom to worry about.

But if I bought the restaurant ...

Whoa! I pictured the Roadrunner from a childhood cartoon screeching to a halt right at the edge of a cliff. Even dreaming of it would only lead to disappointment. I couldn't afford it. End of story.

I sighed and glanced in the small square mirror on my locker door. "Never going to happen, and you know it," I muttered to my reflection, while a single copper spiral slipped out of the clip to droop over my right eye. I blew it out of the way. No time to spare. Slamming the locker door, I turned to hurry back. Pearl was waiting.

***

"Ah, Ms. Campbell," Pearl's throaty growl doused any hope of slipping in without calling attention to myself. "Glad you could *finally* join us. Okay, people. Listen up and take notes."

I had to press my lips together to trap the indignant words that were dying to get out. It was still three minutes *before* our meeting was scheduled to begin. *Let it go,* I thought as I flipped open my spiral bound notebook to where the paper clip marked tonight's menu selections. *Channel your inner Disney theme song.*

Clearing my throat, I began, "I was able to get some wonderful shrimp and crab from Jeb this morning, as well as some beautiful perch and yellowfin tuna, so I worked up a menu featuring those tonight. We'll offer Baja fish tacos, using the perch, and have a nice black bean-mango salsa to go with it."

"Mmmm. Fish tacos are a lot of people's favorite, mine included," Sarah, one of the servers, dared to reply. "It's versatile too, since it can be either an appetizer or a light main di—" She broke off at Pearl's glare.

"Less chatter, people," Pearl growled, and whirled her fingers in 'hurry up' motion. "Next?"

I clenched my teeth behind my fake smile, then continued, "Crab dishes will include Singaporean chili crab, a rich corn and crab pudding, and of course our famous she-crab soup." I glanced at Pearl to gauge her response, but the woman was bent intently over a yellow note pad, scribbling notes at a furious pace.

"The shrimp choices will be spicy prawns over angel hair pasta, as well as a Thai shrimp curry. As for the yellowfin, I thought I'd do tuna steaks with roasted, sliced Jarrahdale, ah … *blue* pumpkin," I clarified at Pearl's questioning scowl. Pearl didn't like it when I used "fancy" words. "How does that sound?"

A chorus of appreciative sounds followed the line-up.

"No lobster?" Pearl arched a dark-penciled brow.

I shook my head and kept the smile on my face with an effort. "I didn't like the looks of them. They seemed a bit lethargic. Usually means they're not fresh. I look for the lively ones."

Uh-oh. Another scowl.

I hurriedly added, "I have some in the freezer as a back-up plan, if it's going to be a game-changer." I knew Pearl was partial to lobster—almost fanatical about it, really—dining on the rich meat almost daily. It was a wonder she didn't have gout.

Pearl just grunted, and scratched some more notes, her mouth pursed in an unattractive manner, emphasizing deep wrinkles that didn't need any help to draw attention to them.

"Would you like my wine suggestions?" I asked, knowing the answer.

Pearl waved her pudgy hand again as if shooing away a pesky fly, rings wedged tightly on every sausage-like finger, including her thumb. "No, no … I'll take care of that." She looked up from her notes, peering around the table. "Any questions? No? Well, let's get to work. Time is money, people."

***

"I don't know why you put up with the way Pearl treats you," my sous-chef, Mia, huffed. With her bandana tied around her head, causing her thick bangs to angle across her forehead, and her uptilted eyes, her face had a slightly geometric look. "If I had your flair and skill," she griped, furiously chopping ripe mango for the salsa, "I'd be out of here so fast, all you'd see was a blur."

I drew a deep calming breath of the tendrils of steam rising from the sauté pan in front of me, the delectable scent of shallots and poblano chilies sautéing in butter swirling around me. "You know I can't do that."

"I know, I know." Mia scraped the juicy, peach-colored fruit into a bowl and reached for another mango to repeat the process. "Your mother would freak in new surroundings, but it's not fair that you're trapped here, practically chained to the stove, turning out gourmet yumminess night after night, making Pearl a wealthy woman while you're getting paid a fraction of what you're worth. How can you be so calm about it? It makes my blood boil!" There were angry flags of color painting her high cheekbones by the end of her diatribe.

"Calm? I seem *calm* to you? Just an illusion, my friend. A papier mâché façade. I'm *anything* but calm on the inside, but I have to keep it bottled up. I *need* this job." I shrugged, then laughed without humor. "At least we're not frying everything to within an inch of its life anymore. And Pearl *is* coughing up the money for good produce, now so we can shop at Farm-to-Table. I absolutely love their herbs and veggies. The colors are so deep and rich they almost *sing*. Unusual, too. Purple bell peppers and carrots, white and jade green pumpkins, blue ones like tonight's Jarrahdales. Colors you don't expect. It took me long enough, but I think Pearl is finally getting the message that fresh, organic stuff makes a difference in the quality and taste of our menu."

"You know ..." Mia peered over both shoulders before leaning closer and whispering, "You should buy this place."

My eyes darted in all directions before returning to glare at my co-worker, angry that her words were an echo to my earlier thoughts. Had I somehow telegraphed my feelings? I hoped not. "Don't say that out loud," I hissed. "Do you want Pearl to hear? She's on my case enough as it is. The last thing I want to do is give her any other ammunition to use against me."

"Chillax! I made sure no one was close enough to overhear, and I'm serious. You should buy it."

"With what? Pray, tell."

"Well," Mia grinned. "You know, banks have these really cool things called 'loans.' I bet you could get one if you use your beach house as collateral—"

"Not going to happen," I interrupted before she could continue her fairy tale. "What in the world do you think would happen if I couldn't make a go of it? I'd lose both, and then what would I do about Mom? Now," I paused, anxious to change the subject. "Did that corn I ordered come in? I need to puree it for this pudding."

Mia shook her head in reproach and clicked her tongue. "Your segue could use some work. And yes, it's ready and waiting. I shucked it and cut it off the cob as soon as it arrived this afternoon. It's in the cooler. I'll get it." She grabbed a towel to wipe her hands and hurried to retrieve the large stainless steel bowl heaped with creamy yellow and white kernels. "Here you go."

"Perfect," I grinned while scraping the corn into the food processor. "Now," I shot Mia a pointed look. "I think we'd better concentrate on tonight's entrees, unless you'd rather have Pearl breathing down our necks and telling us how to do our job."

***

Clouds drifted across the moon that silvered the Atlantic in the distance. Lightning pulsed from a darker bank of clouds to the southeast. The steady breeze, always flavored with salt, also carried the scent of rain with it. I reached up, unclasping the clip that held my hair and it tumbled down, allowing dampness to sift through it like fingers. I took a deep breath, released it slowly, and prayed the tension would join that exhale and wind up somewhere across the ocean.

I took another sip of wine and leaned my head against the back of the deck chair, relieved that my mother had been asleep when I got home. That wasn't always the case. Sometimes Mom got an ornery streak and nothing would pacify her but to wait for me to get home—however late it was—and read her nightly bedtime story. The nurse was more than happy to do it, and usually did, but on those nights when Mom couldn't be appeased, the reading ritual fell on my tired shoulders. I breathed a sigh of relief, thankful that wasn't the case tonight.

Mia's words from this afternoon echoed through my mind. "You should buy this place," I mimicked, then made a face. "Ah ... If only ..." I breathed. My list of "if onlys" was a mile long: if only mom didn't have Alzheimer's; if only Dad were still here to help; if only all of his estate didn't have to go toward taking care of Mom; if only I could sell this place and use the money to buy my own restaurant; if only . . .

Of course I could use the beach house as collateral, like Mia suggested. I was sure the bank would give me a loan. That wasn't it. I had responsibilities—whether I liked it or not. What if the restaurant failed? It wasn't uncommon for new businesses—even established ones—to go belly-up, and that scared me. I wasn't a gambler by nature, and it was a risk I just couldn't take. I had to think of Mom and her inability to cope with change. The monster, Alzheimer's, demanded we stay right here. Was I using it as a cop-out? My altruistic side said no, that I was only thinking of Mom. But was that entirely true? Maybe I was using it as an excuse. Maybe it was partly a fear of failure.

There were some people in town who would've loved to see me fail.

Okay, *one* person: Raine Fairbanks.

Raine was gorgeous—sort of a Victoria's Secret model on steroids, but for some reason *she* was jealous of *me*, which I thought was crazy. It seemed to have started back in second grade during our weekly spelling bees. Every time I won, it sent Raine into a meltdown. Maybe it was because her parents split that year, and her mom got custody. Raine was a daddy's girl, and being forced to live with her mom had to have been hard on her. I think seeing my family remain intact sort of poured salt in her wounds, too.

The biggest problem with Raine feeling the way she did about me was that she knew my secret … that I dreamed the future. Not *about* the future. That would be pretty normal. No, my dreams were prophetic … things that actually happened. This "gift," as some mistakenly called it, had been passed down through the women in my family for as long as anyone could remember.

Yay. Lucky me.

Some might think that having the "sight" was a good thing, something to be desired, a trait that could really help the police solve crimes, maybe even keep them from happening.

If only that were true.

My dreams were always in snapshots. Like a puzzle with most of the pieces missing. Not really useful at all. I'd tried to tell the police once, which was one time too many. I was still paying for it.

The images from that dream were as clear today as when I'd dreamt them in the seventh grade: the red bike with the wire basket on the handlebars, the little girl with a long blond ponytail wearing pink shorts, a white t-shirt with a hand printed on its front, the murky marsh water under the bridge.

Mom had driven me to the police station, and they'd taken the report. I'd never forget the look on the officer's face, the mocking laughter that followed us out of the building.

Then the news was full of a missing person's report: little nine-year-old Becky Simmons with her long blond hair, was last seen riding a red bicycle and was believed to be wearing pink shorts and a white t-shirt bearing the "hang loose" symbol. Becky's mom had demonstrated the sign with her hand when she was on television … the same one I'd seen in my dream.

Suddenly, the police turned all business. Officers stopped by our home, asked me more questions … lots and lots of them, before finally leaving. After three days of intense searching, a little girl's body was discovered in the marsh by a crabber. The same red bicycle had been found in the tall grasses beside the bridge. She'd been murdered and the killer was never found.

Somehow Raine had found out about it, and suddenly the entire population of Fernandina Beach knew—visitors included. The whole fiasco probably would've settled into the backs of people's minds like dust on old library books, but she'd fanned those coals, adding fuel to keep them alive, all the while hating me for the attention it got me.

And if the dream-thing wasn't bad enough, add in the fact that I could win an Olympic gold medal in a klutz competition, and it made the rest of my school years a living hell. It's a wonder I lived through them.

I still cringed at the memory of the worst example of that malady. I'd been in middle school, not long after "the dream," so I was sure it was fresh in everyone's mind. After a football game, where I'd cheered until I was hoarse for one Stafford Jamison—or *Ford*, as his friends called him. I had a secret crush on him twice the size of the Atlantic Ocean, which was pitiful because he didn't even know I existed. He was the best-looking guy in high school and played football. I was "that weird Campbell girl" and in seventh grade, which wasn't an attractive time for anyone.

After the game, Mom had swung by the local burger joint and sent me in to pick up dinner to-go. I couldn't help but wonder how my life might've been different if we'd gone straight home that night.

I was standing in the long line, trying to ignore the loud, bumbling horseplay of a group of high school boys trying to impress a group of girls who giggled behind their hands. I had jumped when someone tapped me on the shoulder. Then I slowly turned and my heart leapt into my throat.

It was Ford Jamison. He grinned down at me; his sea green eyes twinkled and sparked beneath a shank of sun-bleached hair that draped across his forehead.

"Enjoy the game?" he drawled.

I opened my mouth to respond, but realized I couldn't speak with my heart wedged several inches higher than it was supposed to be. I snapped it shut again, dying inside. From the way my face was burning, I was sure astronauts could see the glow from outer space.

He laughed. "I know you have a voice. I could hear you hollerin' during the game."

My face grew hotter. If he'd heard me, then he knew I'd been cheering for *him*. Any hope of coming up with some quick, catchy comeback sank like a diving submarine. I panicked and whirled around to leave.

Unfortunately, my next-door neighbor, Coop, had just stepped directly behind me, carrying his tray in careful search for an empty seat. His nearly colorless eyes and beak of a nose garnered him a lot of teasing, especially with a nickname like *Coop*. When I turned, one of my elbows caught the rim of his super-sized drink. I watched the cup tilt in slow motion. The plastic lid popped off like it had been shot from a cannon, and what seemed like a gallon of soda exploded toward him. Dark liquid cascaded down the front of his shirt and pants, creating a huge puddle on the floor at his feet. He stood frozen in the ever-widening lake of soft drink while his face kept flashing between pasty white and heat-stroke red, changing colors like a neon sign in a diner's window.

There was a moment of silence, then chaos erupted. The crowd of boys howled like a pack of hyenas; the girls squealed, trying to avoid getting their shoes wet. I *wish* I could say I apologized. It's what I *should've* done.

But I didn't.

Desperate to turn attention away from me, I looked straight into those colorless eyes and said in an uncharacteristically loud and scathing voice, "Gosh, Coop, why don't you look where you're going?"

I know, I know. It was mean and nasty and so not me, especially since it was all my fault, but the words were out of my mouth and there was no way to take them back.

If possible, the laughter grew louder and insults followed, predominantly ones about him wetting his pants. Coop's eyes shot death rays at me, then he turned and splashed his way over to the trash bin, dumped his ruined meal, and shoved through the front door so hard it's a wonder the glass didn't break. I could still see those dripping handprints on the doors clear surface. I'd just made an enemy and I knew it.

Ford was still there, laughing with the rest of the crowd, but I could tell by the expression on his face that he knew the truth, and he was laughing at *me,* not Coop. In an instant my emotions did an about face; from school-girl crush to loathing in point-zero-three seconds.

I stared, unseeing, across the room, breathing hard and trying to regain some measure of control. That's when I met the hard blue eyes of the last person I wanted to witness what had just happened.

Raine.

One of her eyebrows rose and she smirked. Without a word, I spun around and flung myself out the door.

It was hard to believe that Raine was related to local legend George Rainsford Fairbanks. History cited nothing but *good* about him. Not only had he been a lawyer, historian, and editor of Fernandina's *The Florida Mirror*, but he also pioneered the citrus industry and helped establish the University of the South in Sewanee, Tennessee. If that wasn't enough, thousands of school children—including *me*—used his "History of Florida" as a school textbook.

Seven or so generations later, along came Raine; she was named after him, but that was where all similarities ended. Now that we were adults, the childish jealousy she'd always shown toward me had grown to a malignant, unhealthy level and festered, deeply poisoning her attitude toward me. Maybe a little jealousy was understandable. Black Pearl was an amazing success, and we'd stacked up an impressive number of restaurant awards, but Raine had those incredible English tea parties at her family's B & B. Immensely popular and sold-out every day … with *waiting lists*. That should make her ecstatic, but it didn't.

I guess what probably sent her over the edge was when the Food Network offered me a timeslot for my own cooking show. If life had been different, and I wasn't caring for a mother with Alzheimer's, I might've taken it. But a reality check quickly put that into the realm of the impossible. I never told a soul about it, but it's hard to keep something like that a secret in a small town. Word had gotten out.

It was right after that when Raine offered me a job as head chef at the Fairbanks House. In hindsight, maybe turning her down hadn't been one of my smarter decisions, but it was too late to change my mind, even if I wanted to, which I *didn't*. I cringed at the idea of having Raine for a boss. Pearl was a *cupcake* in comparison.

"Okay," I muttered before gulping the last of my wine and hoisting myself out of the chair. "Enough strolling down memory lane. Time for bed." I was exhausted, and tomorrow would come too soon. Grabbing my wine glass, I stepped inside the warm glow of the living room, closing the door to the porch, dead-bolting the muffled roar of the ocean outside.

CHAPTER TWO

"Shhh. Don't worry. No one will bother us here," he soothed the young woman as he settled her on the porch swing, propping her up with a pillow. "We have all the privacy we'll need. The shop is closed."

Terrified dark eyes welled with tears above immobile lips, sending a silent plea, begging him in the only way she could.

He smiled tenderly, and smoothed the tears away with a gloved hand before spreading her dark curls out like a fan over her shoulders, adjusting individual tendrils so they lay just right. "Your hair is one of the reasons I chose you. You have to look the part, you know."

"I'm sorry it has to end like this. I really like you, I do, but your role is just a minor one in this play." He shook his head sadly. "Minor, but important. It sets the stage for the rest of the performance. It's not your fault, and it's not personal. It's just the way it is. There," he leaned back and cocked his head to the side, surveying his handiwork. "Perfect."

Thick foliage of a nearby maple tree kept them mostly in the shadows, but flickering illumination from the corner streetlight spotlighted her face, just like he'd planned, strobing through fluttering leaves, silvering the wet paths tracking down each of her cheeks. He'd arranged her pale limbs into the position he desired, like a life-sized Barbie doll: bendable, pliant. Presentation was everything.

"Hush, little baby. Don't say a word," he whisper-sang under his breath, staring into the frantic gaze below him, eyes that were wide with the silent scream her lips couldn't muster. His finger stroked along the side of her head, down her long pale neck to the edge of her blouse, arranging the collar just so. "Mama's going to buy you a mockingbird." He closed his eyes, concentrating on the feeling of his fingers closing around the warm malleable neck, tight, tighter. He continued humming the sing-song tune while his fingers squeezed deep into flesh, bruising, crushing, feeling the rapid throb of pulse grow fainter and fainter, until it stopped altogether.

When there was nothing left, he blended into the darkness like another shadow.

CHAPTER THREE

Lacey

My eyes snapped open like they were spring-loaded, my heart thudding against my ribcage like a trapped animal. The nightmare continued even though I was awake. Scenes flashed in my head like a slide show: a tree crowded with birdhouses, a rust-speckled cherub, a stained pillow with a bird's profile printed on its surface, a weathered iron gate, slightly ajar, a porch swing with flaky green paint, a girl with long, dark, curly hair, terror-filled eyes bulging, a noose of purple bruises around her neck. The lullaby my mother used to sing to me as a child wove between each scene like smoke.

The numbers on the clock on the nightstand were a red blur.

1:22? I'd only been in bed a few minutes. How could I have fallen so deeply asleep so quickly?

I struggled out of bed, stumbling over the blanket that was twisted around my lower body. I was filled with the sensation of being under water, all sounds muted and hollow … echo-y. Fighting my way to the surface, I swayed a little with the effort, then staggered to the bathroom for a drink of water, praying it would wash the remnants of the dream away.

I gulped it down, trying to convince myself that it was just because of the reminiscing I'd done earlier, that it didn't mean anything, even though I knew that was a lie. It was happening again.

After placing the glass back on the counter, I stared at the dim outline of my reflection in the mirror while my hands clutched the cold edges of the granite countertop. Curls flared out in wild abandon, untamed, chaotic, like my thoughts. In the shadows my hair just looked dark … no color … like that of the girl in my dream.

No! Don't think about it.

Stress ... that's what it is. My mind grasped at the explanation. Yes, it was all the stress I'd been under. Entirely understandable. A loved one with Alzheimer's was enough to give anyone nightmares. And when all the drama from the restaurant with Pearl was added in, well, it was a thousand wonders I didn't have nightmares *every* night.

I sighed. Great. Now I was really awake. Chamomile tea might help. I had some that included valerian. A cup of that should do the trick, and the time it took to fix it would give my heart rate a chance to ease back into the normal range.

Once I put the kettle on to boil, I rummaged in the cabinet for the right box of teabags. Chai? Bengal Spice? Blueberry? Peppermint? None of those. Ahh ... there was the one I was looking for.

Dropping the teabag into a mug, I stared at the kettle as if I could hurry the process. *A watched pot never boils.* I remembered my mother repeating the old saying to me on more than one occasion, trying to curb childish impatience.

"Sorry, Mama ... I guess I never learned that lesson," I murmured before turning away from the stove and wandering to the bank of windows overlooking the crashing surf. It was pitch black. That bank of clouds I'd seen to the north earlier had rolled this way, blocking any moonlight that might be out there. Black water blended seamlessly with black sky. The lines of breaking waves provided the only variance of that color—undulating ribbons of slightly lighter gray. The memory of my nightmare tugged at me like an undertow, and I was afraid ... afraid if I let myself think about it, I'd be pulled out into the blackness.

Call the police! My conscience shouted. *And tell them, what?* I countered, silently. As usual, there hadn't been enough detail. Just flashes ... nothing to pinpoint a location.

"Call the police," I ordered myself—aloud this time.

Yeah, right. And how would that go? "Hello . . . Yes. I'd like to report a crime . . . Well, um, a murder. But it might not have happened yet, and actually, it may not happen at all . . . Yes, that's what I said . . .Well, I, uh, I *dreamt* it . . . No, I haven't been drinking . . . Okay, *yes*, I had one glass of white wine before bed, but that was a while ago and it's immaterial to this situation . . . No! This is *not* a prank call . . . No, I'm *not* interested in you sending someone to pick me up."

The teakettle's piercing whistle interrupted my imaginary conversation, and I hurried to turn the burner off, lifted the pot and poured boiling water into my cup. I dunked my teabag over and over, relishing the sweet steam wafting into my face. Telling the police wasn't a good idea. I'd tried it before and didn't care to repeat the performance.

Scenes from tonight's nightmare continued to wash over me in waves, making me quake inside. Birdhouses, cherub, bird pillow, gate, swing, girl … Not enough to tell the location, but the girl … She looked slightly familiar. Was it someone I knew? I didn't think so, but there was something about her.

I shook the thought away, concentrating on stirring a teaspoon of honey and a bit of cream into my tea. Then clutching the mug in suddenly icy hands, I hurried back to my bedroom. I hadn't been able to stop it from happening years ago, so there was nothing to make me think it would end differently this time. The only thing I'd accomplished before was to make the police, and everyone else in town, look at me with suspicion and fear. I did *not* want to live through that again.

Besides, it was possible it was just a dream … a plain ol' garden-variety dream that didn't necessarily have to come true … the same as other people dreamed. Yes, that's what it was. Just a dream.

Once settled back in bed, I forced my mind to stay blank, taking mechanical swallows of tea, followed by long, deep breaths, trying desperately to turn off my mind. *Sip … breathe in … out. Sip … breathe in … out. Sip …*

CHAPTER FOUR

Ford

I leaned back on the park bench and took a sip of coffee, savoring the dark, rich flavor. "Ahh … nectar of the gods," I murmured in a reverent tone, almost a prayer. Most of the time, I swilled my coffee at any temperature, hardly tasting it. It was simply a means to an end, a legal stimulant necessary for me to do my job. When was the last time I'd actually had the leisure to "enjoy" a cup? My last day off? If so, it'd been a while.

Ever since I had moved to Tallahassee from Fernandina Beach, my bosses at the State Bureau of Investigation seemed to think that because I was single, I was automatically available to work all the extra hours they could throw at me. Usually, I didn't mind, but even a die-hard workaholic needed a day off now and then.

Taking another sip, I drew a deep breath. A light April breeze blew across the small lake, mixing the dank "pond-smell" with the perfume of a thousand spring blossoms, while wicking perspiration from my forehead, shorts, and T-shirt, damp from my run. I knew I should be rehydrating with water or Gatorade, but I'd missed my morning coffee in my desire to get out early and pound the sidewalks, wearing running shoes rather than my usual black leather ones. I'd get water later, back at my apartment.

Fingers of morning light reached timidly through spring-green leaves, tracing lacy designs along the sidewalk in front of me. The quiet was almost hypnotizing, punctuated only by annoyingly happy songbirds and the sounds of other runners, taking advantage of the day's coolest temperatures. The steady *thud-thud-thud* signaled the approach of a runner.

The girl looked like an ad for the latest skimpy running gear. She was too tanned, too blonde, and her teeth, when she flashed a smile of invitation my way, too white. Everything about her screamed *artificial*. And she wasn't even sweating.

Uh ... nope. Too high maintenance for me.

I lifted my chin in acknowledgement, then deliberately turned my attention back to the pond. Her expression turned stony and she huffed past me.

Once she rounded the curve and was out of sight, I relaxed, but my relief turned into a scowl. *What in the world is wrong with you? She was hot and you haven't had a date in months. So what if she wasn't sweating? Maybe it's a medical issue. You could've at least gotten her number.*

I shook my head in disgust, and took another sip of coffee, which had suddenly lost its appeal. Heaving myself to my feet, I tossed my cup into a nearby garbage can and turned toward home.

The vibration of my phone against my leg startled me. Retrieving it from my pocket, I glanced at the screen, afraid my boss might've changed his mind and was calling me in after all. I grinned when I saw who it was.

"Jonas!" I crowed. "Wazz-UP?" The pop culture catchphrase from the past had been the college greeting between me, and my best friend, Jonas Holmes.

"Dude!" he answered with a laugh.

"How the heck are you?"

"Living the dream, man! Living the dream. Married life is amazing. You should try it!"

I ignored his suggestion and countered, "How is Cleo?* I haven't heard a word out of you since the weddin'."

"Great! Cleo's amazing, but you should see for yourself."

"What do you mean?"

"I mean, we're in Tallahassee a couple of days, visiting my sister, Sam. Did I tell you she moved here from Charleston when she finally finished grad school?"

* For more on the Cleo/Jonas story, read *Red Curtains*

"What? She's here? In Tallahassee? No, I had no idea. You mean she managed to cut the apron strings from that Civil War kook she grad-assisted for?"

"Good old Dr. Poinsett," Jonas laughed. "He finally retired. She didn't have a choice. I think she would've become one of those permanent students you hear about if he'd stayed. Anyway, she moved to Tallahassee to 'start a new life,' whatever that means. Been here a couple of weeks. She's got herself a job and a place to live, but no friends. Might be nice if someone who knew the area would show her around."

I heard the hint in my friend's voice. "You can give me her number and I'll check on her, but it ain't goin' to happen, man."

"What?" The question was all innocence.

"Have you really forgotten that we've tried this before? It didn't work then; it won't work now."

"Well, why not? *You're* single. *She's* single—"

"No chemistry. Give it a rest."

"But—"

"*No!*"

Jonas sighed. "Well, can't blame a guy for trying." After a beat of silence, he continued, "Back to my story … Sam's move just about killed Mom. *'But it's two states away.'*" He mimicked in a falsetto wail. "Her exact words, emphasis included. The way she said it, you'd think it was out past Pluto, or something. You remember me telling you how she liked to keep all us kids close?"

"Yeah."

"Well, it's worse now. She nearly blew a gasket when I moved from Charleston to Savannah a couple years ago, and that's less than an hour away."

I laughed. "I remember. She even 'mother-henned' *me* while we were in college."

"You're lucky she stopped," Jonas laughed. "Anyway, since Sam just started this new job and can't take off today, I was calling to see if there was any way Cleo and I could meet you for lunch or something? You know, catch up on old times. What do you say? Think you could squeeze us into your crowded social calendar?"

"Social calendar? Riii-ght."

"Oh, heads up, man. Cleo brought pictures from the wedding. She wanted to make sure you saw how 'cute'—her word, not mine—you and Lily looked together."

I groaned. "But I *saw* them. On Facebook."

He laughed like it was the funniest thing he'd ever heard. "You saw *some* of them, my friend. She brought them *all*. Had them printed and bound into a book. Pretty cool, actually. You'll be expected to 'ooh' and 'ahh' in prodigious amounts."

"Thanks for the warnin'. From what I remember, I'm not sure I'd call me and Miss Lily 'cute,' but we definitely weren't your average best man and matron of honor. How *is* she, by the way? Any leftover issues from her gettin' beat up?"

"Nah, she's completely recovered. Tough as nails, even at almost seventy years old. 'Course her husband helps with that—you remember him? The doctor?"

"Oh, yeah. That's right."

"So … lunch? Dinner?"

"Yes," I answered, trying not to sound too desperate. "I actually have today off, somethin' that only occurs once in a blue moon, I might add."

"Great! Name a time and place and we'll be there."

***

"You're what?!" I asked much too loudly, drawing looks from most of the lunchtime crowd at Dave's Pizza Garage.

Jonas winced and cast an apologetic glance around the room. "Uh, could you take it down a decibel or two, buddy?"

Cleo's face glowed bright pink and she looked like she wanted to hide under the table, but she whispered, "You heard him. We're pregnant!"

I swallowed hard. I was jealous over Jonas and Cleo's obvious happiness. A wave of it nearly choked me. "When?" I croaked.

"Around Thanksgiving," Jonas answered carefully. His reporter's eyes missed nothing. I could feel them reading me like a book, seeing more than I wanted them to see. He wouldn't ask about it, though. Guys' code of ethics thing.

Cleo had no such reticence and pulled no punches. "So, don't you think it's time you found yourself a woman and settled down?" Her turquoise eyes pinned me in place, dissecting me like a specimen in biology class. "What? Don't look at Jonas. He feels the same way. You think working yourself to death will impress the SBI? Make you indispensable or something? "

I shot my friend a murderous look, but he was suddenly all about picking the olives off his slice of pizza and transferring them to Cleo's.

She wasn't done yet, though. "You do realize, don't you, that if they work you into an early grave, they'll just find another idiot to take your place?"

"Cleo, honey," Jonas interrupted, soothing her. "Getting upset isn't good for the baby. Look," he pointed to her pizza. "Remember how you've been craving olives? See, I'm helping you with that."

"Thanks, sweetie," she beamed and kissed him on the cheek.

They looked adoringly into each other's eyes for an inordinate amount of time. I cleared my throat. "Uh, still here, guys."

Cleo giggled, and her cheeks turned pink again.

"Ford's a big boy, sweetheart," Jonas continued as if there'd been no interruption. "It's his life. It's up to him to decide what to do with it. Marriage may not be in his cards." He gave me a pointed look. "Right, buddy?"

I clenched my teeth, and fought a sudden irresistible urge to punch my friend in the throat. "Right," I muttered, glowering at both of them.

"Good," Cleo chirped, dimpling at me. "Now, how would you like to be our baby's godfather?"

***

I played tour guide to my friends for the rest of the day, dividing the afternoon equally between the University Museum of Fine Arts for Cleo, since she was an artist, and the Antique Car Museum for Jonas, since he was a guy. It had been a wonderful day, filled with reminiscing over college memories.

After a relaxed dinner of my famous grilled "Ford" burgers, the only thing that I could really cook, Jonas brought up a more serious subject.

"So ... any update on the murder of that girl in Fernandina?"

The mention of my hometown seemed to electrify the air between us. "What murder?" I asked.

"Don't give me that. There's no way that *I* have more information than *you* do," Jonas gave a disbelieving bark of laughter. "You work for the SBI, for heaven's sake. I'm not buying it."

"What murder?" I repeated, while my eyes drilled him for the answer.

Jonas shrugged. "Okay, I'll play along. As you well know, a girl was murdered last night. They found her at a little antique shop; I think that's what they said. Not too far from the river. Strangled." He stopped and studied my face. "You really didn't know? How is that possible? Isn't it sort of your job to be on top of these things?"

"You said it happened last night," I replied evenly. "Today was my first day off in weeks. I haven't had the radio or TV on, haven't checked my email or read the newspaper. How could I have known? And for that matter, how'd *you* know?"

Jonas shrugged. "Some little intern at the *Trib*. No idea how he did it, but he got wind of the story. Even got a photo of the girl. Must've heard me mention my SBI friend who used to live in that neck of the woods. He emailed it to me a little while ago. Just showing off his sourcing abilities, I guess. Probably hoping I'll put in a good word with the boss."

"Local girl?"

"That, I don't know."

"Oh, well, I'll check my email later. Now ..." I pushed the plate containing the last burger toward him with a grin. "... how 'bout another burger?"

CHAPTER FIVE

Lacey

"**G**ood morning, Mom," I said when I entered the kitchen for breakfast. I leaned down to kiss my mother's soft cheek, sending a smile to Bonnie, our live-in nurse, before continuing, "Did you sleep well?"

She gave me a blank stare. No recognition lit those eyes that were so like mine.

"Where's my husband?" she demanded.

I shot Bonnie a questioning glance. She gave me a rueful smile and shook her head.

"Looks like we're having one of *those* days, Miss Lacey. That was the first thing she asked me this morning."

"Oh, boy." I grabbed a mug from the cabinet and poured a cup of coffee, stirring in cream until it was the color of caramel. After Dad's death, the care of Mom had landed squarely in my lap. Thank goodness the rent money from the two apartments upstairs helped cover Bonnie's wages. Lord only knew what I'd do otherwise. Right now, I only had one renter, Mae Branson, a retiree who'd been working on her "great American novel" for the past three years. I had to admit the reliability of having a year-round income from her had shown me just how stressful the seasonal rentals were. I'd never realized it before. It had been a nice reprieve, but I met Mae as I was leaving last Thursday and she informed me her book was nearly finished, that she'd be moving out any day, so I'd soon be back to "flying-by-the-seat-of-my-pants," and I wasn't looking forward to it.

I squared my shoulders and turned back to my mother, touching her shoulder, making eye contact before speaking.

"Daddy's in heaven, Mama. I'm sure he's getting our mansion fixed up for us ... painting all kinds of pictures for it." I glanced up at the large framed seascape on the wall across from the dining room table and barely stopped a grimace. I sincerely doubted God allowed things like that in heaven. It would be much more at home in the other place.

There'd been other "masterpieces" like the one in front of me—*many others*—all over the house, but after Daddy died, I'd stacked them all in the back bedroom closet so I wouldn't have to look at them. Mom had a fit when I did it and made me promise I wouldn't get rid of them. Who knew why it mattered so much to her, but I felt bound by that promise. They were still piled in that closet. This was the only one still up. It would've joined the others, but Mom wouldn't hear of it, so it had to stay.

The colors were garish and thick, smeared on with the palette knife Dad loved to use, though he wasn't good at it. *At. All.*

Now Granddad ... *he'd* been the artist. He'd died before I was born so I never knew him, but I knew his work. His canvases—at least twenty of them, each worth a small fortune—once graced nearly every wall in the house, but they'd disappeared while I was away at culinary school. When I got home at the end of the year, Dad's "art" had taken their place. I missed them, but I knew my father had a huge inferiority complex when comparing himself to his father's work—with good reason—so I never asked where the missing paintings were, just assumed he'd sold them or donated them to a museum. They were his. It was his business what he'd done with them. I only wish I could've chosen a favorite—a small piece of the man I never knew.

My eyes went back to my mother and I forced a smile. *Okay ... time to change the subject.* I crossed my fingers, hoping it would work. Sometimes it did. Sometimes it didn't.

"You look nice today, by the way. I like those shoes."

"What?"

My eyes darted to Mom's ears and my shoulders sagged. Her hearing aids were gone again. Mom didn't like them and pulled them out whenever she got the chance, tucking them away in some new hiding place. Bonnie and I were always on the lookout for the blasted things.

"Your shoes," I repeated, raising my voice so she could hear me. "I like your shoes."

Mom looked down at her feet, and her expression became animated.

"Yes, they're so comfortable, and you know how important that is. I have to have comfortable shoes since I'm on my feet all day, reading to the children."

"You're right. It *is* important," I agreed loudly. It was just easier doing it that way rather than trying to argue. Mom had retired from teaching fifteen years ago, and then volunteered at a local Christian school as the "reading lady." While there, her sole responsibility was visiting each classroom, reading aloud to the kids, teaching by example the joys a book can bring. The students absolutely loved her, and her influence was so great that several of them had gone on to become librarians, or some other book-related profession.

All that stopped when she was diagnosed with the terrible disease intent on stealing her memories ... who she was. Mom couldn't remember where she lived most of the time, but she remembered reading to those children. That was her happy place, her "reality" where she "lived" most of the time. She still had lucid moments when it was easier to pretend nothing was wrong, but those were growing fewer and farther between.

I poured myself a bowl of oat bran flakes and raisins, and made a face. "Why does 'healthy' equal 'meh' in the cereal realm?" I grumbled. "They can make computers that fit on your wrist, but they can't make Cap'n Crunch or Frosted Flakes healthy?" I sighed and continued, "It's just one more thing to take all the fun out of growing up."

Bonnie cocked an eyebrow at me. "That kind of talk doesn't help my attempts at getting someone else at this table—" she tilted her head toward Eve "—to eat a healthy breakfast, you know."

"Sorry," I apologized. "But she can't hear me. She's hidden her hearing aids again."

"I'll find them. They always turn up."

"Yeah, I know," I sighed. "I guess I'm a bit grumpy this morning. Couldn't sleep ... bad dreams." *What an understatement!* The grisly nightmare tried to push into my mind, but I slammed the door. *No! Forget it! It was just a dream. Just a dream.* "Finally had to get up and fix myself some chamomile tea."

"I thought you looked a bit 'raccoon-ish' this morning. You might want to use some concealer on those rings before you go out."

I snorted. "Thanks, Bonnie. I know I can always depend on you to boost my ego." I gave her a wry smile. "It's a good thing you're such an amazing nurse."

"Just keeping it real," she laughed.

I hurried through my cereal before it turned to sludge. "Anything fun planned today?"

"Well ... we need to get a few groceries, then ... uh, wait, Mrs. Campbell," she raised her voice to be heard. "Toast is something you can eat with your fingers. You don't have to use your fork. Yes, like that." She turned back to me. "She's been trying to use her fork to eat everything. Even potato chips and grapes. Anyway, the walk around the grocery store will probably wear her out, so she'll be ready for a nap after lunch. This afternoon I'm going to try to get her interested in the new adult coloring book and pencils I got her."

"Oh, she'll love that. Tell her we'll display it on the fridge so every-one can enjoy it. That's what she always told me When I colored pictures for her and daddy as a little girl. Made me feel like a million bucks when my picture got put on the fridge." I gathered up my bowl and spoon. "I'm sorry to eat and run, but I need to catch Jeb this morning before he heads out, and I have a lunch meeting. Also, planning to get to work a little ear-ly so hopefully Pearl won't have anything to complain about." Leaning over, I pressed a kiss to the top of my mother's head. "Have a good day, Mama. I love you. See you tonight, Bonnie."

"Don't forget to cover those raccoon eyes," the nurse reminded me.

"Got it," I sang over my shoulder.

***

I pulled into my usual parking spot alongside the dumpster tucked beside a weather-beaten structure, my tires crunching over the crushed oyster shells that coastal businesses used in place of gravel due to their abundant availability and low cost. I could see Jeb's fishing boat bobbing and swaying at the end of a rickety dock. Good. He hadn't left yet.

There was a reason I parked where I did, like I was trying to hide. I didn't want to be conspicuous. I considered Jeb's my little secret, and I'd like very much to keep it that way. It wouldn't do for other Fernandina seafood establishments to learn where I got the best seafood in town.

The air breezing through my open window seemed extra heavy with dead fish and diesel fuel, smells always associated with the fishing industry. Seagulls wheeled and laughed over the water, on the lookout for castoffs from fishing nets. The sight of them brought a flash of memory. The bird on the pillow. The girl. The lullaby's echo, *Mama's gonna buy you a mockingbird ...*

No! It was just a dream! I fought the childish urge to put my hands over my ears, close my eyes, and belt out, "La, la, la," in my loudest voice. Not very mature. Singing would help, but how about a real song? My mind clutched at the first tune that popped into it: "Favorite Things" from *The Sound of Music.* Imagining myself as Maria and belting out the list that included roses and kittens, kettles and mittens had a calming effect, and succeeded in chasing the other memories away.

There, I thought with a sigh when I'd finished. *Much better.* Getting out of my car, I began picking a path around the perennial mud puddles that pitted the lot. Some of them never seemed to go completely away, even when it hadn't rained.

Billings Seafood. The crooked letters over the door were hand painted and off-centered. No doubt painted by Jeb himself. Good thing his seafood was the best, since his place had no curb appeal at all. One side of the small sun-bleached structure featured curled, faded gray paint. The shady side was streaked with mildew, its drain-pipes rusted dull orange. Clumps of matted grass and weeds skirted its front, looking more like an overgrown beard than a lawn.

My stomach always clenched a little when I came by here. This wasn't the "postcard perfect" side of Fernandina, and not the part of town I'd frequent if it wasn't necessary, but I'd known Jeb since high school. He was harmless, if a bit scary looking. Heavily tatted and pierced, he usually wore his mane of dark hair in a scraggly man-bun. His long beard was often braided in a single, thick plait; his face—the part that was visible—was tanned to the saddle-leather stage. But despite his looks, and that of his business, I couldn't ask for any better product.

The screen door's rusty hinges screeched an announcement of my arrival, the sound magnified in the tiny space. The entire building was only about three hundred square feet, with most of it behind a plywood wall that separated the "front"—the only part the public saw, which was about the size of a walk-in shower—and the "back," which was mostly coolers filled with no telling what.

Jeb's decoration style would be classified as "minimalist." The unpainted walls boasted nothing but a tide chart, a farmer's almanac calendar with large red X's crossing off the days to the present, and a glossy blue plastic swordfish over the door to the back. Any finish that might've been on the pine floors was long since gone, scuffed off by countless sandy shoes. The ceiling was adorned with urine colored water stains in all shapes and sizes. A short length of worn Formica countertop held a battered set of scales, an antique cash register, a spike stick full of order receipts, and one of those dingers customers were *supposed* to be able to use to let someone know they were there. Jeb's was useless, sounding like it was stuffed with cotton balls. No one was behind the counter.

"Yoohoo?" I called out loud enough for him to hear me in the back.

There was a muffled thump, followed by a string of curse words. I pressed my lips together to trap a smile as he hobbled through the door, rubbing his knee and wincing. "Thought it was probably you."

"You alright?"

"Aw, yeah," he waved my concern away, shrugging. "Wasn't watching where I was going. like to have knocked my da—" He broke off at my look. "I mean, my *dadgum* kneecap off. Come on back." He turned and limped off the way he'd come.

When I joined him, he was already pulling Styrofoam boxes from one of the big walk-in coolers. "Got these in late yesterday. You get first dibs, as usual."

I removed the lid off the first bin. "Scallops, yes. Perfect. Sautéed and served with truffle risotto." I moved to the next cooler, filled with iced crabs. "These will be perfect for my Cajun Crab cakes and stuffed avocados. Do you have some sea bass? Or perch? Or both?"

He grunted and pulled out two more coolers.

"Good. I'll take them, and either swordfish or shark. Either will work for the grilled kebabs. I'll need prawns, clams, and mussels for the Frutti de Mare I'm making for tonight, and calamari, if you have any. I can make do without if you don't, so no worries."

He silently retrieved box after box as I listed them, almost as if he knew what I was going to say before I asked.

"Lastly, please, please, *please* tell me you have some decent lobster. Pearl wasn't happy last night. You know how she is."

Before I'd finished speaking, he plunked two five gallon buckets at my feet. I smiled when I saw the seething mass of creatures, fat claws waving around in a warning. They were so fresh he hadn't even dumped them in his aquarium yet. "Oh, nice! Feisty little boogers, aren't they? This will make Pearl happy." I stopped and rolled my eyes before correcting myself. "Well, maybe not 'happy,' but it'll be one less thing for her to complain about, and that makes me happy. Thank you!"

The parts of his face that weren't covered with beard pinked with pleasure as he began re-stacking the bins in the large cooler.

"I've got to scoot now, Jeb. Just write up my order and someone will sign for it when it's delivered this afternoon. Have a successful day." I turned toward the door. "Happy fishing!" I flung over my shoulder.

***

Back in town, I parked in the art gallery lot and headed for Main Street, smiling like I always did when I saw the large pink and black sign. How could I not? With two fuzzy yellow ducklings running in the rain wearing red galoshes and carrying matching umbrellas, it invited a smile. The shop belonged to my best friend, Olivia Hale. Liv had named her store *Par-a-dux*, a play on the word *paradox*. I thought the name was perfect … a spot-on illustration for the real word's meaning: a person, situation or action having seemingly contradictory qualities. What could be more contradictory than ducks that didn't want to get wet?

It was a store full of toys that weren't just toys. Nothing in it was merely for entertainment. Each item had a deeper purpose: feeding imagination, teaching, and growing kids to be the best they could be. More often than not, it featured items whose proceeds went to help various charities or causes.

I pushed through the door, which triggered the delicate musical tinkling of various wind chimes. Every time I entered the store it was like entering a magical kingdom. Swaths of sequined tulle in shades of purples, pinks, white, and silver draped from the ceiling in layers, sheathing strands of tiny white lights that blinked on and off in random pulses of energy, mimicking thousands of fireflies. Hundreds of fairies and butterflies, in all sizes and colors, dangled from the ceiling by invisible threads. The colors and dazzle were enough to take my breath away. As usual, the placed was packed with potential customers.

"Lacey!" Olivia beamed as soon as she saw me, fluttering over to give me a swift hug. That was Liv's gift: making a person feel as if they'd just made her day perfect.

I grinned at her and asked, "Any photo-ops on the way to work this morning?"

"A couple," she replied. "You'd think no one had ever seen a woman riding a bike before."

I laughed. "Well, probably not a *pink* bike. And let's face it, wearing a tutu, leotard and angel wings, not to mention a halo and a magic wand with a big glittery star at its end—all in bubblegum pink—is kind of asking for attention."

Liv shrugged. "Who knew this get-up would be such a great promotional tool? Um, could you excuse me a sec?" Hurrying over to a teenage girl behind the counter, she leaned close and whispered something in her ear. The girl sighed, stuffed her phone in her back pocket, and shuffled over to help a family choose a puzzle. Rejoining me, Liv shook her head. "If that girl would give customers half the attention she gives that cell phone of hers, she might be of some use. As it is, I believe she's going to have to find herself another job. As busy as we are, I need all hands on deck."

"Sorry. If this is a bad time, I—"

"No, no, no! Judy and Lindsey are here too. I can take a break. C'mon back." She motioned toward the door that led to the back of the store.

"Have a seat." She waved toward my usual stool before plopping down at her desk and sighing. "You're so right about this pink tutu idea. If I'd paid big bucks to some high-faluting advertising outfit, I doubt they'd have come up with a better gimmick. I can't even do a simple errand without tourists snapping pictures of me and sharing them with their friends on Facebook and Instagram. And the YouTube videos ..." She shook her head in amazement. "... some of them have gone viral. The children drag their parents, grandparents, or both, into my shop like mice following the Pied Piper. Hardly a customer comes in who doesn't leave with a pink bag."

I leaned forward and patted her blond mop of curls. "Proud of you, girl!"

Liv's cheeks suddenly matched the rest of her outfit, and she blustered around a bit, fiddling with the star at the end of her wand. "I was hoping you'd have a chance to drop by before heading to work. I wanted to see if you'd heard."

"Depends on which 'what' you're talking about."

"Huh?" Liv looked confused.

"Never mind." I waved the question away. Liv was my best friend and I'd do about anything for her, but she suffered the tiniest smidge of air-headedness. "Tell me."

"That poor woman."

"Do we have to do this every time?" I moaned. "Just tell me."

"Oh, *you!*" she made a face, and bopped me gently on the head with her wand. "The woman they found murdered this morning, of course."

My heart stuttered a bit before thundering ahead in a full gallop. "M-m-murdered?"

"Yes, I heard it from Vanna, who got it from Sybil who heard it straight from Carol's daughter," she gave a solemn nod. "Down on Ash Street. You know ... that little antique shop you like so much?"

"You mean Chateau Debris?"

"Yes, that's the one. They found this young woman, sitting on a porch swing, dead as a doornail."

"On a porch swing, you say?" Black spots started clouding the periphery of my vision, and my skin went clammy. *Oh no! Just like in my dream.*

"Yeah ... hey, you don't look so good, honey." Liv hurried around her desk, and shoved my head down between my knees. "Don't move. Let me get you something to drink." She darted to the small fridge in the corner but kept talking. "I've got Cheerwine. I can't stand the stuff, but since I know you like it, I keep some here for you. Shows how much I love you."

Her voice sounded like it was wrapped in sheep's wool, but maybe it was just my ears in their present state.

She was back in an instant, pressing an icy can against the back of my neck. I gasped, but the shock of it made the black dots dancing behind my eyelids disappear. "Okay, okay. I'm fine now," I exclaimed, reaching back and snatching the can off my neck.

Liv squinted at me. "If you say so, kiddo, but I've seen *dead* people with more color than your face has right now. Here." A single miniature candy bar lay in the middle of her flat palm.

I grunted, and waved it away.

"But it's *chocolate.*"

One corner of my mouth tilted up. "Said like that gives it medicinal value."

"It's *dark* chocolate. It *does* have medicinal value ... or at least it's good for you, and that's close to the same thing. Eat it."

I obediently unwrapped the candy and tossed it in, pressing it to the roof of my mouth with my tongue so it would melt slowly. "And just for the record," I continued after I'd swallowed the thick lusciousness. "... the only dead people you've seen are on TV, and they don't count. Now ..." I popped the top on the can, and took a big swig, hiccuping twice. "... who is she? The dead woman? Do they have any leads? Did they give her name?"

"Dead people on TV do *too* count," Liv argued, still stuck on my earlier comment. "Well, they're not *really* dead, but they make them look so realistic, they're like the real thing." She paused and watched me sip my soft drink, then shook her head. "They haven't notified next of kin, so no name yet, but I heard she's not local."

I stiffened. "Where did you hear that?"

Liv tapped her temple, leaned forward and whispered, "Sources."

"This isn't a game, Liv. You—" I rubbed my forehead in an effort to soothe away an oncoming headache. "Never mind. I need to run. I have a lunch meeting at the Florida House and I don't want to be late."

"Lunch meeting, huh?" Liv cocked an eyebrow and smirked. "Is that code for *date?*"

I snorted, "Hardly. It's some real estate guy named Travis Sterling. He's been bugging me to death, trying to set up a meeting. I've been ignoring him because I know he just wants the beach house. I finally gave in so he'd leave me alone."

Liv's blue eyes went wide and round "Ooh … he sounds nice."

I sent her a *you've-got-to-be-kidding-me* look. "Did you miss the part about him being a real estate guy?"

"It might be a coincidence."

"It might. And pigs might fly if they had wings."

"Well, at least you'll get a nice meal this time."

"That's the plan." I finished off the soda and stood, swaying a bit as I did. Liv reached out a steadying hand, and I gave it a squeeze before leaning over to toss the can in her recycle bin. "Let me know if you hear anything more about the dead woman."

"You got it," Liv answered. "Enjoy your lunch."

CHAPTER SIX

Lacey

As I hurried down to the Florida House Inn, where I was to meet the persistent Mr. Sterling for lunch, the fact that Liv's news and my nightmare were one and the same kept circling in my brain. I didn't want to think about it, because if that were true, it meant I might've been able to save that girl. That wasn't something I wanted to dwell on. Of course, that depended entirely on the time of death, which hadn't been released yet, according to Liv. I'd have to wait and see. Until then, it wouldn't do me or anyone else any good to dwell on it.

Good grief! I thought as a gust of wind shoved me up the steps of the restaurant. *I'm glad I didn't wear a skirt. I'd be battling the updraft like Marilyn Monroe.* I peered up at the cerulean blue sky, nodding when I spied the bank of cauliflower-headed clouds billowing out over the river to the west. We could use the rain. The weatherman said we were still in a deficit. Not enough tropical storms last fall. Of course, I was hearing a lot of chatter about that freak hurricane-like storm that had spun off the coast of Africa two weeks ago. Somewhere out in the Atlantic now. Maybe we'd get some rain from that. The weather-folks weren't calling it a hurricane since it wasn't in-season, but one never knew. *Ahh ... Springtime in Florida. The only thing predictable about it is its unpredictability.*

Loud cracks and snaps drew my attention as I put my hand to the doorknob. Eight flags, colorful emblems of our heritage, flapped from the second story porch railing: French, Spanish, British, Patriots, Green Cross, Mexican Revolutionary, Confederate National, and United States. Amelia Island was the only place in American where this many flags had flown during its history. Opening the door, I blew into the restaurant, my hair swirling in a cloud around my head, obscuring my vision. The insistent breeze tried to follow me in, but was cut off when the door banged shut behind me. I ducked my head, embarrassed by my loud entrance, and ran nervous fingers through my chaotic curls. I tried to bring them under some semblance of order, but gave up, knowing it was a lost cause.

"Ms. Campbell?"

My eyes hadn't adjusted from the brilliant sunlight from outdoors quite yet, so the low voice was wrapped in a shadow. When the man stepped forward, my heartbeat faltered, then hammered away at a furious pace. *Ford Jamison?* The jolt of recognition brought back all those feelings from junior high school. No. A careful, second glance picked out differences: a narrower face, wider set eyes. It wasn't him, but the resemblance was startling. This guy looked enough like Ford to be his brother.

He approached me, hand held out to shake mine. "Travis Sterling. We spoke on the phone yesterday?"

After shaking his hand, I pulled mine away and tried to gather my unraveled wits as I compared him with the memory of the boy who'd changed a bad case of puppy love into a worse case of animosity. He had the same frame, six-foot three or so. The same broad shoulders filling his navy sports coat. The same sun-streaked blond hair, dazzling smile and flawless tan. Even his eyes were the same unique color … intense sea green. But he was one of those men who wore the scruff of a three or four day-old beard, GQ magazine sexy. The Ford I remembered from high school was smooth-shaven. I floundered for a response, wondering if my expression was what was making his eyes laugh. "Y-yes. Please call me Lacey."

"Only if you'll call me Travis," he countered smoothly. "I have a table for us … right over here."

C'mon, Lace, I ordered myself while walking to the table. *Get a grip. Yes, he's handsome, but it's not like you haven't seen handsome men before.*

Maybe not, but it's been a while, my other side argued.

Well, for heaven's sake, try not to gawk.

As soon as we were seated, a waitress appeared like a genie, doling out menus and taking our drink orders before flitting away.

"So, any recommendations?" Travis asked, perusing the menu with interest.

"Honey Child," I blurted without thinking.

Surprised eyes shot my way; his eyebrows disappeared under the hair feathered across his forehead. "Excuse me?"

I gave a nervous laugh, my cheeks burning. "It's the name of their chicken salad sandwich. They serve it on fresh croissant that's been glazed with a yummy, buttery-honey mixture. You get two sides with it. I recommend the onion straws and the fresh fruit."

He closed his menu and laid it on the table with a grin that made my heart trip. "Decision made. That was easy."

As if on cue, the waitress was back with our drinks, and was soon gone again with our orders.

I opened my mouth to speak, but he beat me to it, almost as if he knew I planned to cut this lunch short. "So tell me a bit about your town."

"You mean the birthplace of the modern shrimping industry?" I laughed at his expression. "Never mind. Do you like history?"

"I do."

"Then you've come to the right place. Fernandina practically oozes Old-Florida ambience. Our little town has fifty-plus blocks that are on the National Register of Historic places. Over four hundred houses, businesses and churches are on that list."

His eyebrows rose again and he nodded. "Impressive. So, where did Amelia Island get its name?"

"It's named after Princess Amelia, Britain's King George II's daughter." I held up my hand to stop the next question. "Mr. Ster—" I broke off at his look. "Sorry, *Travis* . . ." I gave him an apologetic smile then continued, "The ladies down at the Welcome Center would be overjoyed to let you know what kind of tours are available if you're interested in town history, but right now, I think we should stick to the purpose of this lunch. What is this proposition you mentioned on the phone? Or do I need to ask?"

"Uh, are you always this direct?"

"Sorry, but I have something I need to do this afternoon, and I wanted to get to work a little early today."

"Well, I hope you don't have to go that way," he tipped his head toward the left. "They've got the road blocked. Police tape and everything. Place is crawling with cops. What's going on?"

"I heard they found the body of a woman there this morning."

"What? You mean, *dead?*" his voice sounded surprised. "Natural causes, I hope."

I shook my head. "They're saying murder."

"Here? In this sleepy little town?"

My smile was grim. "Unfortunately, bad stuff can happen anywhere, even places like Fernandina Beach."

He took a sip of his tea, a slight frown etched between his eyes. I reached for my own glass for something to do, while visions from last night's nightmare tried to sneak into the silence. I was busy trying to shove them back into the box I'd stuffed them into, and only realized I'd missed his question when I looked up and saw him wearing an expectant look.

"I'm sorry. What?"

"Where do you work?" he repeated.

"Oh, I'm chef at Black Pearl, a restaurant here in town."

He nodded, and those disconcerting green eyes never left my face, flattering me with their attentiveness. It had been a *long* time since anyone had looked at me that way.

I mentally shook the thought away. It wasn't real. He was only after my property. Time to put a stop to this. I knew just how to do it. "And you're … what? In real estate?"

The question was asked on purpose. I knew it would bring the reason for this lunch to a head, resulting in an abrupt end, which was exactly what needed to happen. The simple fact that I wasn't sure that's what I *wanted* was reason enough.

"*Developer*," he stressed the word.

"Right." I stared at the table. It was easier to think straight that way. "Look, I'm sure the only reason you wanted to meet with me was for my beach property. I don't know how you found out about it, nor do I care. You probably have some grandiose scheme of tearing the house down and putting up a bunch of cookie-cutter type condos or a big ol' high-rise hotel." I smiled grimly at his surprised look. "This isn't my first dance, Mr. Sterling."

One of his eyebrows rose at the same time the corners of his mouth went down.

I gave him an apologetic smile. "Oops. Sorry, *Travis*. Anyway, the list of people who want that property is a long one, but I'll tell you the same thing I told them: I'm not selling. Not now ... not ever, and I won't change my mind." I finally looked up to meet his grave eyes. "Is that too blunt?"

"Okaaay, folks," the waitress' reappearance was ill-timed to say the least. Her voice seemed extra loud and *way* too cheerful. "I have two Honey Child —" She broke off and giggled. "Would that make them Honey *Children?* Get it?" When she got zero response, she cleared her throat and continued, "Right ... two Honey Child plates, with onion straws and fresh fruit." She set one in front of me, then Travis. "Here you go. Enjoy." In an instant, she was gone.

"Where were we?" he asked after a short, but uncomfortable silence.

"You mean I have to repeat it?"

"No, I heard your speech, loud and clear ... and blunt, but I can handle blunt. At least I know where I stand. By the way, how many times did you have to practice that before you came here today?"

My eyes dropped to my plate. I could feel my cheeks warm. Darn my inability to keep from blushing.

He surprised me by laughing. "Okay. You don't want to sell. Fine. But I like what I've seen of Fernandina Beach, so far, and I'm thinking I just might want to stick around for a while ... see what else it has to offer."

What? I raised wide eyes to stare at him, and felt a slow smile stretch across my face.

"C'mon, Lacey, dig in," he urged, waving an onion straw in front of me like a maestro leading an orchestra. "I know chicken salad is served cold, but I'm certain these are better when eaten warm."

***

I glanced at my watch at the bottom of the Inn's steps. Lunch with Travis had taken longer than I'd planned, but there was still time for my detour before going to work. The extra walk would allow me time to mull some things over, too. Turning left, I headed south.

To say the meeting with Travis had surprised me would be greatly understating the obvious. He had said he wanted to see me again, said he'd call in a day or two. Of course, that could very well be a line. But what if it wasn't? What if he *did* call? What then? I hadn't really dated in years ... nothing serious, anyway.

Life had been too busy. Helping Dad care for Mom while getting my culinary degree had left no time for dating. It was worth it though. That degree enabled me to have a decent-paying profession in Fernandina Beach so I could continue to help Dad. Then he got cancer and died, leaving Mom and all that entailed. My life consisted solely of taking care of her and working at the restaurant. There was no time for a social life. There still wasn't, but for the first time in what seemed like forever, I found myself missing it. Might there be a way to squeeze it in? The thought caused a nervous tremor in the pit of my stomach.

It was definitely something to think about.

My footsteps slowed as I neared the corner. It was cordoned off with police tape and barriers, just like Travis had said. Media vans from several local news stations were parked along the street, as well as an assortment of law enforcement. Tripods topped with cameras were aimed at an angle across the street. I was sure they were zoomed in to the max, hoping for some little something that might give them the edge on tonight's ratings. Uniformed men milled around the Victorian house-turned-antique store, like worker bees around a hive. There were so many of them I was sure they were mostly getting in each other's way. Curious onlookers crowded the sidewalks, overflowing into the street, pressing as close as possible to the scene of the crime. It looked like I just might be able to squeeze through and follow the sidewalk over to Second Street and on to work, which was good. If I had to backtrack the way I'd come, it might make me "late" again, and Pearl would have a fit.

A space between the shoulders of two thrill-seekers allowed me a view of the house. The commotion seemed to be concentrated on the left side, which was almost entirely blocked by a huge maple tree and the coroner's van. At that precise moment, a gurney was wheeled out, bumping over the uneven sidewalk. Glimpses of a black plastic body bag showed through the throng that surrounded the wheeled cart. The instant I saw it, scenes from my nightmare began flipping through my brain in repeat mode. I squeezed my eyes shut as a wave of guilt washed over me. Could this girl have been saved if I'd called the police last night? Probably not. The clues were too vague; not enough for the police to go on, but that knowledge did nothing to assuage the guilty feeling that I was at least partly responsible for this girl's death.

I turned away, feeling a little queasy. Bleh! Maybe I shouldn't have eaten all those onion straws at lunch. Food that had tasted so delicious while eating it now felt as heavy as a brick in my stomach. But queasy or not, I had to get to work. There were only two reasons Pearl would tolerate an absence: one, if you were in the hospital, and two, if you were in the morgue. A shudder rolled down my spine at that last thought. Understandable. One shouldn't think about such a place this close to a murder scene.

I pressed forward, weaving through the bodies that clogged the sidewalk. I made a blind right at the corner of Second Street and crashed headlong into someone pushing through from the opposite way.

"Oh, I'm so—" I broke off, and my heart sank when I realized who it was.

"Well, well, well." Raine Fairbanks looked like a cat that'd just caught a canary. "Fancy meeting *you* here."

She looked strikingly beautiful, as usual; tall and long-limbed like a model, but with curves that didn't match her greyhound-thin frame. Her mane of thick dark hair was pulled up into a messy bun on top of her head. Well, on anyone else, it would be a "messy bun." Raine wore the look with panache, exuding "casual elegance." It wasn't fair.

"Sorry, I-I can't stop and chat," I stammered, inching around her and backing up. "You caught me on my way to work." Ugh. I winced as soon as that final word left my lips, wishing I could snatch it back. Why did I add that? It only served as a reminder of the job offer I'd turned down. Raine's expression turned icy and twin death rays shot from her glacial blue eyes. Her mouth pressed into a grim line, which was quite an undertaking for those plump Angelina Jolie-like lips.

"Raine! Over here!" a masculine voice shouted from somewhere behind us. Her glare continued a beat longer, silently promising a reprisal before her expression changed. A fake smile lit her face, and she turned and hurried forward to greet her admirer.

I sagged in relief, but wasted no time with self-congratulations. My goal was to put as much distance as I could between me and my nemesis, and to do it as quickly as possible, just in case Raine changed her mind. Being this near the scene of a crime, with all those news teams might turn into too much of a temptation. It could cause Raine to blurt out a reminder of the last time I'd been linked to a murder, twisting this present scene with tales from the past until folks weren't able to tell one from the other. Nothing good could come of it.

I didn't breathe easy until I walked through the restaurant's front door.

***

"Another night in paradise," Mia groused as she minced shallots for the creamy sauce that would go over the perch fillets. "You'd think Pearl would be happy. After all, she's got her lobster tonight."

I ignored my sous chef's grouchy attitude, busy with preparing tonight's Frutti di Mare, which literally meant "Fruit of the Sea." I added shrimp and scallops to the shallots and garlic I'd just sautéed in olive oil and stirred, breathing in the yummy smells that steamed into my face. Jeb hadn't had any calamari, but I'd made this dish without squid before and no one had been the wiser. There was no reason tonight would be any different.

"Once you're done with those shallots," I told Mia, after adding the crabmeat and turning the heat down low. "I need the swordfish cut into chunks for the kebabs, the zucchini—"

"Already done. In the cooler with the mushrooms."

"Okay, good. You can go ahead and start loading the skewers so we'll have them ready in the cooler. After that, start on the mango salsa. Emile can help." When he wasn't unloading trucks, Emile was the one who usually chopped ingredients all afternoon in preparation for the dinner rush.

"No, he can't."

I shot her a startled glance. "What? Why?"

She shrugged. "His non-slip shoes didn't live up to their name in the freezer this afternoon."

"Oh, no! What happened?"

"He fell. Feet flew right out from under him, and the way his wrist was bent, I'm pretty sure it's broken. Pearl went with him to the hospital."

"Human emotions? Pearl?!"

Mia laughed. "I know, right? Seems like an oxymoron."

"Hmm." I shook my head in amazement. "Sorry. Having a hard time wrapping my head around it. Well, good. He probably needed a translator. He doesn't know a lot of English."

"Don't kid yourself. Pearl went to keep herself out of trouble. Emile's not here legally, and she hired him knowing that."

"How'd you know that? No, never mind." I bit my lip, worry creasing a line between my brows. Emile's absence would leave a big gap. I finally shrugged. "I guess we'll have to manage. I'll start the truffle risotto."

Mia rolled her eyes, but kept her snarky comments to herself, which was good. I didn't have the time or patience to deal with it tonight. Every second counted. According to Pearl, we were booked solid for the whole evening, which meant tensions would be high. It was up to me to keep my kitchen running like clockwork.

"Clockwork?" I snorted under my breath as I reached for another pan to sauté more onions. "More like 'controlled chaos' … barely controlled, that is."

When things were this busy, all it took was one little "unknown" to send everything into a tailspin. Finding out about Emile definitely fit that category, but I was determined not to let it be a catalyst for disaster.

I glanced up when Sarah hurried in with the first order of the evening. "Okay, ladies and gentlemen," I raised my voice to be heard over the noisy kitchen. "It's showtime."

***

Ten minutes before closing, while we were in the process of cleaning up and shutting things down, Pearl herself pushed through the door like a barge through a sea of icebergs, waving a slip of paper she had pinched between her thumb and forefinger. "One more order, people."

My tired shoulders slumped. "What? I thought we'd already served our last reservation."

Spots of indignant color rose on Pearl's cheeks. "You're right, Ms. Campbell. We *did*, but I decided to accept one more. Do we have a problem?"

Tension drew my sagging shoulders up into a taut line. "No, no problem. We'll have the order up straight away."

"That's better," Pearl answered primly and turned to leave. "I hope you have two more servings of that seafood stew left. That's what they ordered," she flung over her shoulder just before exiting.

The kitchen was silent as all eyes watched the doors swing shut behind her. My grip tightened on my knife handle, so hard my knuckles turned white.

"She's not worth it, you know."

"What?" I blinked back to the present.

Mia gestured toward my clenched hand. "I know how you are about your knives. She's not worth damaging them. You're gripping it so hard, I'm afraid you'll bend it."

I drew a deep breath and deliberately loosened my hold, one finger at a time. "I was fighting the urge to throw it at her," I muttered. "Ugh! We're advertised as a 'reservation-only' place. Why does she keep letting no-rez people in? And *this* late?"

Mia just rolled her eyes.

I turned the heat back up under a pot of water to boil some fettuccini, and then studied what was left of the Frutti di Mare in the enormous pot.

"I'm glad we hadn't scrapped the rest of this yet. Two servings will be tight, but I'll give them extra pasta and make it work."

Mia stared at me with brooding eyes. "I still think you should buy this place."

"Not again," I scoffed. "Leave it alone, Mia."

"I heard that Pearl might be putting the place on the market, that she wants to move to the mountains, where it's cooler."

"Where do you get this stuff? I haven't heard a thing."

"Can't remember, but I'm serious. You'd do a better job of running it than Pearl ever thought about doing."

"That'll never happen, my friend. Okay, the water is boiling. Hand me that fettuccini, will you?"

Mia passed me the box. After a few minutes of working in silence, she asked, "Why not?"

"Why not what?"

"Why wouldn't you buy the restaurant?"

I sighed. "Believe me. I'd love to. It's my dream to own my own restaurant, but the problem is the same answer as before: M-O-N-E-Y ... or in my case, the lack thereof."

"I thought your dad was some famous artist ... his paintings worth thousands of dollars a piece. You could probably sell a few of them or at least use them as collateral to get a loan."

"Like I said before, where do you get this stuff?" I gave an incredulous laugh. "In the first place, it was my grandfather—not my dad—who was the painter. Well, the *real* painter. Dad tried to follow in his father's footsteps, but that didn't work out too well for him. And secondly ..." I dipped the al dente noodles onto two plates, then ladled the stew over both. "... all of the paintings are gone, so there's no sense talking about it." My tone let her know that the topic of conversation was closed for further discussion. Thankfully, Mia got the message and didn't press further. After grating Parmesan and placing a sprig of fresh basil atop, I sighed with relief. "There. Done. Let the server know, please."

***

I groaned as I stood in my shower, letting the hot water pulse against my back and taut shoulders, praying the steam would melt away the tension.

Though we'd been insanely busy, it wasn't the night, as a whole, that had my muscles, as well as my mind, in a tight knot. No, it was the fiasco that followed Pearl admitting those last two customers that did it. I groaned again, bending my head forward so the water would beat my neck more effectively, and then muttered through clenched teeth, "If I'd known it was Raine and her date, it never would've happened. I'd have made sure of it."

"Ugh." Water coursed off the tip of my nose, tickling it. I blew an angry puff of air out with my bottom lip and a stream of water spurted like a rooster tail. "I served that stew—*without* calamari—all night, and no one even noticed. Leave it to Raine to cause a ruckus. She's always spoiling for a fight where I'm concerned."

Sarah was the unfortunate server at whose table the couple was seated. According to her, Raine immediately began picking through the entree, almost as if she knew something was missing. "Impossible," I growled. "How could she know?" But whether she knew it or not was immaterial because when she couldn't find any calamari, Sarah was on the receiving end of the first attack. Raine began berating the poor girl, who was completely innocent in the whole ordeal. But that wasn't enough. No, she demanded to see Pearl, screeching like a banshee the whole time. And of course, Pearl, being her typical self, insisted on dragging me out of the kitchen so I could explain why such an "important ingredient" was missing from a recipe that "*always* called for it," according to Raine.

The scene that followed rattled me so, all I could do was to stutter and stammer about how I couldn't get any that was fresh and how frozen calamari wouldn't work. But my explanation had been pointless. Drama-queen Raine refused to listen. The only good thing about the whole mess was that there'd been no other customers in the restaurant to witness the debacle. Well, other than Raine's poor, dumb date.

But it wasn't over. After exacting my red-faced apology, Raine proceeded to insinuate how it was only right that she and her date not have to pay for their meal—*including drinks*. I almost laughed. Pearl did *not* do gratis meals, for any reason. There were actually dollar signs in Pearl's eye's rather than irises. Most people didn't look at her carefully enough to see them, but it was true.

"But she gave it to them," I whispered, still in shock. "The stupid cow gave it to them." The anger and astonishment surged all over again at the memory of the humiliating and confusing experience. "*Of course* there'll be no charge," I could mimic Pearl's throaty purr because my throat felt nearly raw from pent-up emotion. "Please consider it my *gift*. And how about I throw in a complimentary dessert, too?" Then she flicked her hand at me, motioning me back to the kitchen. I could tell by the look she gave me that she wasn't finished with me, not by a long shot.

My ears burned with shame as I remembered what followed in the kitchen. Pearl hadn't even had the decency to take me into her office where there'd have been some level of privacy for my subsequent chewing out. No, Pearl let me have it in front of my co-workers, informing me, in no uncertain terms, that the cost of the two meals would be deducted from my next check. Raine had probably heard it in the dining room, and was no doubt *still* smirking about it.

I turned the water off and watched soapy water swirl down the drain, feeling like it was an apt illustration for my life. I'd get over this. I knew I would … *eventually*. People didn't die of embarrassment. At least, I didn't think so.

Reaching out of the shower stall, I groped for my towel, briskly rubbed my skin dry, wrapped the towel around my head like a turban, and donned my pajamas. It was late. Hopefully, sleep would provide an escape until the morning.

CHAPTER SEVEN

Lightning forked across the black sky, turning the landscape black and white, an x-ray of physical reality. Thunder boom-boom-BOOMED right behind it. Then the clip replayed over and over. The wipers chunked at full-speed, unable to keep the windshield clear enough to see. Water flowed, inches deep, across the road. Tires sent spray in sheets higher than the car.

"I'm sorry about the weather," he raised his voice to be heard over the noise of the storm, glancing in the rear view mirror to the shadows and stillness of the back of his car. "But it's serendipitous, don't you think? I was worried about the streetlights. Too much light wouldn't give us the privacy we need. But this thunderstorm has taken care of that little problem. Power is out all over town."

A guttural grunt was the only response. He smiled. "I know, I know … but it's not much farther. I promise."

The darkness between flashes of lightning was absolute. The only other light was the twin beams from his headlights, slicing through the shadows like blades. One gloved finger reached up and pulled the collar of his shirt away from his neck. The darkness was closing in, smothering him … reminding him of long ago. Webs from the past. Sticky strands that clung, wound tight, wouldn't let go. Nights when his mother was stoned out of her mind, allowing her sadist boyfriend to press a cigarette's glowing tip or a live electric wire against his young, unblemished skin, laughing while he writhed, the stinging slap if he dared to cry out.

"Hush, little baby. Don't say a word," he sang the lullaby softly, more to himself than the shadows in the back seat. The familiar words both calmed and infuriated him, just like they had for years. He continued humming the sing-song tune, relaxing in the repetition of it until he was pulling into the deepest shadows of his destination. Unbuckling his seatbelt, he patted his shirt pocket and smiled at the reassuring lump. Good. He had everything he needed.

He was soaked the instant he stepped out of his car, but the complete darkness made that discomfort worth it. Once darkness was his enemy; tonight it was his friend.

He'd disconnected all interior lights in preparation, so there was no danger in opening the back door. Reaching in, he pulled the young woman out, lifting her, draping her over his shoulder like a sack of feed. Lightning strobed around him as he moved with a purpose to the bench he knew was there, but could only see in the intermittent flashes. He leaned down, carefully depositing his burden onto the bench, leaning her against the bronze statue on the right end, working as quickly as possible, feeling vulnerable out in the open. He fished in his pocket for the lump, placing it like a prop in a play.

Another flash of lightning—they weren't happening as often now. The storm was moving out to sea. He smiled tenderly at the dim shape in front of him, savoring the look he could see in the brief bursts of bluish light, terrified eyes staring up at him, tears blending with rain wetness dripping from her chin. Again, a flare, not as bright this time. He pushed the sodden mass of her dark hair back from her face, away from her neck, and began humming the lullaby again. "Hush, little baby. Don't say a word . . ."

His fingers circled her throat, resting there a moment like a necklace, thumbs just below her larynx, then they tensed, constricted, squeezing harder, tighter ... until the frantic pulse on the side of her throat went still.

He was gone before the next bolt of lightning.

CHAPTER EIGHT

Lacey

I jerked awake. My hands went to my throat, clawing at the chokehold that wasn't there. It took several minutes for me to untangle the nightmare from reality. I could still hear notes from the lullaby. I sat up and pushed my hair out of my face. It was still damp. I hadn't taken the time to blow it dry before collapsing in bed earlier. The dampness made it harder to separate myself from the dream of the girl ... dark hair, sodden by the storm.

It had happened again. I couldn't tell where. The darkness hadn't divulged that secret, but I knew they'd find another body in the morning.

Wait! That bench. There'd been statue sitting at one end. I'd seen it awash in one of the blue-violet flashes of lightning. There was only one place in town that had a statue like that. The Welcome Center downtown. The life-sized bronze of David Yulee! Incongruous tidbits of history shot through in my brain, confusing me with the timing of it all, clouding reason. David Yulee, the first Jewish senator appointed to the United States Congress. David Yulee, who chose Fernandina Beach's harbor as the beginning point of the first trans-peninsular railroad in Florida, that allowed trade to reach the Gulf of Mexico and created a worldwide network. David Yulee, who was imprisoned at Fort Pulaski after the Confederate surrender, and released ten months later thanks to General Ulysses S. Grant. A great Floridian every child in Fernandina Beach learned about in elementary school . . .

My dazed thoughts trickled to a stop. Now wasn't the time for a history lesson. If there was the slightest chance I could help stop this madness, I needed to call the police. *Now.*

Without hesitation, which might give me time to talk myself out of it, I reached for my phone, impressed 911, and waited impatiently for the reassuring ring.

All I got was silence.

I pulled my phone away from my ear and stared at the screen. The three numbers glowed and the little circle was spinning around and around, but nothing was happening. The battery icon at the top right showed only the tiniest sliver of red. Uh-oh. My phone was almost out of power. How was that possible? I'd plugged it in to recharge before going to bed.

I pressed *done* and tried again.

Again, nothing but silence.

My eyes darted to the digital clock beside my bed. Uh-oh. The screen was blank. No reassuring red numbers shining in the darkness. I felt across the top of the nightstand until my fingers found my watch.

2:11.

With a sinking feeling in the pit of my stomach, I stumbled to the window, pulled back the curtains and groaned. No streetlights either. A flash of lightning outlined a palm tree on the other side of the glass, fronds nearly horizontal in the wind, leaf streamers twisting and flapping like a ragged-edged flag. Water flowed in the street, a misplaced creek moving fast enough to have a current.

A storm … just like in my dream. Bad enough to knock out the electricity. But why wasn't my phone working? It still had a little juice. Had lightning struck a cell tower?

As my brain roiled with questions, one thought emerged from the confusion, and my shoulders slumped in despair. I wouldn't be calling the police tonight.

CHAPTER NINE

Ford

I wheeled off Lime Street into the Fernandina Beach police department's parking lot, staring at the building's blue awning while my car idled.

Five years ... and the place hasn't changed a bit, I thought with a wave of nostalgia.

When I'd left here, I thought I was headed for glory. I guess it was kind of a big deal for a small-town Florida cop to get a job with the Florida State Bureau of Investigation. So I'd torn out of Fernandina Beach, leaving it in the proverbial cloud of dust, anxious to make my mark in the world, and especially glad to put as many miles as possible between me and my former boss, Chief-of-Police J.D. Craig. Everyone in the department knew Craig had tried—and failed—for the position I'd snagged. As a result, let's just say I wasn't included on his Christmas card list.

There were times—and it seemed to get worse with every passing year, though I hated to admit it—when I missed living in a place where everyone knew everyone else and folks looked out for each other; where the pace was less hurried; where the extent of crime was usually nothing more serious than jay-walking, and parking in a no-parking zone.

I sighed. I knew when I'd volunteered for this case that I'd have to talk to Chief Craig, feel him out, maybe get him to fill in some blanks that weren't in the emailed report. I hoped five years had mellowed him a bit, but I wasn't holding my breath. Shoving the car into park, I got out, chirping the doors locked.

I strode across the pavement, stepping across puddles mirroring blue, but veering widely around swaths of Spanish moss that had been ripped from nearby water oaks by last night's storm. Though it lay around in innocent clumps of dirty rags, I couldn't help shuddering. Looks could be deceiving. The stuff was full of chiggers - tiny insects from hell whose bites caused itching that nothing could remedy. Believe me, I'd tried them all during a number of youthful run-ins with the little devils. Nail polish, kerosene, castor oil, vinegar … the list went on. *Never again,* I thought grimly. *Not if I can help it.*

Once through the doors, I flashed my badge and my grin at the familiar face behind the desk. "Hi, Midge. Long time, no see."

"Ford!" the receptionist squealed in a highly unprofessional manner. Her high swirl of platinum hair still reminded me of a vanilla ice cream cone. It hadn't changed either.

"Shh," I murmured, under my breath, taking note of some raised eyebrows and disapproving looks on faces I didn't recognize. "You're gonna get yourself in trouble."

"Psh!" She waved her hand as if waving away a bad smell, but she waited until the hallway was empty both directions before hurrying from behind the desk to give me a quick hug and then scooting back to her desk before someone saw her. She rolled her eyes at the look I gave her. "Rules are made to be bent."

"Not words one generally expects to hear in the police department," I admonished, laughing. "You'd be in a heap of trouble if your boss happened to be within earshot."

"Heard they were calling in the SBI." She adroitly changed the subject. "But I never dreamed they'd send you."

"This is my old stompin' grounds." I shrugged. "Thought it might give me inside track … something an agent unfamiliar with the area wouldn't have. My boss agreed."

"Hope your theory is right," she replied, "'cause this thing's giving everyone the willies. "Well,"—she turned brisk and all-business—"Chief Craig is expecting you. Well, an *agent*, not you, personally. FYI,"—she leaned forward and added in a whisper—"he's not happy about the SBI butting in." Then she was back to all business. "I'll let him know you're here. You can have a seat." Lifting her chin toward the chairs in the lobby, she pressed some buttons on her switchboard. "Sir? Ford Jamison is here to see you."

***

"Jamison!" Chief Craig boomed theatrically, and his meaty right hand wrapped around mine, giving it a vigorous shake while clapping his left one on my shoulder, a little harder than necessary. "Tallahassee treating you well?"

I winced inwardly, then answered, "Yes, sir. It's good to see you. You haven't changed a bit. Well, maybe a bit grayer around the muzzle."

The chief rubbed his short goatee with a rueful laugh; sweat glistened on his billiard ball-smooth head. "My wife tells me it makes me look 'distinguished,' which is code for 'old,' I think, but getting old beats the alternative, right?"

"Right."

He sobered immediately. "Sorry your trip back here is under such grim circumstances."

"Yeah, it's hard to believe somethin' like this happened in little ol' Fernandina."

Craig gave me a shrewd appraisal, as if trying to determine whether I'd just insulted his town. I mentally rolled my eyes. *C'mon, man*, I wanted to say. *I'm not dissin' Fernandina. This is my hometown, too, for cryin' out loud!* I hadn't needed Midge's warning. It was always the same. Even in the best-case scenario, local law enforcement chafed when the SBI was called in. Sometimes it got downright hostile. And with the history between me and Craig, this *wasn't* a best-case situation.

The older man finally replied, "Well, the rest of the state seems to be going to hell in a handbasket so why should I think we're immune from it? You got that I report I sent, right? Hey, shut that door, will you?"

"Yes, sir," I answered, closing the door with a soft *click.* "Another body showed up?"

He nodded, motioning me toward the chair opposite his desk and then took his own seat, leaning forward, elbows atop the various papers strewed across the surface. "No prints. We dusted everything at both scenes, even though the rain at last night's scene would've destroyed any that might've been there. The perp probably wore gloves."

"The girls local?" I asked.

"No." He shook his head. "The first one … Natalie Winters," he supplied the name by glancing at one of the papers on his desk. "… is from Jacksonville. Coroner put the time of death at 2 a.m. We don't have a name for the second one yet, but I don't think she's from around here either. No one recognized her. Her TOD is 2:45." He picked up a file and handed it over the desk. "They just gave me a set of photos on her. Notice anything?"

Opening the folder caused the knot in my gut to tighten. The likeness between the second and the first victim was eerie. Both were slender and long-limbed; both had long curly dark hair; both had been beautiful young women, and both had almost identical dark bruising around their necks. "Cause of death was strangulation," I choked out, feeling strangled myself.

My comment wasn't a question, but the chief answered anyway. "Yes. Well, at least with victim number one. Coroner has confirmed it already. His preliminary report on this one suggests the same. She has the same petechial hemorrhaging, same crushed hyoid." He paused, then added in a lower voice, "They found enough Rohypnol in the first one to incapacitate someone twice her size."

I winced. "Any sign of sexual assault?"

Chief Craig shook his head, eyes on his desk. "No, which is strange. That's not usually the case. Whole reason it's called the 'date rape drug,' you know. Poor thing didn't have a chance. She couldn't fight, so there was nothing under her fingernails. That much drug in her system, she wouldn't have been able to scream either."

I didn't bother commenting. What could I say? I continued flipping through the crime photos, stopping when I got to the sealed plastic bag that held a brass ring set with an almost comically large stone. "What's this?"

Craig nodded. "Figured you'd have a question about that one. It's a ring."

"I can see that, Chief." My answer was clipped short. "What's it doin' in with the evidence photos? It looks like somethin' you'd get out of gumball machines."

"It was at the crime scene, sitting on top of the statue's pocket watch Maybe it has something to do with the murder, maybe some kid left it there and it's totally unrelated. Either way, we bagged it just in case. No prints, so I think it's linked."

When I'd gone through the photos twice, I tucked them into the folder and sat back in my chair. A tense silence stretched between us for a long minute. I was sure we were thinking the same thing: *serial killer.*

"Two bodies in two days?" I finally blurted. "Almost identical in appearance, with the same M.O.? You know what you're lookin' at, right?"

"I'd rather not label it quite yet, if you don't mind," the chief replied with a grimace as he massaged his temples. "The press is rabid over this as it is."

I ignored that. "No witnesses? With either of them?"

Another head shake. "No one's come forward."

"How is that even possible?" My question came out a bit sharper than I intended, surprising me, as well as the chief, but once I started I couldn't seem to stop. "The little shop on Ash Street? I could see that … maybe. It's off the beaten path a bit, not a lot of traffic, foot or otherwise, but the Yulee bench is right in front of the Welcome Center! In the heart of downtown, on the main drag! How did no one see anything? He obviously *wants* the bodies found. No hidin' them out in the woods or marsh where we have to hunt for them. It's front and center with this guy, and he's stagin' the crime scene like a movie set, for God's sake. Practically throwing it in your face! Flauntin' it!"

"Well, guess it's a good thing you've ridden in on your white horse to take over then, isn't it?" Craig snapped, temper tinting his whole head hot pink, a balloon of barely-suppressed anger.

I had my retort ready, but someone rapped loudly on the door. Probably a good thing. It provided time for both of us to go back to our corners and cool off a bit.

"What?" Craig barked.

I didn't recognize the young officer who stuck his head in, cowering a bit at the scowl on his boss' face. "Uh, someone … a woman … just came in who said she tried to report a murder last night, but the phones were out, due to the storm."

"*What?* " Craig cursed. "Well, what are you waiting for? Bring her in!"

"Y-yes, sir. Right away, sir."

"Well, Jamison." The chief's smile was grim, and his skin color was fading to a much more subdued shade of pink, almost normal. Looks like we might have a witness after all."

I didn't answer, listening to the sound of footsteps getting louder as they neared the door, the officer's voice saying, "Right this way, ma'am." Then the door swung open.

"This is Lacey Campbell, Chief."

Lacey Campbell? The name sounded familiar, but I couldn't quite place it.

She stepped into the room, her hand held out to shake Craig's. "Chief … thank y—" She broke off when she saw me, jaw dropped in surprise. Eyes the color of blackstrap molasses, widened in shock before narrowing into almost a glare; a blush—more the color of anger than embarrassment— stole up her neck and bloomed into her cheeks, clashing with her auburn curls.

Ah … Lacey Campbell. I remembered her. Though the irate young woman in front of me—stunning in spite of clash of reds—bore little resemblance to the gangly, awkward little thing who'd spooked so badly the one and only time I'd ever talked to her that she dumped about a gallon of drink all over that poor guy in the diner, then tried to make it look like it was his fault. I'd known the truth—had even laughed about it, but she wouldn't be mad about that, would she?

"Good to see you this morning, Ms. Campbell," Craig greeted. "Though I wish the circumstances were better. What's this I hear about you trying to call 911 last night?"

Lacey's mouth finally moved, but no sound came out. She shook her head as if shaking off a stun, then tried again. "I dreamt it." Her voice was barely a whisper.

"Another dream … I—" Craig broke off and drew a deep breath, blowing out in a noisy huff as he looked every direction except at her.

Oh, yeah. She was the one who'd dreamed about that little girl they'd found in the marsh. The chief was remembering, same as me. I could almost see the wheels turning in the man's head.

The story had spread quickly, with practically the whole town label-ing her as crazy, that is until that crabber came across the bike, and then the little girl's body showed up. After that, there were all kinds of rumors and theories thrown around. The most common? That she was some kind of a witch … her mother, too. Second place was the crazy theory. That's the one I went with, though I wasn't exactly sure how it might work. I mean, could a crazy person even *have* accurate dreams? Oh, well. It was easier to believe than witchcraft.

That was my freshman year in high school. She was a couple of years behind me so … probably seventh grade—everyone's least favorite year. The best thing you can do at that age is to hunker down and try not to draw attention to yourself until you can muddle through it. The fact that she did the exact opposite must've made middle school hellish for her.

But she *had* made it through. The rumors had died down and she'd grown up … quite nicely, I mentally added while my eyes swept her from head-to-toe. So why in the world was she here reporting another dream? Maybe I'd been right and she *was* crazy.

Craig dragged another chair over in front of his desk and motioned her into it. "Why don't you have a seat and tell me about this dream of yours."

She flicked a nervous glance my direction, and this time I felt a jolt when our eyes met, as if my heart was attached to jumper cables.

What the heck was that?

Maybe I needed to rethink the witch theory.

The chief noticed her unease. "It's alright. Detective Jamison is here by my request." His tone belied his words. He was ticked off and wasn't hiding it well. "The SBI will be joining us on this case. He needs to hear whatever you have to tell."

I could see uncertainty all over her face; her whole body was rigid with it, fight or flight —the survival instinct hardwired into every living creature. Then she swallowed hard, set her shoulders, and took her seat.

"It's actually been two dreams . . ."

CHAPTER TEN

Lacey

*F*ord is back.

Just thinking the words sent anger coursing through my veins while my stomach performed a series of loop-dee-loops.

C'mon, girl, I urged myself, as I practically squealed out of the parking lot. *Harboring anger for this long can't good for you. You'll end up with an ulcer. Get over it and go home.*

Home ... right.

Monday was my only day off, and I'd planned to spend it with my mother. In the past, when Dad was still with us, Mom had loved outings at Fort Clinch. That's where I was going to take her. A picnic in the park. It'd been a long time since we'd done that ... too long. It would just be the two of us, too. Bonnie said she wasn't coming; said we needed some mother/daughter time, that Mom's "on" days would get fewer and fewer as this disease progressed so I needed to take advantage of them when I got them, to think of them as gifts.

Thank goodness for a day off. After last night's fiasco with Raine, and then Pearl raking me over the coals, mixed with liberal amounts of stress produced by the nightmare and another girl being killed—I needed some time to recuperate, maybe a week ... no, more like a *month*.

Ford is back . . . My mind circled back to the forbidden subject, like a vulture over roadkill.

Ugh. What was wrong with me? He was here to do a job, to head the investigation into the murders of those two girls, and that was all. His actions only reiterated that. Our eyes had connected twice, and though my blood pressure had rocketed into the danger zone, it hadn't seemed to affect him. Admitting that bothered me more than it should.

I took a deep, cleansing breath, and exhaled. "Get over it," I said, turning into my driveway and pulling to a stop at the foot of the wooden stairs. "It's time for a picnic."

***

The weather was perfect. No remnants of last night's storm, no sign of the unusually early tropical storm churning and gaining strength out in the Atlantic. Vivid blue sky stretched from horizon to horizon, the water reflecting its color in a darker shade. A white lacy froth scalloped along the waterline that was crunchy with millions of tiny shells in at least as many colors. Broken bits of sand dollars, whitened by the sun, stood out among them like bits of bleached bones. The crash and thunder of the waves blended with the cheerful squabble of seagulls. Nimble sandpipers chased back and forth between the waves like they didn't want to get their feet wet.

"Spindly-legged things," my mom laughed. "Backward knees. Cartoon birds."

I grinned at my mother's rosy cheeks, her brown eyes that snapped and sparkled under the brim of her big straw hat, so unlike yesterday, when she could hardly speak in sentences and kept asking me if I knew where her daddy was. Grandpa had been dead for years. Alzheimer's was like riding a rollercoaster in the dark. You never knew what to expect. It could change in an instant, but now was a gift.

Mom giggled like a little girl as the pipers darted and danced with the surf. A spent wave washed over her feet and they disappeared under the sand as the water receded. She wiggled her toes like a child. "... doesn't make mistakes," she murmured, watching minnows investigate the bright red that I'd painted her toenails.

"Who doesn't?"

She motioned toward the birds. "God doesn't make mistakes. I can't remember things, but God makes no mistakes."

I gasped in surprise. *She realizes what's happening to her? She understands? She recognizes that Alzheimer's is stealing her memories?* "I know," I croaked in a voice gone hoarse. "Thanks, I needed that reminder."

I reached for her hand, and we strolled along in a warm silence, awash in the crash of waves, leaving two trails of footprints in the damp sand.

"I have more problems than a math book," I quipped once we'd reached the curve of the beach, then followed it with a shaky laugh, trying to lighten the moment. "That used to be one of Dad's favorite things to say." I felt my attempt at a smile fade, then I shrugged. "Besides not sleeping well lately, I had a rough night at work last night."

Her expression invited me to continue, so I did. "My boss was being her usual sunny self and we had a difficult late customer. You remember Raine? Raine Fairbanks?"

A little "V" pulled between Mom's eyebrows. "Doug Fairbanks was a nice boy. I went to school with him."

I scoffed. "That's her dad. He must've kept all those genes to himse—"

A Frisbee skidded to a stop in front of us, scattering crumbs of wet sand over our feet. Mom leaned down to retrieve the toy while I scanned the direction it came from. My eyes widened in alarm. A black Lab, only slightly smaller than one of those Smart cars, barreled our direction, pink tongue flapping from his huge doggy grin.

"Mom, look out!"

Grabbing her arm, I managed to whirl her out of the line of impact, but the motion propelled us both in a wide teetering circle of flailing arms, before plopping us into an ungraceful heap.

"Mom!" I scrambled, crab-like, over to her in an instant. "Are you okay? Do you hurt anywhere?" While running anxious hands over her limbs, I noted with relief that our crazy dance of trying to regain our balance had moved us inland a bit where the sand was looser ... softer. Had it cushioned Mom's landing enough?

Her eyes sparked in anger as she stared after the dog, which was dashing back to its owner with the Frisbee clamped in his teeth. "Duke!" she gasped. "That dog! I've *told* Dan we don't need a dog that big! I can't control him. Oooh ... just wait 'til your father gets home!"

What? Dan? Duke? My dad had been gone for two years, and Duke had died the summer before I started middle school. Had the shock of being almost plowed over by this dog, so similar to the one she remembered from years earlier, flicked Mom's "on" switch to "off"?

No! We were talking, having a conversation. Real words that made sense. I didn't want it to be over. I helped her to her feet, watching her carefully. *Oh, please don't let it be over. Please ... please ...*

She just stood there ... not brushing the loose sand from her shorts, legs, and arms, not ranting more about the dog, who had conveniently disappeared, along with its owner. She just stood there, swaying a bit. Then her eyes suddenly clouded with confusion, her whole body outlined in uncertainty. When her fingers started the familiar nervous pleating of her shirttail, my heart sank and I swallowed the lump of disappointment that rose up in my throat. She was gone again, and I was left with someone who *looked* like my mother, but *wasn't*.

I sighed, blinking back tears. "C'mon, Mom, let's go home."

CHAPTER ELEVEN

Ford

My keys clattered on the counter by the television, then I tossed my go-bag and the case files on the end of the bed. Shrugging out of my sports jacket, I found one of those annoying "hookless" hotel hangers in the tiny closet and mechanically hung it up, my mind busy cataloging the overload of information I'd received since arriving back in my hometown.

When Lacey first started describing her dreams, Chief Craig and I were on the same page. Humor her. Let her get it out of her system so she'd leave and we could get back to work on the case. Yes, there was a history. She'd dreamed the death of that little girl years ago, but that had to have been some kind of fluke.

But the more she talked the more my opinion changed. I felt my almost-smirk disappear. My focus grew more intense. None of the information about either murder had been shared with the press, but Lacey had described the crime scenes down to the color of the paint on the porch swing, and not only that there'd been a ring, but exactly where it had been found; things she had no way of knowing. My preconceived notion of her morphed. She went from being a looney-tune to quite possibly the key to this case. It was too early to know that for sure, but as far as I could tell, there were really only two explanations for her to know what she did. Either she'd "seen" the murders in her dreams like she said, or she was the murderer or played some part in the killings. I was willing to go with number one. I wasn't so sure about Chief Craig.

Of course, the real problem was he had a burr under his saddle because the big boys had been called in, same as all the others I'd dealt with over the years. He'd take an opposing viewpoint for everything I said, on principle alone.

Typical.

After Lacey left, with the chief's advice, "don't leave town" ringing in her ears, I'd spent an excruciating couple of hours debriefing with Craig, which accomplished exactly nothing, as far as I was concerned.

On second thought, maybe we *did* accomplish something. Although we still disagreed on Lacey's part in it all, we'd pieced together a possible time correlation using the approximate time of her nightmares compared to the TOD from the coroner. Near as we could tell, her first nightmare occurred about forty minutes before the actual murder. The second one was around thirty-five minutes before; five minutes *less* time between. That could mean nothing or everything. And unfortunately, we wouldn't know which until the next murder.

When I could take it no longer, I decided enough was enough. I excused myself to grab a sandwich and a Pepsi from the vending machine, then I headed to an empty conference room. Once there, I spread the file contents around me like a fan and started scribbling notes.

Two hours later, my head was splitting, and the only thing I was sure about was that the vending machine sandwiches hadn't gotten any better since I'd left five years earlier. In fact, I wasn't convinced they weren't the same sandwiches. That's when I'd decided I needed a change of scenery and cut out.

I shook my head impatiently. A run … that's what I needed … a good, long one. When I got into my "zone" with all those endorphins racing through my bloodstream, my mind switched into high gear, and new ideas began sparking along my synapses. I wasn't sure *how* it worked, only that it *did*. If I wanted my brain to be on its A-game, I needed to put in a few miles on the beach.

I quickly changed into my running gear, zipped my room key into my shorts pocket, and slipped out of my room.

***

I glanced at my watch. Almost seven miles. Time to turn around. An hour out meant an hour back. Probably more than that, since I'd be running into the wind on the return trip. Sweat ran down the sides of my face, dripping off my chin. Man! What I wouldn't give for some water. I should've grabbed a bottle before starting, but I'd been too intent to get out on the beach.

The shoreline was hard-packed and crunchy, littered with shells at ten or so feet from where spent waves rippled in. Just like I liked it. Perfect to run on. Perfect time to think.

The problem was instead of focusing on the case, my brain kept re-running that moment when Lacey and I made eye contact. What the heck was that jolt about? I'd never felt anything like that before. Maybe she'd caused it. That witch theory was looking more and more likely.

I scoffed. "Stop letting yourself be sidetracked. You're here to find a murderer. Period."

Executing a wide U-turn around a huge sandcastle that was directly in my path, I slowed, admiring the construction. The engineer/architect was a boy about seven or eight years old. His hair was stiff, spiky with salt, sticking up in a dozen directions. He wore a goofy pair of bright red goggles, and his nose was slathered white. Smelled like Noxema. I smiled, remembering how my mom used to smear the stuff on my nose too.

The boy was focused, intent on digging a moat around his master-piece and humming a sing-song tune to himself. The castle's thick walls bristled with an oyster shell armor designed to protect the multiple turrets and towers. There was even a flag flying from the tallest of those towers, flapping in the strengthening breeze. I had to admire the kid's single-minded determination, then I looked up.

Uh-oh. In the distance a thunderhead sent rain to the ocean in showers that moved like gauze curtains over its surface. The ocean looked bruised, the color of loneliness and resentment and regret. White caps chopped the surface. While I didn't believe I had to worry about getting wet—the storm looked like it was heading out to sea—the trip back was going to be harder. The wind was picking up and I'd be running right into it.

Just as I was starting to hit my stride again, the thought struck me like a thunderbolt.

The music.

Maybe it came from hearing that kid humming, maybe it was simply the endorphins flooding my brain, but whatever it was, I zeroed in on part of Lacey's story and gave my mind free rein.

She'd said there'd been music in the background during both of her nightmares … a lullaby, one that her mother used to sing to her when she was little. "Hush, Little Baby." The murderer had sung that to each of his victims. The second line of that song said the mama would buy a diamond ring. A diamond ring … There was a ring found at the crime scene—not a diamond, but clear plastic or glass, cheap costume stuff, made to *look* like a diamond. And hadn't there been some kind of bird in one of the photos from the first murder? Could it have been a mockingbird?

I sped up. I needed another look at those photos.

***

The song is the clue.

The thought came to me in a flash of certainty as I flipped through the crime scene photos for the umpteenth time. I'd bet my life on it. In the first verse of the lullaby the singer promises the baby a mockingbird. I sifted through the photos from the first murder, found the one I was looking for, and studied it. There, on the swing beside the strangled girl, was a pillow with a bird's profile clearly visible. I laid it aside.

The second verse's gift to the baby was a diamond ring. I picked up the photos from the second murder and chose the close-up photo of the gaudy ring, laying it next to the first photo. They might as well be outlined with blinking neon lights and a siren blaring out, "*Clue, clue, clue!*" How else could I interpret them?

Now … what did the third verse promise? I fast-forwarded the song in my mind, slowing on the third stanza. *And if that diamond ring turns brass, mama's gonna buy you a …* "Lookin'-glass!" I shouted. "That's next."

My elation was short-lived, and my shoulders sagged as the realization hit me. "So?" I asked myself with disgust. "And that narrows it down, *how?* There are probably a million mirrors in this town. That useless scrap of information and a dollar might get you a cup of coffee somewhere, but that's about it."

I groaned and ran a frustrated hand through my hair, springing to my feet, pacing the length of the room, back and forth, unable to sit still. If the pattern held—and there was no reason to think it wouldn't—another girl was going to die tonight, and there was nothing I could do about it.

The tempo of my pacing increased in direct correlation with my turmoil. I hated not being in control. The feeling of helplessness was overwhelming. In the midst of the madness of the things I *didn't* know, I clung to the two things I *did* know. One—we were, in fact, dealing with the killer. I knew that just as sure as I knew my own name. And two—the lullaby was our clue—our *only* clue—a map, if you will, leading from one victim to the next. There would be a mirror *on*, or *near*, the next victim. I was sure of it. I just had no way of *stopping* the next murder, or the next, or the next . . .

My groan was more like a growl this time. Yes, there was a third thing I was certain of. Unless we caught a lucky break, we'd have *seven* victims on our hands, one for each verse of the song. Seven young women's lives cut tragically short.

Chief Craig was suspicious of Lacey. I had my doubts, but it was worth keeping an eye on her. Craig mentioned she rented out the upstairs apartments of her beach house. Made sense to see if one was available. My motel room was several miles away from her house, so being in one of those apartments would make surveillance a lot easier

It was spring now, before the glut of tourist season. Chances were good that at least one of the apartments wasn't being used. If I could rent one of those units, it would kill two birds with one stone. One, I'd be nearby to keep tabs on Lacey, and two, I wouldn't have to live in a motel. I could buy groceries ... well, ramen noodles and TV dinners, but I could cook for myself rather than eat out every meal. I knew those items were cheap. They were staples of my diet in Tallahassee. I'd save money, and that in itself would thrill my boss.

It would be tricky, though … watching her without letting her *know* that's what I was doing. I knew, without being told, she wouldn't appreciate it. She didn't like me. That was obvious. But she was involved in this case, and since I had no other leads at the present, she was it. Now … to see if one of those apartments was available.

I glanced at my watch and winced. It was late. After eleven already. Maybe I should wait until tomorrow morning. An internal debate raged a whole minute before I shrugged. She might still be awake, but if she was already in bed, I'd just leave a message.

I sorted through the papers I'd gotten from Chief Craig until I found what I was looking for, then pulled out my phone. After entering her number, I stared at it a few seconds before pressing *send*, then waited for it to ring, wondering why my heart was pounding like a dryer full of wet sneakers.

"Hello?"

"Lacey? This is Ford … uh, I mean Detective Jamison." Better to keep things professional.

The silence at the other end of the line was so profound, I checked my phone's screen to see if the call had been dropped. "Hello?" I prompted.

"I'm here," her voice sounded a little shaky when she finally replied.

"Sorry it's so late. I was just gonna to leave a voice mail."

Silence.

"Right," I blustered. "I'll get right to it. I heard you live in a beach house."

"Uh … yes."

I could hear the question in her voice. "Good. And that you rent out the apartments upstairs?"

"Ye-es."

"Good," I repeated, noting even more hesitancy. "Would you be interested in rentin' one of them to me? If it's available, that is." I hurried on, before she could turn me down without hearing me out. "Looks like this case might keep me here a while and I really hate the idea of stayin' in a motel for any length of time, and I thought of those apartments and just wondered …"

Silence.

"Look, I won't bother you, if that's what you're worried about. You won't even know I'm there unless we bump into each other comin' or goin'. It's strictly business—nothin' more—but I'd count it as a huge favor. What do you say?"

I checked my phone screen again during the continued silence to make sure the seconds were still counting off.

They were.

"Lace—"

"Okay, I'll do it," she blurted. "By the week. Pay in advance. And it's only because I could really use the money. That's all. Come by in the morning … first thing. I have to see Jeb before he heads out. You'll—"

"Jeb? *Billings?*" I interrupted, startled. "What are *you* doing around *him?*" I winced as soon as the words were out of my mouth. It was none of my business who she saw or didn't see. But really … *Jeb?* He was the conspiracy theory guy from high school. Russia using cell phones to spy on us, and all that.

I waited through another lengthy pause before she finally responded in a voice so icy I could feel the chill through the phone. "Not that it's any of your business, but I buy seafood from him."

"Oh, yeah?" I tried to smooth the tension away, using the same technique I'd use to keep a suicide jumper from jumping. "That's right. Seems like I remember he was tryin' to buy him a boat before I left. Commercial fisherman … his dream vocation, right? But why would you need to place an order with him? You plannin' a luau or somethin'?"

"No luau." Another pause, then her voice thawed a little, "Look, you're sure to find out, so I might as well tell you. I'm a chef. I need the seafood for my dinner menu."

"I'm livin' on ramen noodles and you're a chef?" I laughed. "Now, there's some irony. Where do you work? Maybe I could come by … give it a try."

"Black Pearl, down on Second."

"Must be a new one. The only place I remember on Second was that little dump where simply breathin' the air would clog your arteries. *That* place wouldn't need a chef, though. Any person capable of dumpin' everything in a deep fryer would do. What was its name? You know the one I mean?"

"Pearl's."

I could hear the smile in her voice and it sent another little jolt sizzling under my skin. "Wait! *Pearl's?* Pearl's is Black Pearl? How in the world did that happen?"

"Just a different business plan, is all. Reservations only." A slight pause, then, "All organic ingredients, fresh seafood, nothing deep fried."

She sounded almost flippant, but a sixth sense told me that wasn't the case. "So what about the name change? How'd you manage that?"

"Serendipity. I found a black pearl in an oyster I was shucking and broached the idea of changing it, arguing that a classy restaurant needed a classier name."

Before I could respond, her voice was suddenly back to all business, "Make sure you're here by seven in the morning. You'll need to fill out some paperwork, pay me, and I'll give you the key to the apartment."

"Right," I replied, reeling from the rapid change. Hot to cold in an instant? She *was* crazy, after all. "I'll see you in the mornin'."

CHAPTER TWELVE

Lacey

I glared at my phone. My heart felt like something wild, hammering at my ribcage, trying to escape. My mind whirled with the velocity of an F-5 tornado. I'd been on my way to take a shower, thankful my mother's window was dark when I got home and that I didn't have to deal with her. I was coated with smells from the evening's menu. My white chef's jacket bore a large greasy stain that my apron hadn't caught. It needed treating with some Spray n' Wash if I expected it to come out, but that was before. All thoughts of stain removal and showers spun to the four winds the instant I'd answered and heard his voice.

I still stood in exactly the same spot as when my phone rang, my feet frozen to the floor. I was too stunned to do more than gaze at the screen where his number and the length of the call still showed. Green letters and numbers against black. It had been less than a minute. Forty-three seconds, to be exact. Forty-three seconds to send me into a dither and I didn't even understand why.

It wasn't until the screen faded that I was able to break out of my daze and force my feet to scuff down the hallway toward my bedroom.

Once I was in the shower, with hot water needling my scalp and steam billowing around me, I squirted some shampoo in my palm and started sudsing my hair, letting my mind go where it wished. He wanted to rent one of my apartments. Why? To save money? I scoffed. Right. It might save him in food, but the rest of his expense would probably be a wash. So what else?

I closed my eyes, tilting my head back to rinse out the suds. The "hotel" smell? Did *eau de hotel* bother Ford as much as it did me? How did they get their rooms to smell like that? Was it a spray? A particular carpet cleaner? The detergent they used to wash the linens? Ugh! I'd never figured it out, but every hotel room I'd ever stayed in smelled exactly the same.

I squirted a blop of body wash on my loofah, and began scrubbing away the kitchen smells. Of course, the apartment had a washer and dryer, so he could take care of his own laundry. That was an issue since he said he might be here a while. In a hotel, he had two choices: either sit for hours in a sketchy Laundromat or get the hotel to take care of it. Either way, there was added cost.

Turning off the water, I reached for a towel, dried myself off, turbaned my hair, then donned my pajamas. A couple of swipes with the hand towel took care of the fogged up mirror. "The apartment would be homier and have more room," I spoke to my pink-cheeked reflection. "Both plusses for an extended stay, but are any of these 'reasons' legitimate enough to warrant the change?"

The girl in the mirror stared back at me a long minute. Then I shook my head, made a face, and ordered myself, "For heaven's sake, stop questioning it to death! That scene in the diner was a million years ago. He probably doesn't even remember it. It's pitiful that it still bothers you so badly. Get over it and be thankful. You know Mae left you that note in the mailbox tonight. She's finished writing her novel. She's moving out tomorrow. That means no more rent money. You can make it with one apartment vacant, but not two. this is a godsend. Perfect timing, and all that. Dad would say, 'Don't look a gift horse in the mouth.'"

After brushing my teeth and combing out my wet hair, I met the wary brown eyes of the girl in the mirror again, noticed the faint dark smudges under them, and winced, thinking about the night to come, the fear of another nightmare, another girl dying. "Maybe you'll sleep better with a cop upstairs," I whispered, before turning off the light and heading to bed.

***

Knock, knock, knock-knock, knock.

Though I'd been listening for it, the rapping startled me. I glanced at my watch. 6:58. I'd told him "by seven." At least he was punctual. Grabbing the clipboard bearing the necessary leasing agreement and the pen I had waiting on the foyer table, I took a deep breath to prepare myself and swung open the door.

"Good morning," he said, before I could open my mouth.

"Good morning back." My greeting was cool and I avoided eye contact, looking *toward* him, but not *at* him. It was a good plan. The memory of our eye contact in Chief Craig's office was burned indelibly in my mind. "Here," I thrust the clipboard at him. "You need to fill these out, and initial where I've highlighted. That's the amount for your check." I pointed at the figure near the bottom of the first page.

"You want me to do this *here*?" He gestured, indicating the porch.

I gave him a jerky nod. "If you don't mind. I'm on my way out. You can use the railing to press on."

My eyes flickered from just over his head, to his face then quickly back again. Even that brief look spiked my heart rate and my cheeks burned. He shrugged before bending to rest the clipboard atop the railing, scratching his information onto the appropriate lines in hard, irritated strokes. Once completed, he pulled out his checkbook and hurriedly filled that out as well, slipping his check under the strong clasp of the clipboard, leaving it resting on the railing, and then holding out his hand for the key.

"Thank you." I dropped it into his outstretched palm, glad the action didn't require me to touch him. "Let me know if you need anything."

A strange look chased across his face, but was gone before I could figure out what it was. The corner of his mouth quirked up—half-smile, half-grimace—then he turned to leave, muttering something I couldn't understand under his breath.

I glanced at my watch again. Seven on the dot.

I watched him back his car out, turn around, and crunch over the crushed oyster shells out to the hardtop road. After several cars drove past, he wheeled out to the right, tires chirping slightly, and disappeared.

It took several minutes for my heart to get back to its normal rhythm. I tried to convince myself it was because I was still angry, but was beginning to wonder if that was the case.

***

Breeng-breeeng.

The familiar sound roused me from an internal debate over whether or not I'd done the right thing in renting that apartment to Ford. I whirled around, laughing a greeting to the man riding an old-fashioned bicycle. "Obadiah Marsden!" I scolded. "You better watch where you're going with that thing. The police will force you to park it if you keep riding on the sidewalks."

His dark face split in an impish grin as he braked, motioning to the wire basket on his handlebars, which was piled with fresh pineapples. "Miss Laaa-cey," he sang. "Do you need some piiine ap-pulllls?"

"As a matter of fact," I answered, digging in my purse for my wallet. "I do." I handed him two dollars and chose the nicest one in the bunch. "I'll take this one for us at home. You can deliver the others to the restaurant. Same as usual. Thanks, Obie."

He nodded, grin still in place, then continued down the sidewalk as before, regularly flicking his little bell with his thumb, warning pedestrians of his approach.

I shook my head, still smiling as I watched him go, his impressive headful of dreadlocks bundled under a red and blue striped Rasta cap bobbing through the crowd. What a character. He was a common sight around the historic district. Everybody knew him and couldn't help but love him. Well, maybe not the Fernandina police force. They had tried, repeatedly and unsuccessfully, to get him to ride with traffic along the road, *not* on the sidewalks. They'd issued warning after warning, but threats of fines and the confiscation of his ride had done nothing to change his ways.

Other than the cops, though, he'd endeared himself to the citizens and shopkeepers of the historic district with his rolling pineapple market and his singing conversations. Obie had a stuttering problem so severe he couldn't speak to save his life, but it was a different story if he put the words to music. I didn't understand exactly how it worked. Something about the brain functioning differently for singing than it does for talking. I'd Googled it the first time I experienced the phenomenon, discovering that it was more common than I would've imagined. Some pretty famous singers had stuttering problems—Carly Simon, B.B. King, and Mel Tillis were three that I remembered—but you'd never know it by their music.

Anyway, Obie hadn't talked for as long as I'd known him; he sang ... everything. Conversations with him were something to be experienced. His rich baritone turned even the most mundane subject into a sort of mini-opera. Not the high-browed vibrato kind; more like a beautiful story set to music. I found myself wanting to sing with him when we talked, turning his solo into a duet. He was one of the many reasons I loved living in this town. Just thinking about it made me smile.

Then my thoughts returned to my earlier encounter with Jeb at his shop and the smile faded. I'd stopped to place my seafood order, like I did almost every morning, but he hadn't been himself. Everyone knew Jeb Billings was a man of few words, rarely speaking more than a handful of sentences. That was normal ... the way he'd always been. I was the one who did most of the talking. This morning was no exception, but he'd been ... "off." I couldn't quite put my finger on it, but something had been different; tension in the air, something about his posture. And he'd become especially agitated when I told him Raine's reaction to the lack of calamari. I frowned and shook my head, frustrated with my inability to pinpoint what it was.

His eyes were dark, like obsidian marbles, something that came from Indian blood somewhere in his family tree. That was nothing new, of course. They'd always been open, *friendly* marbles, at least with me. Not today, though. Today they were more like a limousine's windows—closed and black. He could see out, but I couldn't see in.

I shrugged. Everybody had problems—me included—and that was *without* counting the Ford situation. After two nights in a row of nightmares that came true, I had actually dreaded going to sleep last night. I tossed and turned, flipped and flopped, fearful of the nightmare I was sure would come if I dared to shut my eyes. Same scene, different actress.

But eventually, I lost the fight. My tired eyelids quivered shut, and I fell, exhausted, into the arms of Morpheus, and … slept like a rock.

When I woke up to the sun pouring like melted butter through my window this morning, I was surprised and relieved. What did it mean? I had no clue, but no nightmare meant no dead girl, and I was fine with that. Maybe it was over. One problem I could check off my list.

Thinking the word, "problem" circled my mind back to Jeb. Maybe he was just going through a down time in his life. Maybe *he* hadn't slept well. Maybe he'd gotten some bad news. Maybe his boat needed a new gear or belt, or maybe he was facing some other issue I knew nothing about. I didn't *really* know him. He was a loner, always had been, and he seemed to prefer it that way. Yes, we were friends, but not *close* friends; he ran in different circles than I did, but I considered us friends nonetheless. We'd known each other our whole lives, were in many of the same classrooms from elementary through high school, but in spite of that, I had no idea what he did when he wasn't fishing or in his shop. Did that make him any less of a friend? No, it just made him private. Everybody was entitled to that, right?

Oh, well. Whatever the case, I missed his mime-like camaraderie and hoped things would be back to normal tomorrow.

***

When I pushed my way through the swinging doors of the Palace Saloon, it was like stepping back in time.

The doors' heavy leaded glass caught the sunlight and refracted rainbows across the same mosaic tile that had graced the floors of the Prescott building since it was completed in 1878. It's first and only other business had been a haberdashery. Then Louis Hirth bought the building in 1903, replaced shoes with booze, and started The Palace on its way to owning the title of the state's oldest continually-operating drinking establishment. It boasted the original pressed tin ceilings, a forty-foot bar lit with hand-carved mahogany caryatid gas lamps, and six commissioned murals.

"Hi, Todd." I waved at the grizzled man behind the bar, who had a mug tilted under one of the many beer taps. I glanced at my watch.

Hmmm. "A little early for that, isn't it?" I motioned toward the tap with my chin.

He shrugged, tilting his head toward the two guys at the end of the bar.

My eyes followed the gesture, noting the safari hats, the almost-matching Hawaiian-print shirts paired with Bermuda shorts, dark socks, and bright white New Balance walking shoes. TOURISTS! Their outfits screamed the word, and if I'd had any doubts, the wide-strapped cameras hanging from their necks would've dispelled them. I swallowed back my laugh. "Is my lunch order ready?"

"You bet," he answered as he slid two foam-topped mugs down the bar to the waiting patrons, then grabbed two brown paper bags off the counter behind him. "Right here. They just brought them out." He checked the tickets and added a handful of napkins. "Yep … your extra guacamole is in there. Here you go, darlin' … give Olivia my best."

"How'd you know I was having lunch with Liv today?" I laughed, surprised.

He grinned. "Because while you'll mix it up and try new things, Liv *always* gets the Southwest dog. Every time." He barked a gruff laugh. "Good thing you don't come more than once a week. Her blood pressure couldn't take it."

I smiled as I tucked a dollar in the tip jar, then gathered my bags. "Don't think it'll change anything, but I'll tell her you said so. Bye, now!" I turned, muttering under my breath, "No secrets in this town."

"I heard that!" Todd hollered.

I didn't bother to turn around, just waved a hand in the air, shaking my head as I paid the cashier and pushed back through the swinging doors.

I'd taken about two steps when a low voice rumbled just behind my left ear, "I've been looking for you." Startled by its proximity, I jumped, whirled around, and nearly dropped the lunch bags. My wide eyes met the set of mocking sea green ones that danced with suppressed laughter and mischief.

"Travis!" I gasped. "Give a girl some warning next time, will you?"

"What? And lose the element of surprise? Where's the fun in that?"

My grin matched his, and my galloping heart settled into a steady trot. "Haven't seen you around lately," I said, mentally wincing as soon as the words left my lips. Would he think I'd been sitting around looking for him? I studied him carefully. He showed no visible reaction to my observation. Good.

"Yeah, I was gone yesterday. Some things to take care of in Jacksonville. Just drove back up this morning, because I needed to talk to you and, lo and behold ..." he spread his hands in a theatrical 'ta-dah' motion. "... here you are."

I couldn't help but laugh. "So, why do you need to talk to me?"

"You're heading somewhere." He ignored my question, gesturing to the bags I clutched in sweaty hands. "May I walk with you?"

"Oh," I glanced down at the bags as if wondering where they'd come from. "Um ... yeah. Sure, but I'm just going across the street to Liv's." At his blank expression, I elaborated, "My best friend, Olivia Hale. She owns Par-a-dux, the toy store."

"Perfect." He fell into step beside me. "This won't take long."

I opened my mouth to respond, but he hurried on. "Like I told you at our lunch meeting the other day, I like what I've seen of this town and have decided to try it out a while. I know your beach house has a couple of apartments that you rent out. I was wondering if either of them are available."

"How'd you know—? Oh, right. You're a realtor."

"Developer," he corrected.

I gave him a distracted smile. *First Ford and now him?* The shock of his request, coming right on the heels of Ford's, was stupefying, freezing me into a complete standstill right in the middle of a crosswalk. My head was spinning. I felt as if I were wading through wet cement.

An impatient driver tapped his horn, breaking the spell. I stumbled forward, but not before sending a scowl at the offender. He probably referred to right and left as east and west when he gave directions, too. *Didn't your mama teach you any manners?*

"Well?" he questioned once we'd regained the sidewalk. "What do you say?"

An approaching train blasted its horn as it approached the crossing at the end of the street. It gave me a moment to gather my thoughts. Still somewhat dazed, I turned to stare at him, then mustered a smile. "I just rented my vacant apartment this morning, but the other tenant is actually moving out today if you can wait until I can get it cleaned. How does this weekend—?"

"Cleaning's not necessary," he interrupted. "I'd prefer to move in sooner rather than later."

"Um …" I wasn't sure what to say. "I rent by the week, and you pay in advance."

He nodded his agreement.

"Right," I nodded once, feeling uncertain. *O-kaaay. Whatever floats your boat, buddy.* "Come by in the morning, early. You'll need to fill out the paperwork and pay me. As soon as that's done, I'll give you the key."

"Deal. See you in the morning." Then he turned and sauntered away.

I stared after him until his head was lost in the jostle of the sidewalk's crowd. When I could no longer see him, I shook the stun off as best I could before turning and hurrying the last few steps to my friend's shop. "Liv's not going to believe this," I muttered as I swung open the door. The tinkle of wind chimes announced my arrival.

***

"Then what did he say?" Liv asked around a bite of hot dog. It really sounded more like den-*whut-dee-shay*, but we'd been friends a long time. I was fluent in "hotdog."

"He wants to move in immediately. Tomorrow. He doesn't even want to wait until it's cleaned."

Liv chewed thoughtfully a few seconds, her blue eyes staring off into space. Who knew what she was seeing. Then she washed the bite down with a swig of sweet tea and focused back on the present. "Weird."

"Weird? That's all you got? C'mon . . ."

She shrugged. "Looks like your financial problems are taken care of for the time being. One less thing for you to worry about."

"Yeah, but ..."

She held up a hand to stop me. "Don't look a gift horse in the mouth."

I groaned while I used my finger to scrape up a dollop of guacamole that had dropped onto the paper wrapping of my sandwich, before popping it into my mouth. "Now you sound like my dad."

"Well, it's good advice."

"But . . ."

"No 'buts.' You need to change your mindset. 'Don't borrow trouble,' is what my grandma used to say. This is business, pure and simple. Two renters for two apartments." She arched an eyebrow at me.

"What's that look for?"

"It means ... I'd *kill* to have two handsome, single guys living right upstairs from me. What a waste," she sighed.

"I thought you said 'this is business, pure and simple.'"

Liv rolled her eyes and shook her head then continued, "Frankly, with all that's going on, it might not be such a bad idea to have a couple of guys close by. Could come in handy."

My eyes shot up to meet hers while my heart rate spiked. "You haven't heard about any other bodies showing up, have you?"

She shook her head, but her eyes narrowed as she studied me. "Is there something you're not telling me? You seem to get really nervous whenever anything about those murders comes up."

"That's hardly abnormal," I said, avoiding her eyes. "Murders *should* make people nervous."

She just gave me a that's-not-what-I'm-talking-about-and-you-know-it look.

I swallowed hard. She was right. I hadn't told her about the dreams yet. "Well . . ."

"There *is?*" Her mouth dropped open, then she pouted, looking upset. "But we tell each other *everything.*"

I sighed. Now I had to deal with Liv's hurt feelings too. "Okay, you're right. I apologize. I guess I was hoping that ignoring it would make it go away."

"Make *what* go away?"

"The dreams."

"What dreams?" she began, then her eyes widened. "You *dreamed* the murders?"

I nodded.

"*Both* of them?"

Another nod.

"Tell me." Her voice brooked no argument.

"I saw every detail of the crime scene, saw the guy kill them."

"You *saw* him? What did he look like? Did you recognize him?"

I shook my head. "It was dark. All I could see was a sort of black silhouette. And he whispered so there's no way to know his voice."

"He talked?"

"Yeah. Sang too. He was sort of whisper-singing the words to that lullaby, 'Hush Little Baby.'"

She was silent for a long minute before taking her last bite of hotdog. She chewed slowly. I could almost hear the hamster on the wheel squeaking inside her head.

"Have you told the police?" she finally asked.

"Yes, that's how I knew Ford was back in town. He was there. They called the SBI in to help with the case."

"Well?" She whirled both hands in the air, urging me for details.

"The reaction was about the same as eleven years ago. They treated me like I was a crazy person."

Liv's expression turned sympathetic and she reached for my hand, gave it a squeeze. "Well, you didn't dream last night. That's a good thing. Maybe there won't be any more murders."

"Yeah, maybe."

She made a face. "Well, *that* was convincing."

I shrugged. "I don't think it's over."

"Why do you say that?"

I shook my head. "I don't know. Just a feeling."

She gave my hand another squeeze. "Well, if that feeling is right, then I'm *especially* glad you'll have two guys nearby. You might very well need the protection."

CHAPTER THIRTEEN

Ford

"**W**ell?" Chief Craig asked, his voice decidedly belligerent. "I'm just fine, thanks, and you?" I answered, turning away and rolling my eyes heavenward. Great. His attitude hadn't improved overnight. I drew a deep breath, trying to count to ten for control, and almost choked. *Gah!* It smelled like Chinatown in July in here. Craig must've had takeout for lunch. No … more likely it was the microwavable stuff. I knew General Tso's when I smelled it. The General and I went way back, first name basis. I sniffed again, tentatively. Smelled like this one was *way* past its expiration date, though. Better breathe through my mouth.

"Don't believe I appreciate your tone, son." Craig sat like a Buddha statue, glowering from his tilted back desk chair, arms folded and shelved atop his belly. Finally he scoffed, "Will we be seeing those SBI superpowers anytime soon?"

The fluorescent light over Craig's messy desk must have had a ballast going out. It was doing a good imitation of a strobe light, making the removal of papers from my messenger bag look jerky, almost robotic. "No new bodies last night." I tried to give him a pleasant smile. "Somethin' to be thankful for."

"Not that we've *found* yet." The chief's retort escalated toward the combative range.

"Tryin' to be positive, here," I replied, keeping my voice as even as possible. "Judgin' by what we've seen so far, if there *was* another body, we'd know it. The perp puts them where they're sure to be found."

Craig's response was a grunt.

"I talked to the parents." *Ahh ... that got his attention.* "Of both girls ... several friends and workmates too. Nothin' in common so far, other than the similarity in appearance, of course."

"Wow," Craig smirked. "Glad to see that our tax dollars are being spent so well. All that special SBI training is really paying off."

I clenched my jaw so hard I was afraid I might crack a tooth. I used the beat of silence to calm down. The last thing I needed was for this to escalate. We were supposed to be on the same team, after all.

"They both used a datin' service," I finally continued as if he hadn't spoken. "But I'm not sure if it's the same one, yet. Winters used, 'Perfect Match.' It's legit. I'm still workin' on which one Jessica O'Neill used."

Craig's brows rose in silent question.

"Victim number two?" I prompted.

Fuming at his continued blank look, I opened the O'Neill file, not because I needed to refresh my memory, but because I needed to think of something besides my desire to jack-slap the chief. I knew I'd already emailed this information. "Jessica Denise O'Neill. We used dental records. Contacted the mother. She'd already filed a missin' person's report. She gave a positive ID."

I reached for a different file, opened it. "I was able to obtain the girls' laptops, and your department's computer genius is attemptin' to get into them, as we speak. It might be nothin', but since it's the only thing I have to go on right now, that's where I'm startin'."

"Just *gave* them to you, did they?"

It was my turn to look blank.

"The laptops," he added.

I met Craig's sneer with a level gaze. "As a matter of fact, they *did*. I could've gotten a court order, but seein' as both the Winters and the O'Neills were anxious to help in any way possible, it saved a lot of time."

"Why don't you just compare phone records? See if there's a common number."

"Already did. We got nothin', but all that might mean is that the perp used one or more burn phones."

"So what are you thinking might be on the laptops?"

"Don't know. But our first step'll be seein' if O'Neill has a 'Perfect Match' account. If she does, then we'll compare the names of any potential date candidates. If we get someone who shows up in both girls' account history, then we've got ourselves a 'person of interest.' That's when we'll bring them in for questionin'."

"And if you don't?"

"We'll go to Plan B."

Craig cocked an eyebrow. "Which is?"

I gave him a grim smile. "I'll have to let you know."

***

I was on my way out to the apartment after stopping for a few groceries. I'd already been there once today. The appointment with Lacey had been early … before seven, like she said. I'd signed the papers, paid her, and got the key and the Wi-Fi password, but hadn't stuck around to check the place out. She'd been as stiff as jeans dried on a clothesline, treating me like a vacuum cleaner salesman. No … worse. Maybe a Jehovah's Witness vacuum cleaner salesman. She hadn't even let me inside the house. We'd conducted the entire transaction out on her front porch, no small talk, no eye contact, then she'd practically 'shooed' me off. Sort of a *here's-your-hat-what's-your-hurry* mentality. I drove away wondering what in the world had just happened. The only thing I was crystal clear on was this: any settling in I needed to do, I'd have to do *later*.

Later was *now*. I'd deliberately waited until after three because I figured Lacey'd be at work. My aim was to avoid a replay of this morning if at all possible. Move my stuff and get settled in without any drama. There wasn't much to move: one suitcase, a messenger bag full of files, and now a few bags of groceries. That was it. Ah, the beauty of traveling light.

My tires crunched up the oyster-shell driveway and rolled to a stop. I hadn't taken time to study the Campbell home this morning. Too intent on seeing Lacey, and then leaving as quickly as possible. Now I had the time, and let my eyes roam to their heart's content. This place had weathered probably sixty years or more of time and tide, but it looked exactly the same, solid and familiar. The two-story structure was built on thick wooden stilts, like so many coastal homes, perched above the reach of all but the most severe flooding. Palm trees and oleander bushes softened the harsh lines of the boxy building. The paint was the same as I'd remembered. No pastel Caribbean colors so commonly seen on coastal homes. Just generic white with black shutters framing each window. The shutters weren't just for decoration, either. They provided protection for the windows whenever a hurricane or tropical storm rolled onto shore. I could remember a few such disasters. Hurricane Matthew was the most recent. I wasn't here then but I heard it was a doozy. Winds around 115 miles per hour. Many less-substantially built places crumbled and were swept out to sea. Hopefully, that super-storm the weather guy kept mentioning would stay far enough out to sea that we'd not get anything but a couple inches of rain.

I eyed the first floor, where I assumed Lacey lived. Wonder how her parents were doing? Were they even still alive? I toyed with the idea of knocking on the door just to see, but decided not to. The last thing I wanted to do was make Lacey any angrier than she already was. Besides, some of my groceries needed to get in the fridge.

I glanced at my key. A small round metal marker, sort of like a dog tag, was engraved with 2-A. That was the apartment on the left. I pulled under the left side, into the parking space labeled with the corresponding number. A wooden staircase led upstairs, but to get to the apartment, I'd have to follow the covered porch around to the left side of the building, where there was a second staircase. An identical set of stairs on the right side led to 2-B.

There was a dark blue Prius parked in one of the stalls of the separate garage that would be for the Campbells' use. No other vehicles. Maybe it was Lacey's boyfriend's car, or her fiancé, or … her *husband. Sheesh. Imagine … being married to that looney-tune*, I thought, and was surprised at the way I felt … like a giant hand was squeezing my heart.

Of course, it was possible for her to be married, *entirely* possible. If you overlooked the crazy factor. She was a beautiful girl. She'd probably had guys standing in line for a chance to go out with her. She could take her pick.

I scowled at that thought. Why would that make me angry?

I tried to shake the feeling off, but it clung like gum on my shoe, which made me even more irritated. I thrust the key into the door's lock and turned it a little harder than necessary, then swung the door open.

The place looked exactly as I would've imagined. Light, airy curtains at the windows overlooking the ocean, whitewashed paneling, pale pine floors, oriental rug in hues of navy, silvery gray, and touches of turquoise, soft and squatty navy-and-white striped easy chairs, and a dark blue sofa.

Hurrying to the kitchen, I put my meager assortment of groceries away. It was mostly the same stuff I bought in Tallahassee: cheap microwaveable entrees that were quick to fix. What they lacked in nutrition, they made up for in sodium and preservatives. I winced as I scanned the dietary information on the side panel of one of the boxes before shoving it out of sight, into one of the cabinets. "You need more *food* in your food," I grumbled to myself. "Stuff with actual *nutrition* in it. You're a runner, for heaven's sake. Runners are supposed to eat *healthy*." The healthiest thing I fixed was probably my Ford burgers, and I'd hardly call those a "well-balanced diet."

I grabbed an apple, and took a self-congratulatory bite before heading to the small, glass-topped white wicker dining table I'd decided would be my desk. See? Healthy. An apple a day and all that. I took a seat and opened my laptop, typed in the Wi-Fi password, then checked my email.

The very first one was from the computer nerd down at the police station. Already? Good. Or at least I *hoped* it was good. I quickly clicked it open.

It *was* good. Not only had the guy unlocked all the password-protected files, he'd created a spreadsheet of all the file names, complete with the necessary user IDs and passwords. Genius! We could use this guy in Tallahassee.

Since we already knew victim number one had a Perfect Match account, that's what I wanted to check first. I scanned the second victim's list, looking for the p's, while reminding myself not to get my hopes up, that the chances of her having the same account were slim-to-n—

My jaw dropped. The bite of apple I'd just taken almost fell out. There it was. Perfect Match. She actually had an account with them too. Of course, it could be nothing, but it was a starting point and it could actually be significant. I'd discovered in my line of work that coincidences usually weren't very coincidental. I needed to check to see if there were any common contacts on each of their profiles.

No, wait. Looked like the computer rat was a step ahead of me. Wow! I definitely needed to see if this guy was interested in relocating to Tallahassee.

Three commonalities? I frowned, wondering at the odds. I knew the girls *looked* similar, but did it go deeper than that? I shrugged. Similar tastes in men, anyway.

The usernames were listed in alphabetical order: fridaynightlights, lookinforlove, and whoareyou? No real names or contact info. The guy must still be working on that, and it might take him a while. These dating sites could be downright junkyard-doggish when it came to guarding their clients' privacy. Made it almost impossible to get vital information at times. This was great for the bad guys, but hard on us good guys. We'd probably have to get a search warrant. I groaned, thinking of all the red tape that endeavor would entail.

Wait. Maybe we could hack into Perfect Match's database. This computer guy—*Myron*—he probably had such a skillset. It'd be a piece of cake for him. Though technically bending the rules, hacking would be a lot easier than another undercover operation like that one down in Orlando. We had infiltrated that company, actually getting a girl on the inside as an employee so we could get to their records. Got the guy though, so it was worth it.

Since I was unfamiliar with how these dating sites really worked— I'd never personally used one before—I figured I needed to educate myself a bit before delving in any deeper.

It didn't take me long to discover that this stuff has been around a lot longer than I would've guessed. The first site, Match.com, was launched in 1995. Now it was so big, it operated in twenty-five countries. And if you didn't like that one, there were about 2,500 other sites and apps to choose from. The number blew my mind.

Even more mind-boggling? More than 70% of adults in the U.S. used dating sites.

Good grief! Why were so many people opting to date this way? Hmm. The article must've heard my question. Apparently, it boiled down to folks wanting to take all the guesswork out of dating. If one's goal was to find someone with shared interests or backgrounds, all they had to do was list their preferences: age, location, hobbies, political views, religious affiliation, physical appearance, etc. Then algorithms performed their magic, coming up with a pool of potential candidates that met those preferences.

Personality-based dating sites encouraged members to fill out questionnaires that matched them with other like-minded users. The questions used emotional and psychological information to determine compatibility, so they were better suited for those whose end goal was the wedding altar.

I shook my head in amazement. It seemed messed up to me. Human beings were too complicated for this to really work. People weren't like math, where one plus one always equalled two. Because of that, I didn't think you could have a "magic potion" no matter how advanced the algorithms were. Even though we lived in an "instant gratification" society, it didn't mean that was the answer to everything … especially not dating. There was something to be said for getting to know another person gradually. I preferred good old-fashioned dating, but then, what did I know? My dating track record was pretty bleak. I was in no position to criticize anybody's method. Maybe I needed to rethink my view of online dating.

At any rate, it looked like I'd have to create an account for myself in order to be able to do any digging. Company policy insisted I have an account in order to do a search. No problem, I could set up a bogus profile. I was sure I wasn't the only one on their site who did this, which was another reason I preferred the old way of dating. Yes, people could pretend to be someone they really weren't, even keep the charade going for a while, but you had a lot better chance figuring that out face-to-face than in the cyber world. I took another bite of apple and flexed my fingers, preparing to create a convincing persona.

It didn't take me long. I skipped loading my photo. I didn't want to take the time to find a fake one. I could add it later. Right now, all I wanted was to be able to search out the three common denominators of the two victims.

I typed in the first name on the list: *fridaynightlights*. A blurry photo of a relatively good-looking guy wearing a cheesy grin, a Florida State football jersey, and a backward ball cap popped up. I didn't know how the other sites worked, but this one didn't allow real names, addresses or phone numbers to show up. Probably so members had a measure of protection in case someone turned out to be a psycho-date. It put individuals in control of how much information they felt comfortable giving out, depending on their overall impression of a potential candidate.

Good policy. I nodded to myself, studying the profile on my computer screen.

Looks could be deceiving, but this guy appeared harmless; an ex-jock, longing for his glory days, but harmless. I might even know him. Hard to tell with the blurry photo, but he looked vaguely familiar.

Lookinforlove was next. I found myself humming the tune from the 80s movie starring John Travolta while the profile loaded, then snorted a laugh as soon as his picture appeared. Yes, he was actually wearing a cowboy hat and a bandana handkerchief tied around his neck. I squinted at the photo, studying it carefully. How old *was* this guy? Hard to tell. Either he was just a weird Urban Cowboy aficionado, or he was from that era, pushing fifty—or *pulling* it. I'd bet a bundle he was bald under that hat. How had he appealed to the two victims? What about him had created any interest whatsoever?

The guy was obviously into fantasy, or at least play-acting. Not crazy enough to pretend to be a superhero, but maybe crazy enough to strangle women of a certain type. I'd be investigating him more.

The last guy was *whoareyou?* Not only the name of a Who song, but a question. A hidden message? I shrugged. Only one way to find out. I typed it in the search box.

The first thing I noticed was there was no photo, just the generic faceless outline that showed up when a photo isn't available. *Who are you, indeed?* I queried silently. A red flag rose in my mind.

I scanned his profile information. It was generic, too, though it did state he was recovering from a broken heart and was looking for the right woman to help him heal. The whole thing was a bunch of gushing, painful, sentimental verbiage, irresistible to women, creating a Florence Nightingale syndrome. It was classic. I'd seen it before. Stuff like this brought out a woman's mothering instinct. All they wanted to do was make the suffering to go away.

I took another bite of apple, chewing thoughtfully as I re-read the information, studying it clinically, without emotion. The username and the lack of photo created an air of mystery. Add in the almost poetic sentimentality as bait, and hundreds of women were sure to bite. It was the perfect lure. The guy could take his pick.

I leaned back in my chair, tossing the apple core at the garbage can at the end of the bar that separated the kitchen from the dining area, and it disappeared inside. Two points! My theory was plausible, but I was stuck for now, until Myron got me the rest of the information. I could list suppositions all day, but without hard evidence, that's all they'd be.

I closed my eyes and massaged my temples. It had surprised me when no third victim had shown up this morning. No new dead body was a good thing, yes, but what did it mean?

Was the perp just trying to be unpredictable? To throw me off? Something else? It'd be nice if the killing spree were over ... that there'd be no more bodies, but I knew that wasn't the case. There were still several verses of the song to go. I knew the type. He'd keep going until he'd finished the song. The only way he'd stop was if he was *made* to stop. It was up to me to do just that.

CHAPTER FOURTEEN

He grunted as he bent clumsily to deposit the young woman into the darkest corner of the walled lot. Her head *thunked* against the stuccoed surface like a ripe melon, eliciting a single soft groan that came from deep in her throat, but that was all.

"Sorry about that, my dear," he panted, hands on his knees for support as he tried to catch his breath. Carrying her from his car, making sure to stay concealed under the trees at the edge of the lot and then in the shadow of the wall, took more effort that he'd counted on. He squinted at the corner, then continued without empathy. "The good news is, it won't hurt for long."

Once his breathing was back to normal he murmured, "You're heavier than the other two were. I'll have to be more careful in choosing the others. Mustn't repeat that mistake."

He heard a faint whimper of protest, but the only thing he could see in the blackness behind the wiry ornamental grass was other shades of the same color. He frowned in annoyance, rising on tiptoes to peer over the wall.

Across the street, the nearest streetlight glowed like a beacon, and strips of light shot through the regularly-spaced openings in the wall, striping the courtyard. Unfortunately, none of them penetrated the darkened corner where he was, and his mouth twisted in rage at his error in judgment. He'd been meticulous, as usual, thinking everything through, down to the exact place the victim would sit. Of course, he'd never come here at night. And why should he? There were streetlights! He'd expected them to live up to their name and *light the street*. What good were they if they didn't do what they were supposed to do, what their name implied?

He'd made a mistake ... a *big* one. Without light, he wouldn't be able to pose her, and "presentation" was his calling card. The display—how his victims *appeared* to the police when they were discovered—was almost as important to him as the actual act of killing them. He wanted them to see the similarities between the victims. It was why he was so careful about his choices. Not so much for them though; he wanted *her* to know what was coming, needed her to be afraid.

This messed everything up! How could he have been so stupid? How was he supposed to look into her eyes while his hands tightened around her neck? How could he watch the flame of life extinguish? He shook his head in disgust, cursing silently. And the mosaics—the beautiful mosaics—after finding the perfect place for this verse of the song, he wouldn't even see them. Not a single glint. Just ... *blackness*. Of course, the brilliantly-hued patterns would frame the girl beautifully in the morning. She'd wear a rainbow-colored halo just like he'd planned, but that knowledge gave him little solace now. He'd have to wait for the Tweets, for the pictures on Facebook and Instagram, just like everybody else. Until then, he'd have to imagine it, and that infuriated him.

Heat rushed through his veins, filling him with abnormal recklessness. He had a flashlight on his phone. He could use that. It would only take a minute. No one would see. No one was even awake. He hadn't seen or heard a single car on the drive over, and nothing since he'd been here. Even the neighborhood dogs were quiet.

He knelt, slipping his glove off. One trembling finger touched the screen of his phone and a blaze of light filled the corner, reflecting off of each piece of glass. Shards of mirror multiplied the brightness a hundred ... a *thousand* times over. Brighter than he expected. No time to waste. No time to savor the rush of power that came from seeing the terror-filled eyes pleading with him.

He placed his phone on the ground, hurriedly pushed some mulch up behind it so the beam of light would aim the right direction, then pulled his gloves back on, smiling when he saw the tears welling up in her eyes.

"Oh, don't cry," he whispered, wiping the wet streak from her cheek. "I can tell you from experience, crying never helps. But look," he motioned at his phone. "I fixed the light for us so you don't have to be scared of the dark like I used to be. I know bad things happen in the dark. But we have to hurry now. Mustn't keep the light on too long. Someone might see. Shall we get started?" He paused as if waiting for an answer, then nodded eagerly and leaned forward, placing his hands around her neck. "Good. I'm glad you agree. Hush, little baby. Don't say a word. Mama's going to buy you a mockingbird." His low voice was barely audible, his lips hardly moved. "And if that mockingbird don't sing, Mama's going to buy you a diamond ring." His fingers tightened.

As the pressure built, the woman's face slowly darkened … red, crimson, burgundy and finally purple. One of the tiny veins in her bulging eyes burst while he squeezed, creating a smudge of magenta that spread against the white.

Why was it taking so long?

Then he noticed the expression shining from her bulging her eyes: determination, not resignation. She was fighting death the only way she could … with her mind.

Stop fighting!

His hands constricted, pressing harder, deeper.

Her tongue pushed out through her full lips, but still she clung to life.

Sweat beaded on his forehead. *Die. Hurry up and die!*

Finally, her eyes began losing focus. He clutched harder. *C'mon … come on! Before someone sees the light.*

He ground the next line of the song out through clenched teeth, "And if that diamond ring turns brass …" He was panting again, but triumphant when he saw her pupils finally dilate. "Mama's going to buy you a looking-gla—" He broke off suddenly, flipped his phone over to douse the light. *What was that?*

It was only a whisper of sound, and it took him a minute to determine what it was—the *whir* of tires against pavement. He wouldn't have heard it at all, had his ears not been set at "high alert," tuned to pick up the slightest abnormality. Now, he could barely hear it over his pounding heart. As it got closer, he could pick up a soft melody.

"Swing low, sweet chariot comin' for to carry me home …"

With utmost care, he settled the girl's head back against the wall, making sure she wouldn't topple over before rising to his feet and peering again over the top of the wall.

A person on an old-style bicycle with fenders and a wire basket pedaled out of the shadows and into the streetlight's glow. The rider hit a rough spot in the road, causing the bike's wire basket to rattle. Though it couldn't have been loud, it sounded deafening in the still night air.

Oh! He felt his tense shoulders relax slightly when he recognized the striped Rasta cap. It was that guy he'd seen riding all over town singing and selling pineapples this morning.

Okay, he knew who it was now, but the bigger questions were *why* was he riding the streets at this time of night? And *where* was he going?

Almost as if the cyclist had heard the silent queries, he made a right turn … directly into the parking lot that lay on the other side of the wall, the same lot where his car was parked alone in the shadows underneath the trees at the farthest edge. Anxiety rippled up his spine. Oxygen seemed to freeze in his lungs. Panic thrashed for control. Had the rider seen the light from his phone? Was he coming to investigate?

His breathing came in rapid, shallow gulps as he watched the bicycle glide across the lot, nearing the gate. His gloved hands tightened into fists, his whole body tensed as if ready to spring. The closer the biker got to the gate, the slower the tires rolled, and the more his brain scrambled, without success, for a "Plan B."

Not the gate, his heart tapped out the letters, a telegrapher's dots and dashes.

Not. The. Gate.

He held his breath, willing the guy to keep going.

Don't … stop . . .

He stared, wide-eyed and intent. His eyes burned, but he dared not blink. The shadow drew nearer the gate … nearer . . .

Then passed it.

His eyes closed, and he sagged in relief. The cyclist was bumping along a short length of sidewalk, pulling to a smooth stop in the inky blackness beside a two-story block building. *Now what?*

Silence.

The air was heavy with tension, almost too thick to breathe. The blood was pounding so hard behind his eardrums it was hard to hear anything else, but still he strained to listen, staring into the gloom but seeing nothing.

There were a few unintelligible *clanks* and *thumps*, then the sound of boots clumping up wooden stairs, a jangle of keys, a door creaking, creaking again.

Another silence, this one longer than the first.

A minute crept by, one hesitant second at a time. It was only after he saw a rim of yellowish light leaking from the edges of a small window, that he was able to draw a deep breath.

He needed to leave this place. It was too dangerous to remain. He was too exposed, but his legs were suddenly too shaky to hold him up. He fell against the wall, sliding down the rough surface, sinking to his haunches, his shirt clammy against his back, his mind racing at the close call. Too close.

Had the guy seen the light? Had he?

No, he would've investigated it if he had. A light? In the middle of the night? Where no light was supposed to be? Of course, he'd check it out. Anybody would. It would be unnatural not to.

No, everything was all right. The guy was harmless. All was safe, and he'd finish what he set out to do. The song had seven verses, and the job wasn't done until he'd sung to seven women. He had four more to go, and then the grand finale. He couldn't stop until—

He broke off, listening to the distant hum of a car engine that quickly grew louder.

Someone was coming.

A burst of adrenaline gave his legs new strength. Snatching up his phone, he jumped to his feet, turned and raced into the shadowy corner of the parking lot where his car was parked. He was gone in an instant.

CHAPTER FIFTEEN

Lacey

Strands of the nightmare unraveled through the darkness, wrapping around and around my neck. My fingers tore at the binding I felt, even though it wasn't there. I bolted upright in my bed, eyes wide and staring, sobs rasping through a throat that felt raw.

It was happening again.

My eyes were open now, but the nightmare continued, on replay. I saw it again and again the way the tiny vessel burst in the young woman's eye, blood spreading out from the pinpoint, blossoming into the white—pink at first, then red.

Brilliant light flashed against blackness, shimmering and glinting off fragments of glass in every color. Prisms created rainbows. Hand-painted bits of pottery, a face, a flower, a book. Shards of mirror reflected dazzling light, but also bits of a man's face ... a bridge of a nose, an ear, an eyebrow. Picasso-like, puzzle pieces. And in the background, the now-familiar husky voice singing the lullaby.

I gasped for breath, still unable to get enough oxygen into my lungs. I struggled to a sitting position, hoping that would help. A glance at the clock told me it was 1:38. Ford had stressed the importance of noting the time, though he hadn't told me why. Instinct had me snatching up my phone from the nightstand, only to put it down again.

Who was I going to call? The police? What good would that do? I couldn't give them a location. The only thing my report would accomplish would be to let them know they'd find another body in the morning. Unless I had a place to send them the call would be for nothing. It would be better for me to try to work through the details on my own, figure something out, give them something concrete. Well, at least as concrete as dreaming a murder can be.

The flashes of light confused me. The other dreams had been dark. What did the light mean?

No! Focus, I ordered myself. *There was something that stood out. What was it?*

My mind raced through the things I knew, trying frantically to put the puzzle together. I had to make the jumbled mess make sense, but it didn't.

Or did it?

I zeroed in on one of the remembered pieces: Ernest Hemingway's *The Sun Also Rises.* I'd seen that before. Bits of colored glass pieced together to look like a book ... a mosaic of red, blue, white, gray. But where?

I gasped, then grabbed my phone again, pressing my finger to the name of the last person who'd called.

It rang twice, and just started into the third one when a low, sleepy voice answered. "'Lo?"

"It's happening again."

I heard a faint fumbling, then a groan. "What's happenin' again? Who *is* this?"

"It's Lacey," I snapped, angry at the way I was shaking inside, praying my voice wouldn't tremble. I wasn't sure whether it caused by reaction to the dream or Ford's gruff voice suddenly sounding sexy. Though I was trying to convince myself it was the former, I was afraid it was the latter. "We don't have time to play twenty questions. I just had another nightmare, but I know where this time. Maybe you can catch him."

"Tell me."

***

There'd be no more sleeping tonight, a fact I'd be sorry about later, but there was nothing I could do about it now.

I stared blankly at the phone still clutched in my hand, and replayed the shaky, abbreviated version of the dream and its location that I'd given

Ford. The whole conversation had taken a couple of minutes … at most, five. I was still on the phone with him when I heard the thunder of his feet down the outside stairs, the revving of an engine, the screech of tires on pavement, and his barked order of "Stay inside and keep your door locked," right before he hung up.

"Hurry," I urged, whispering in the dark.

CHAPTER SIXTEEN

Ford

I put in a call to Chief Craig while I raced from Lacey's beach house toward downtown. It rang so many times it went to voicemail. I ended the call and immediately redialed, impatiently counting the rings. One … two … three … four …

"What?" the gruff voice barked.

"Sorry to bother you, sir—"

"Jamison? Do you have any idea what time it is?"

"As a matter of fact, I do, sir," I replied, anger rising. Man! This guy had a Sequoia-sized chip on his shoulder. "I thought you'd want to know there's been another murder."

Silence gaped from the other end of the line. I briefly wondered if I should've made sure there *was* the body before calling Craig—but dismissed the worry. If Lacey had dreamt it, I was willing to bet it happened.

"Where?" Craig's voice sounded ragged.

"The courtyard by the art gallery. I'm almost there."

"*Almost* there? You mean you haven't seen the body yet?"

"No, Lacey just called me. She had another dream."

Craig's grunt held a lot of opinion. "Right," he finally replied.

There was another long minute of silence before I heard him mutter, "No, honey. Nothing to worry about. Go back to sleep." A lot of rustling and groaning followed. Guess it takes a lot to hoist something that size out of bed. "Gimme ten minutes. I'll locate some backup, put a call in to the coroner, and then meet you there."

I hung up just in time to wheel into the public parking lot adjacent to the art gallery's walled courtyard and cut the engine. I glanced at my watch. 2:18. Lacey said it'd been 1:38 when she'd looked at the clock after waking up, though she hadn't called me until almost two. Though, I understood why she waited, thinking about it had me grinding my teeth. Now, if my time calculation premise held true, that would make the murder happen a few minutes after two. So, it was possible the guy was still there. I scanned the area with my senses on high alert. The lot was dark and empty.

Grabbing a flashlight from the glove box, I got out of the car, unholstering my gun. The air was cool, almost syrupy with moisture from the river. It was like pushing through velvet curtains perfumed with fish and mud. I could almost taste it. I paused at the gate, listening for a moment. Wraiths of mist crept up the nearby river banks, muffling all sounds, making the silence absolute, as thick as molten tar.

He was gone. I knew it with a bizarre certainty that I couldn't explain. I'd missed him, but I also knew it hadn't been by much.

The only movement I saw was overhead, a glow from a red-eye flight, moving steadily south, probably toward Jacksonville. A solid wall of blackness loomed to the east where the storm lurked, but overhead, a billion stars stitched the black velvet banner behind it.

My gaze dropped to the buildings around the lot. No lights shone from any surrounding windows. Wouldn't stay this way long, though. Once the crime scene was taped off and law enforcement vehicles starting arriving with their flashing lights and squawking radios, there'd be no more sleep for anyone unfortunate enough to live nearby.

I dreaded what I knew I'd find on the other side of the wall, another hapless victim, wearing a necklace of bruises. I drew a deep breath, blew it out. Okay. No sense putting it off any longer. Craig would be here soon, and I couldn't afford for him to find me loitering on this side of the wall.

I reached in my pocket, retrieving a pair of latex gloves and snapping them on before flipping the gate latch. I didn't want my prints to be among those left at the crime scene. I was nearly certain we wouldn't find any of the perp's prints—he hadn't left any at either of the previous scenes—but he'd slip up eventually. Maybe it would be this time.

I scanned my flashlight across the courtyard, from left to right, wide beam illuminating everything in bright bluish glow.

Though I knew she'd be there, I still jumped when the light found her in the right corner closest to me. She had the same dark hair, long curls draping loosely over her shoulders, same pale skin. She was propped up, tucked snugly in the corner, head held erect in the wall's crease, not leaning to the left or right. Posed … just like the other two. All around her was a mosaic design plastered to the wall, colorful pieces of glass, chunks of pottery, and bits of mirror that sparked and reflected the light.

Mirrors.

"Mama's gonna buy you a lookin' glass," I whispered while frustrated anger pulsed through my body. I should've known … I *should've*. *How* I was supposed to know? Well, that was the million-dollar question, but it didn't stop the accusatory thoughts hammering away in my head, battering me with their futility.

My eyes dropped from the rainbow of glass above and around her, to the girl herself. Her dark eyes were open and staring. I could see where the blood vessel had burst in one of them, just like Lacey said. The technical term for it was scleral hemorrhage —a common sign of strangulation—as if I needed any other confirmation. The dark line of bruising circling her neck would've been enough.

I clenched my jaw, noting again the similarities between this victim and the other two. Though a little heavier, victim three could be a sister to the others. How'd this guy keep finding women who all favored each other?

Perfect Match. The name of the dating website flashed neon-bright through my mind. That was it. I knew it. I felt it in my gut. It was a flawless way for this sleezeball to scroll through photos of women, culling out all but a particular type. No one would suspect a thing. All he had to do was begin a nice, safe computer relationship with the unsuspecting girls and then woo them with pretty words. "Or make them feel sorry for him," I muttered, thinking about the *whoareyou* character common to both of the first two girls' profiles.

All this creep needed to do was get them to agree to a date with him. One date. Once he got them alone, they'd signed their own death certificate.

So why did he choose girls who looked alike? It must be important or he wouldn't bother. I mulled this thought, staring at the victim as if the answer might suddenly appear written on her forehead. The only person who knew that was the murderer.

The roar of a high-horsepower engine speeding down the road toward the gallery interrupted my thoughts. I glanced up to see headlights sweeping across the trees lining the parking lot, heard tires screech to a halt on the other side of the wall. A door slammed, followed by the urgent staccato of heels against the sidewalk, then Chief Craig burst through the gate, looking haggard and like he'd dressed hurriedly in the dark, which he probably had.

Show time.

***

Yellow crime scene tape fluttered in morning light. Thin clouds had moved in from the west, providing a canvas for a magnificent sunrise. Flaming magenta bled upward into crimson and higher into purple, the color of grape Kool-Aid. Everything the light touched glowed pink.

Apropos, I thought, musing on the sailor's warning. *Red sky in the morning* ... It certainly fit the situation. I took a gulp of truly horrible coffee and winced. No one should be required to drink coffee this bad, and I wouldn't if there was any other way I could get caffeine into my body.

The coroner had put the TOD at 2:12, which was almost exactly when I'd estimated it. I'd have to tell Lacey what I'd figured out. She needed to know, but I had to tell Chief Craig first.

A sudden commotion just outside the gate caught my attention. Obadiah Marsden ... I'd recognize that knit Rasta cap anywhere. Obie was being dragged along the sidewalk, his arm clutched in the vice-like grip of a cocky uniformed officer, who looked barely old enough to shave, let alone carry a gun.

I hurriedly stepped forward to intercept his intended route toward Chief Craig, who was huddled near the far wall with the coroner. "Here, Officer …" I glanced at his nametag, "… Hembree." I gestured toward Obie. "What's this all about?"

"I brought him in for questioning, sir," he announced proudly.

"You did, did you? And why is that?"

"Following orders, sir. Chief Craig told us to check around the neighborhood. See if anybody saw anything suspicious. This man indicated that he had, and then when I asked him what he'd seen, he started singing. Like he thinks it's a joke. I had to bring him in, sir."

"Ah … I see. You new around here, Hembree?"

"Yessir!" He stood a little taller, chest swelled with pride. "It's only my second day, sir."

Clearly, he thought he was about to earn a commendation. *Mmm, sorry to disappoint you, Baby-face.* "Officer, is this man in custody?"

"Uh … no, sir." His expression changed at my tone. He licked his lips and swallowed. Nervous eyes flickered toward Craig.

I stepped between him and the chief, blocking his line of sight, causing him to deflate a bit. Baby-face Hembree suddenly wasn't so cocky. "Well, you want to tell me why you're treating him like he is, then?"

"Sir?" He swallowed again, sending his Adam's apple bobbing up and down like a fishing float.

I fixed him with a stern look. "Let go of this man's arm, Hembree."

"But …" He stretched his neck to the left, trying to see around me again.

"Or," I continued, shifting a little in order to keep blocking him. "Maybe you don't want to advance in your chosen profession. I could always write up a report, detailin' how you directly disobeyed an SBI detective, and how you harassed a town citizen who *can't* talk, officer, not *won't*. He can sing, but he can't talk. I'm sure that would look real good in your file."

If Obie's arm had suddenly turned into a live coal, the young officer couldn't have dropped it any faster. He scurried away like a whipped puppy, proverbial tail tucked between his legs. Obie stood there, rubbing circulation back into his arm, beaming at me. I only hoped he didn't start singing his thanks.

Before I could open my mouth, I sensed a presence behind me and knew, without turning, it was Craig. I barely kept from groaning. I wasn't up to anymore verbal sparring with this man.

"What did you say to my officer, Jamison?" He lifted his chin toward the figure rapidly disappearing down the street. "And what's Marsden doing at a crime scene?"

"Evidently, no one bothered to tell 'your officer' about Obie. He was followin' your orders, questionin' nearby neighbors, and when Obie was asked if he'd seen anything unusual tonight, he must've nodded that he had, then started tellin' what he'd seen the only way he can."

Craig's shoulders slumped. "By singing?"

I nodded. "By singin'."

He sighed and turned to Obie. "Okay, Marsden. What'd you see?"

Obie glanced at me first, as if for my permission. I could feel Craig bristle. The air around him seemed to super-heat, nearly turning to steam. "A liiight," Obie's baritone voice rang out in the morning air. "A liiight in the gaaar-den where no light is s'posed to beeee."

My eyes met Craig's suddenly alert ones. "A light, Obie?" I asked. "You saw a light in here?"

He nodded enthusiastically.

"Did you see anybody?" Craig barked.

He shook his head, smile fading.

The chief took a step closer, threatening Obie's personal space, practically nose to nose with him. "Let me get this straight, Marsden. You saw a light ... *here* ... in the middle of the night, and you didn't think you might ought to check it out? With all that's been going on in this town? For God's sake, we got girls being murdered right under our noses, and you didn't think you ought to investigate?" His voice grew a bit louder with each word. "Are you out of your ever-loving mind? What is *wrong* with you?" He roared the last sentence.

Obie cowered in the face of Craig's rage, looking like he'd like to be anywhere but here. "It was there, then it wasn't," he sang very quietly. "A flick of light, then it was gone. Did I reeeally see it, or was it my imagin-aaa-shun?"

Craig shook his head in disgust, turned and stalked away.

I patted Obie on the back. "It's okay, man. You didn't do anything wrong. But if you happen to see anything else that looks suspicious, call me." I fished a business card from my pocket and handed it to him. "Or …" I added, picturing that scenario. "… maybe you ought to text me, instead."

Obie nodded, and he stared sad-eyed at the mosaicked corner where the latest victim had been found. "Did this one look like Lay-ceee too?" he asked in a tune so soft I could barely hear him.

I glanced at him sharply. *What?* I felt like I'd been tased. Of course! That's why they all looked the same. *They looked like Lacey.* How had I missed that? The realization was like a hammer banging nails into a coffin. I didn't want to think, "Whose?" If I believed in coincidence at all, that's what I'd be trying to convince myself it was. But I'd been at this job long enough to know there was no such thing as coincidence. If it looked like a duck, waddled and swam like a duck, quacked like a duck—it was a duck. Judging by the evidence at hand, there was a real possibility that someone was targeting Lacey-lookalikes. The conclusion that Lacey was in danger wasn't a stretch. I gave him a grim nod.

Without another word, Obie turned and walked back through the gate. I paused a minute before following him. Someone needed to let Craig know this newest development, and I guessed that "someone" was me.

CHAPTER SEVENTEEN

Lacey

The change was both gradual and sudden. One minute I sat staring at shadowy representations of bed, nightstand, chair, and dresser, dark blobs of varying sizes that blended with the surrounding darkness while wondering, for the millionth time of my sleepless night, why I hadn't heard back from Ford yet. Then I blinked, and pink light the color of strawberry sorbet tinted the room, defining and bringing each item into focus.

I drew a deep breath, the first one in hours, it seemed. The action broke the sort of hypnotic trance I'd been in since I'd made the desperate call to Ford. I tried to move and groaned. My muscles had seized up from not moving for so long and now had all the elasticity of iron. A sudden bump in the hallway halted me, mid-stretch, and I listened so hard, I thought my ears might explode. Time seemed measured by the rhythmic pounding of both surf and my heart rate, the latter of which had ratcheted up several notches.

It was only a couple of seconds, but felt more like an hour before I recognized the familiar *slap-slap* of flip-flops against the floor and relaxed. It was just Bonnie heading to the kitchen to start coffee and her day before Mom woke up. I sighed, then threw the covers back. It was time for me to get up, too. Travis would be here soon to sign the lease papers and get his key to the other apartment.

Heading to my bathroom, I continued my attempt to fit the remembered reflected bits of the killer's face into some kind of a lucid whole. But the results, so far, were nothing but a puzzle with most of the key pieces missing. Not even Picasso-worthy. Maybe, if I'd had Granddad's artistic skill, I could've transferred those flashes of memory to paper and possibly come up with a composite sketch to aid the police with their investigation, but unfortunately, I'd inherited even less of his talent than my dad had. That is to say, none at all.

Flicking on the light produced another groan the instant I saw myself in the mirror. Shadows draped under my eyes like funeral swags, tattling loud and clear about my lack of sleep. I made a face as I smoothed on moisturizer, then reached for the tube of concealer. Better take care of the dark circles *before* breakfast this time. I didn't think I was up to any of Bonnie's wisecracks about "raccoon eyes" this morning.

Once I'd hidden the damage as best I could, I headed to the kitchen. If I was going to be able to get through this day, I needed coffee, and I needed it *now*. The way I was feeling at the moment, I should've been wearing the T-shirt I saw recently: *I hate morning people, and mornings, and people.* Usually, that wasn't the case, but after a night like last night …

Bonnie already had her cup and was bent over the notebook that held her daily plan for my mother, busily scratching away. She made it a point to keep copious notes on Mom's progress, or decline. Mostly decline. "Mornin'," I grunted as I poured my own cup of coffee.

"Good morn—" she broke off when she glanced up from her notebook.

Uh-oh. Here we go. Guess I didn't do as good a job with the concealer as I thought. I cocked my eyebrow and gave her my best don't-mess-with-me look over the rim of my mug. Her lips pressed into a straight line, as if trapping whatever it was she wanted to say behind them, then she turned her attention back to her notes.

Wise move, I thought wryly. I was surprised, though. Bonnie was notorious, not only for her excellent care of my mother, but also for her outspokenness. She rarely kept her opinions to herself. If she *thought* it, I'd *hear* it.

I studied the top of her silver-dusted head, wondering if I should say something, but before I could think of anything clever enough, she said, without looking up at me, "Worry often gives a small thing a big shadow."

I knew she wouldn't be able to stand it. "Been reading your fortune cookie collection again?" I quipped, rolling my eyes, and turning to snatch a bowl from the cupboard. I shook in some cereal before pouring on milk and grabbing a spoon from the drawer. Leaning against the counter, bowl in hand, I shoveled in a mouthful, frowning at her while I crunched. "For your information," I continued once I'd swallowed, "it's not a small thing. It's large and there are quite a lot of them. So yes, if I lump them all together, they cast a pretty big shadow."

"It's a Swedish proverb, not a fortune," she answered, then gestured to a chair across the table from her. "You want to talk about it before your mother comes in?"

"No. I don't have time. I need to finish getting ready. I have another renter coming by this morning. He wants the other apartment."

Bonnie's mahogany face gleamed like freshly polished wood. "Both of them rented? During the off-season? That's great!" She studied me a minute, then added, "Isn't it?"

I took another bite of cereal, chewed a while, swallowed, then sighed. "It's complicated. Lines up with everything else in my life right now." I scraped up another bite of cereal and muttered, "As if having a mother with Alzheimer's isn't complicated enough."

Bonnie sent me a sympathetic look. "Speaking of your mother …"

My shoulders sagged in despair. "Uh-oh. What now?"

"Well, we need to get a new lampshade in her room. She's succeeded in destroying the old one."

"Destroying it? How in the world did she destroy it?" I studied her expression, then added, "Do I even want to know?"

"She's reached the 'picking' stage."

"There's a picking stage?"

She nodded. "It's a normal progression. All Alzheimer's patients exhibit some level of it. But just because it's 'normal,' doesn't mean it's not aggravating."

"But what is it?"

"They get fixated on something: a spot, a place where the paint might be chipped, maybe a label on a bottle. You noticed her picking and peeling the label off the salad dressing the other day, right?"

I nodded.

"Well, it can be 'bout anything, really. Then they pick and pick and pick at it some more, until either they lose interest in it or they destroy it. Far as I can tell, the lampshade had a spot or something on it, and it attracted her attention. That's all it took. She kept at it until the plastic shade was in pieces. I kept finding little shards of plastic in the floor, but I couldn't figure out where they were coming from … until the damage was done, that is. Now one side of the shade is practically touching the light bulb. I'm afraid it's a fire hazard. I unplugged the lamp so she wouldn't try to turn it on."

"Great." I looked at my bowl of cereal, and made a face. It suddenly lost all appeal. I turned and dumped it down the garbage disposal, then resumed my position, leaning against the counter, this time with my arms crossed, as if protecting myself from another blow. "I'll try to get by a store and buy another one today."

"Look on the bright side."

I stared at her, gimlet-eyed. "Are you trying to make a pun?" At her questioning look, I elaborated. "Lamp? Bright side?"

"Nope," she chuckled. "Not this time, though I need to remember that one."

I scoffed. Now I'd given her ammunition. "Okay … what's the bright side?"

Bonnie nodded. "At least it's not her skin she's picking at. They can do that, you know."

"Okay," I replied with difficulty, trying to erase the mental picture her words evoked. "Thankful for that."

She rose from the table and patted my arm with a gentle smile. "You're doing fine. This is hard, but you're doing fine. You go finish getting ready. I'll get her up and dressed."

I blinked away a sting of tears and sent her a wobbly smile. "Thanks, Bonnie."

***

I had just enough time to get dressed and try to tame my hair when there was a knock at the door.

Ford?

My heart jumped to my throat at the thought. I'd been halfway expecting some sort of update from him, something to let me know if he'd somehow gotten there in time, but he hadn't called. Maybe he wanted to tell me in person instead of on the phone. That would work even better. I needed to apologize for how I'd treated him yesterday morning. Making him fill out the rental papers outside on the porch was a tacky thing to do, even though my reason had been valid. I hadn't wanted Mom to see him, or vice versa. I knew he thought I was crazy. I didn't need Mom to do or say something that would give him more reasons to think so.

I hurried to the door and peered through the peephole.

Travis.

My shoulders sagged and for some unexplained reason, I felt sort of deflated—like a balloon with a pinhole in it—which was stupid. I was about to rent the second apartment. I should be happy. I wouldn't have to worry about finances for a while. The reminder didn't seem to help, but I didn't have time to analyze why that might be. I pasted on a smile and opened the door.

"Good morning and come in," I greeted him. "I have the papers all ready. You can fill them out in here."

***

"Okay," I said later, when we were standing in front of the closed front door. "I have your check and everything here seems to be in order." I flipped through the papers to make sure all the blanks were filled in. "Here's the key and the Wi-Fi code." I dropped the key into his outstretched palm, but the slip of paper with the code fluttered to the floor. We both bent to retrieve it at the same time.

Thunk! Our heads collided, sounding solid, but hollow, like two melons. He grunted on impact, wincing and rubbing his head a little. My reaction was a bit more dramatic.

"Yeow!" I cried, hand going immediately to my throbbing skull where a goose egg was already forming. Stars danced and twirled behind my eyes and I staggered a step sideways, peering at him through slits. "Oh, my gosh! Are you alright?"

He waved off my concern and grinned. "It's fine. I guess I must have a harder head than you."

"Hmph," I snorted, still rubbing my head. "If my dad were still alive, he'd argue that point. Here ..." I bent over and gingerly picked up the slip of paper, careful to place it, with precision, in the middle of his palm, then reached for the doorknob, laughing. "Don't want a repeat performance of that fiasco."

"I should say not!" he said, chuckling.

I swung the door open and nearly jumped out of my skin, laughter dying in my throat. Ford stood like a statue, with his hand raised, ready to knock. My stomach did a funny little swoop at the sight of him. But then his eyes narrowed, bounced from my face to Travis' and back again, turning stony when he spied the folded lease agreement, and the apartment key dangling form Travis' fingers. The metal tag with "#2" stamped on it glowed with the pale grayness of a worn-out dime, drawing attention to itself.

One of his eyebrows lifted in a censorious manner and the swooping feeling in my stomach disappeared. I pressed my lips into an angry line. Though he hadn't said a word, I heard the question loud and clear: why did Travis get to fill out his papers inside while he'd been relegated to the porch? His attitude infuriated me. The fact that I'd intended to apologize for that very thing evaporated in a puff of steam.

"Ford! Perfect timing," I chimed out over-loud. "I'd like you to meet your new neighbor, Travis Sterling. He just rented the other apartment. Travis, this is Ford Jamison."

If anything, Ford's eyes only turned harder, but Travis' weren't looking too friendly either. They practically glared at each other, each sizing the other up like male wolves trying to determine who would be Alpha and who was going to have to die.

My eyes rolled heavenward. What was next? Marking territory? I *so* did not need this right now. *My kingdom for a water pistol!* I inwardly groaned. If one happened to magically appear in my hand, I'd let them both have it ... right between each pair of baleful eyes. The stare-down continued, and I was considering the idea of running downstairs and grabbing the water hose, when Mom's bedroom door opened and she shuffled down the hall toward us, with Bonnie right behind her. She stopped abruptly when she reached the vestibule and saw us.

Great. It just kept getting better. Oh, well, at least her appearance called a halt to their silent feud.

A second or two passed, then she beamed ... yes, *beamed*, "Haven't seen you in a while, Ford."

"Been 'bout five years, ma'am." He smiled, stepping forward to take the hand she held out to him.

My mouth dropped open and I stared in amazement. What? She remembers *Ford*? Had she ever even *met* him? She can recall the name of someone who's practically a stranger, but can't remember my name half the time? This disease was the most frustrating thing I've ever had to deal with. And another thing, why could she hear him? I have to repeat everything—almost screech like a banshee—and he hadn't even raised his voice! If I didn't know better, I say she had selective hearing. Before I could gather my senses, she turned to Travis. "Been even longer since you've been around, David."

David? Uh-oh. She had him confused with her nephew. "No, Mom," I corrected loudly. "Not Aunt Danni's son. This is Travis. Travis Sterling? He just rented one of the apartments upstairs." I sent him an apologetic smile. "This is my mother, Eve Campbell."

Mom frowned at me, storm cloud building on her face. I tensed, waiting for the lightning strike.

"Nice to meet you, Mrs. Campbell," Travis jumped in before she got started, then turned to me. "Lacey, I hate to sign-lease-and-run, but I need to go. I have an appointment I can't be late for. I'm a neighborly kind of guy, so I'm sure I'll be seeing a lot of you." He shot Ford a cold look, and dipped his head ever so slightly. A silent farewell ... and a challenge.

Ford served the gesture right back at him, and I fought the urge to roll my eyes again. *Boys!*

"'Til next time, David," Mom called after him sweetly.

He'd already turned and I saw his back sort of stiffen. He tossed a smile over his shoulder, which seemed a bit fake. "Bye, now."

Ford stared after him, wearing a brooding expression, looking as tired as I felt.

A minute crept by, one slow second at a time, and still he stared, watching Travis' SUV speed down the driveway, chirp out onto the hard-top, and roar away. I cleared my throat. "Um ..."

That broke the spell.

"I'm beat," he said with a grimace. "I'll catch you up on everything later. I can't think straight now."

"But what about—"

"I'll call you later."

His tone of voice let me know there was no sense arguing. He gave me a final, inscrutable look before turning toward the staircase leading up to his apartment.

CHAPTER EIGHTEEN

Ford

I punched my pillow so hard in my effort to make it comfortable, some of the stuffing puffed up into the air, tiny feathers floating and twirling in an unseen current. I blew them away from my face. I was still fuming. Angry blood pumped furiously in my veins, which is why the pillow kept turning hot and clammy against my neck. I needed a couple of hours of shut-eye in order to function the rest of the day, but my brain wouldn't stop replaying what had just happened downstairs.

I'd arrived home, prepared to wheel into my designated spot as usual, but had to hit the brakes to keep from rear-ending a luxurious Audi Q7 parked in my spot, its midnight blue paint spotless. I'd sat and fumed, engine idling, debating on whether or not to return the favor by parking behind him, blocking the bozo in, or just pulling into the other space and be done with it. With a growl, I'd whipped into the apartment-two spot and yanked my car into park. I'd glared at the other vehicle, muttering uncomplimentary things about its driver, then stomped up the stairs, right up to Lacey's front door.

I'd had my hand raised to knock when the door swung open, revealing a suave, GQ type guy sporting a spray-on tan, and a Miami Vice scruff-of-a-beard that was probably always the same length. He was wearing a pricey golf ensemble—something you'd see in an ad for a country club in one of those high-end magazines—down to the pristine-white sweater knotted at his neck. Ooh-la-la. Very Ralph Lauren-ish. But even worse than all that? They were laughing together ... *laughing*. I don't know why that bothered me so much, but it did.

As much as it startled me to see them, I think it startled Lacey worse to see me. She jumped visibly, then stood there, looking guiltier and guiltier by the minute. It went downhill from there.

The level of comfortableness between them seemed a little too cozy in my book. It didn't take a rocket scientist to know they'd spent time together before this morning. Thinking about what *that* could mean had me punching my pillow again.

I tossed over onto my side. Okay, maybe it was my imagination. Maybe it was just that she was glad for another renter. There'd been no sign of her dad. Only two cars in their garage—I hadn't seen more than two since being there—a Prius that seemed to always be here, and Lacey's. Mr. Campbell would be retired by now and should've been home this early in the morning. Maybe he'd died sometime during the five years I'd been away.

If he'd died, that meant all the financial responsibility was on Lacey's shoulders. Mrs. Campbell had been a teacher at the elementary school for as long as I could remember, which would give her a decent retirement income, but the cost of owning beachfront property was enormously high. Lacey would need all the money she could get to keep up with it. I was glad she had another renter, but I was suddenly even *gladder* that I'd be living right next to him. Better to keep an eye on him. Though why it mattered so much was beyond me

What if it was more than just needing extra cash flow? Was she interested in this guy? Maybe, but what could she possibly see in him? Okay, yeah, I guess he could be considered handsome if you liked the fake, pretentious look, but Lacey didn't seem like the type who'd go for that kind of thing. No, she seemed more down-to-earth … a genuine kind of girl who would be more inclined to go for a genuine kind of guy, someone who'd protect her, keep her safe.

"You mean someone like you, Jamison?" I asked aloud in a mocking tone, then ran an exasperated hand through my hair. "When did she go from being a grade-A looney-tune to … to … whatever this is?"

Okay, time to think about something else. My brain issued the order and I tried to obey.

My thoughts lit on her mother. Eve Campbell was just as beautiful as I remembered her: graying auburn hair and brown eyes exactly like her daughter's. If Lacey ever wanted to know what she would look like when she got older, all she needed to do was look at her mother.

But there was something different about Mrs. Campbell. I couldn't put my finger on it, but it was there. She'd shuffled down the hall. That was different for sure. The Mrs. Campbell I remembered had always walked kind of fast ... like she had lots to do and needed to be doing it already. And who the heck was that black woman who'd followed her out of her bedroom? What was *that* about?

She'd greeted that jerk as David, too. Seemed sure of it. I narrowed my eyes at the memory of the way the man's shoulders had tensed, the way his eyes had hardened. It was obvious that it bothered him ... a lot. But some people were like that. They didn't like it when people got them mixed up with someone else. And Travis seemed to suffer with a "Great-and-Mighty Oz" complex, so such a faux pas would probably get under his skin.

"Gasp!" I widened my eyes theatrically. "Forsooth and verily! Someone hath confused my superior personage with that of someone of lesser standing!" The back of my hand went to my forehead in despair. "Alas ... the horror of it all!"

I scoffed and flipped over onto my back with a sigh. It was no use. Sleep wasn't going to happen. It was overrated, anyway. Might as well get some work done.

I got up and headed to kitchen. If I was going to be awake, I was going to need coffee and lots of it.

***

Settling myself at the kitchen table with a big mug of strong coffee, I picked up my phone and called Myron, the FBPD's computer geek. I had an idea that might get me the identity of victim three sooner rather than later. Sooner was better.

"*Yell*-ow," a loud, over-the-top-cheerful voice sang out from the other end.

I held the phone away from my ear and made a face at the ridiculous greeting. Why did people do that? It made me want to retort, "Purple!" Or, "Orange!" I shook my head in disgust.

"Myron, please?"

"You got him."

Professional. I rolled my eyes, then shrugged. Guess computer geniuses don't have to bother with things like proper phone etiquette. "Ford Jamison ... SBI, here. I have an idea that might get us the name of victim three a little quicker. Since none of them have had ID on them, I know we've had to use facial recognition software, and then dental records if that didn't work. It can take a while. I thought we might be able to hurry this up a little."

"I'm listening."

"So what if we could narrow the search parameters? Use a smaller database. It wouldn't take as long, right?"

"Riii-ght?"

"Bear with me. First two victims had Perfect Match profiles. What if we do a search on that website, using physical traits? We could type in say ... 'long, dark curly hair,' enter a desired weight and age and then search a specific part of the country; in our case it would be northeast Florida to maybe even include southeast Georgia, since we're so close to the state line. Once we got results from that search, we could run it through our facial recognition software using one of the crime scene photos of victim three for comparison. A lot less data for it to weed through. You think that would work?"

"It would, but it'd just give us her username. I'm working on that part of their security, and hope I can get in to the real names soon, but until then, I think you might have something." Myron's voice sounded excited and I could hear the tappity-tap of computer keys in the background. "You want me to create an account, or have you already done that?"

"I've got one," I responded, quickly giving him the particulars.

"Okay, I'm in," he said seconds later. "It'll take a few minutes, but I'll shoot you what I find as soon as I have something. Oh, and ... *killer* idea, man."

I hung up, smiling. I'd just impressed a computer nerd.

***

Fifteen minutes later, my phone dinged, letting me know I had a new text message. It read: Got her. No name yet. User name – dyin2meetu.

I quickly logged back into my account, then typed her screen name into the search box.

There she was. She wore a contagious smile and her eyes sparkled from the photo ... the epitome of life. So different from the girl I'd found this morning. I scanned through her profile. Ah ... a beautician, and with a sense of humor, too. User name *dyin* ... as in a "dye job." Something a beautician would do.

Oh no! I groaned, as I read further. She had two kids ... two kids who were now without their mom. How old were they? And who had them now? A grandmother, perhaps? Their dad? A sitter? Or were they by themselves? I grimaced at that thought. It happened. More often than I liked to think. Single mom has a date, but can't find or can't afford a sitter, so she leaves the kids alone with a stack of DVDs to babysit them. In this case, she never came home.

I leaned back, thoughts churning. Knowing there were children involved threw everything into urgent mode. We needed to find this woman's real name ... *now.*

CHAPTER NINETEEN

Lacey

I backed into my usual spot at Jeb's place and was reaching for my purse, ready to run in and place my daily order, when I glanced through my windshield and froze.

Raine was just exiting the shop. *What was she doing there?*

Even though she was wearing a floppy hat and large sunglasses, I knew it was her. She had her own set of trademarks—that is to say, significant parts of Raine exited a building before the rest of her did, and she was very proud of those parts.

'Nuff said.

With the hat and glasses, and being all "incognito," she was acting worse than I did when I came here. But then again, this was Raine we were talking about, so it could just be a case of Drama Queen-itis. I watched from the safety of my car, scrunched down so low I was peeking between the steering wheel and the top of the dashboard. For some reason I was suddenly very glad I'd parked where I had. Glad she couldn't see me. She kept scanning the lot like she'd been recruited for a surveillance team, scoping it out, glancing repeatedly over both shoulders in search of who-knew-what. What was that about? Hurrying to her car, she slipped inside and was gone in a flash, leaving a spurt of oyster shell dust that hung, suspended in a cloud, slowly dissipating in the still morning air.

I puzzled over what I'd seen, curiosity gnawing at me like a hamster on a carrot. Of course, it was possible she might need some small amount of seafood for a brunch she was planning, not so likely for a tea party. Those festivities generally required sweet, not savory treats. But why the cloak-and-dagger act? Hmm . . .

It made me nervous to realize she knew about Jeb's. Not that his was an underground business or anything. It's just that I considered him, and the seafood he got for me, sort of a secret weapon ... my ace in the hole, so to speak. The fact that he was on her radar made me uneasy.

The tiniest fear started niggling around in my head the second I'd seen her sneaking out Jeb's door. I prayed it was nothing, but I had to find out, and there was only one way to do that.

I got out of my car and hurried across the lot to the front door.

No one was behind the counter, which wasn't a surprise. That was rarely where I found him. I strode around to the door that led to the back, calling out, "Yoo hoo! Jeb? You here?"

"Yeah, c'mon back," his gruff voice hollered.

I pushed through the door, searching for his familiar bushy head.

He was leaned over doing some kind of adjustment on the lobster aquarium's air pump. I knew you had to keep the water oxygenated so live lobsters would stay that way, so it was vital he kept it in good working order.

"Did I catch you at a bad time?" I asked.

"Nah. Just trying to get this clog out of the air-line. Not enough output." He wiped his hands on his jeans, leaving damp marks. "What you need today?"

"Here," I said, handing him a list. "I noticed you've been a little ... well, not yourself the past couple of days. I thought a list might make it easier for you."

His dark eyes met mine for the briefest second, making me think of the "limo windows" comparison, again. Then he scanned down the list, grunted, and got to work.

"What do you think about the storm that's been all over the news?" I asked, changing the subject, trying to make small talk. Conversations with Jeb were always one-sided. I knew it was all up to me unless I wanted to wait in total silence. "I heard they've finally given her a name. No pretending and calling it an "Atlantic disturbance" anymore. I don't know what was the big deal, why they didn't want to call it a hurricane. Everybody knew that's what it was—all you had to do was look at the shape of the storm on the radar—they just wouldn't admit it. Maybe it's that an April hurricane is so unheard of, it scared them."

I leaned against one of his worktables in order to watch Jeb fill my order. His sinewy arms were almost completely covered with tattoos. Scary ones … skulls and crossbones, mostly, but there was also a preponderance of scorpions, spiders, and various other things one might see in a horror flick or a nightmare. He removed lids from the storage boxes to see what was inside, then replaced them, moving them either to the side or to my stack. He seems content with me carrying on our "conversation," so I kept going.

"They named her Audrey. Can you believe she's already a Category Two? Ever heard of an April hurricane?" I asked, not expecting an answer.

"No hurricanes. Been a couple of tropical storms, though."

What? A response? I was struck speechless for a minute. "Well," I began again, after recovering. "Let's hope we're not starting a new trend."

No reply this time. Back to normal. I bit my lip, wondering if now was a good time to ask about my niggling fear. As good a time as any, I guessed.

Okay … here goes. "Can I ask you something?" I tried to keep my tone casual and nonchalant.

I took his silence as an affirmative and barreled on. "Remember the thing with Raine pitching a fit over there not being any calamari in the entrée she'd ordered?"

He still didn't say anything, but I saw his shoulders tense and my heart sank. My niggling fear might be a reality after all. "You … uh … mmm … you didn't happen to say anything to Raine about me not having calamari for that dish sometime during that day, did you?"

My question made him pause—right in the middle of lifting a cooler. He looked like a statue with his arms suspended, mid-air. It was for only a couple of seconds, then he continued with what he was doing: locating and stacking the last of the coolers full of product I needed for the night's menu. I didn't press him, just waited until he was done.

He finally turned and faced me. His dark eyes were wary, with maybe a flicker of shame behind the smoked glass. "It's my fault you got in trouble. I know that. The part I'm not clear on is, *how*. I know you told me you'd made that Fruity Mare dish without calamari many times and that it would be fine, no one would know. What I don't know is, how did she wrangle that piece of information out of me and into a conversation? You know how I am. Not much for chit-chat, so how'd it happen?"

Finding out my fear was a reality was one thing, but it was his sudden burst of words that had me struggling to think of a response. I'd never heard him string that many words together in my life. "I was wondering that myself," I finally said, then I shrugged. "She's sneaky. Simple as that. You have to watch out for her. Anything you say can, and will, be used against you."

He shook his head as if disgusted with himself and muttered, "Think I'll stick with keeping my mouth shut. Conversating is overrated."

"You coined a new word," I giggled. "I like it. And as for the talking part ... I don't think fish are big conversators either, so you're fine."

He gave me a genuine grin and I knew we were back to normal.

He handed me my list. "That's the lot of it. Nothing missing this time. I'll get it delivered by noon. Lobsters included."

"Thanks, Jeb. You're the best. See you tomorrow." I turned to leave, then smacked my forehead and swung back around. "Almost forgot ... I saw Raine leaving just as I pulled in. What was she doing here?"

He shrugged. "Needs some stuff for a big party next weekend." His expression turned quizzical. "How come you didn't tell me?"

Now it was my turn to look quizzical. "Tell you what?"

"That she's buying your restaurant."

It took about a minute for his words to register, but when they did, all the blood left my head, and was replaced by a loud roar. If I hadn't been standing in the doorway, with its sturdy frame to clutch on either side of me, I would've dropped like a stone. In two long strides, Jeb was at my side, helping me wobble over to perch on a lobster pot. I bent over at the waist, trying to get blood flowing back into my head. He grabbed a bottle of water he had nearby and sloshed it over the not-too-clean bandana he'd snatched from his pocket, pressing the cool, damp cloth to the back of my neck, then my forehead, then my neck again. The bandana smelled fishy.

Sheesh! The other day it was Liv, now Jeb. I needed to get a grip.

I finally sat up and stared at him. All the horror I felt at his announcement was there for him to see.

"Guessing you didn't know."

"No," I gasped, feeling like someone had poleaxed me. "I didn't. I heard a rumor a few days ago, but I blew it off as just that ... a *rumor*." I seized his arm in a death grip, my fingernails digging into one of the tatted skulls. "Could she be lying?"

He looked doubtful. "I don't know ... she ordered a bunch of shrimp."

"Oh, God!" I groaned. "What am I going to do? I can't work for her. I *can't*. She'll make my life a living hell. The calamari fiasco will be a walk in the park compared to what she'll do."

Poor Jeb wore a miserable deer-in-the-headlights look, clearly out of his element. He didn't know what to do with a woman in the throes of a meltdown.

I jumped to my feet so abruptly, the lobster pot on which I sat crashed over. I stared at it in confusion, not comprehending why it was lying on its side or what I should do to fix it. "I need to talk to Liv ... *now!*" I shoved his bandana into his hand. "Thanks for your help. I have to go. I'll see you tomorrow."

I wheeled away, staggering through the door, then across the lot to my car. Somehow the key went into the ignition, though my hands shook so badly it took three tries. The engine roared to life and I fishtailed out of the lot, screeching back toward town. Just before I rounded the curve, I glanced in my rear-view mirror and caught a glimpse of Jeb standing in the doorway of his shop. I couldn't see his face, but was sure he looked worried.

***

I wouldn't be able to park in my usual spot. They'd have the gallery lot and surrounding streets cordoned off. Choosing the next closest place to both Par-a-dux and the restaurant, I found a spot in the waterfront lot, locked my car, and practically ran the block to Liv's shop, making sure to avert my eyes when I passed the David Yulee statue. I couldn't think about the murders right now.

Since nothing but the coffee shops were open yet, there weren't too many early birds out and about town. My audience wasn't a large one. The few brave souls who were venturing down this street crossed carefully to the other side, giving me—the crazy woman—a wide berth.

Oh, no! The door was locked. Panicked eyes went to my watch. She wasn't open yet! I rattled the knob, attracting the attention of a jogger who goggled at me. I ignored him. Pounding on the glass, I pressed my nose against the window, shielding my eyes so I could see into the darkened interior.

"Please be here," I whispered, still pounding, but starting to freak out. "Please, please, please!"

Movement! She was here!

The frown of annoyance she wore when she pushed aside the curtain from the back room turned into a mask of concern the instant she saw it was me. I wondered what I looked like. Must be bad if it painted *that* much worry on her face.

She turned the deadbolt and opened the door, then dragged me inside, wrapping her arms around me. "You've heard?"

"What?"

"The new murder."

"Of course I've heard. I saw it happen!"

"How'd you—" Liv drew back and blinked at me. "You had another dream." She pulled me close again, patting me soothingly on the back. "You poor dear. I can't imagine how awful that must be."

I pushed away from her, shaking my head. "That's not why I came. I found out something even worse than that."

Liv's eyes widened in horror. "Worse than murder?"

I scoffed, waving my hands impatiently on either side of my head. "No, that's not what I meant. It's not worse than a murder, but at the same time, it almost is."

"You're not making any sense," she answered, wearing a perplexed expression. "Let's go to my office. I'll make us some chamomile. You need something to calm you down."

It's going to take more than chamomile, I thought grimly, but I allowed her to pull me through the curtain and into the back room that served as her office, as well as storage.

Shelves lined three walls of the narrow room, each one stuffed to capacity with haphazardly stacked cardboard boxes full of stock items, seasonal decorations, office supplies, and a multitude of other things, creating a veritable horseshoe of stuff. Her desk squatted against the fourth wall with stacks of papers covering almost the entire surface. On one corner sat a scented candle, its flame releasing some flowery scent into the air. The other corner was home to her electric teapot.

As soon as she sat me down, she hurried to fill the pot with water from the bathroom sink. Returning, she set it on its base and flipped the switch. Once this was done, she grabbed two mugs, unwrapped a teabag for each cup, and dropped them inside. I watched her movements as from a distance. It was like watching a ballet from the last row of the balcony. The fact that she was wearing a tutu just added to this illusion.

"When I went to the gym this morning," Liv said, as she finished her tea preparations, "I saw some idiot put a bottle of water in the Pringles holder on the treadmill. Can you believe that?"

I smiled in spite of myself. She beamed when she saw my smile, and continued. "And he got all huffy when I tried to explain its correct use."

I chuckled and helplessly shook my head.

"You know ..."—her blue eyes sparkled—"some days you just have to put on the hat and remind them who they're dealing with."

"Liv ..." By now I was laughing out loud. "You're wearing a halo. How threatening can you be?"

She shrugged, grinned and then shoved a hot mug into my hands. "Drink."

I took a sip and sighed, closed my eyes, breathed in the sweet steam. When I opened them, I met her concerned blue gaze. "Better?" she asked.

I nodded and took another sip, cupping my icy hands around the mug.

We sipped in companionable silence until I swallowed the last drop of mine. "Okay," she leaned forward, removing the mug from my hands and setting it, along with hers, on her desk. She fixed me with a take-no-prisoners kind of stare and ordered, "Start talking."

It was as if a dam broke. Everything gushed out. I told her about my dream, about calling Ford, and the sleepless night that followed. I told her about Travis coming by to sign the rental agreement and how Ford had showed up, how they'd practically circled each other like rabid dogs. Then I told her about stopping at Jeb's, how he'd admitted he'd been the one to rat me out about the calamari, how he hadn't meant to tell Raine.

With every word that passed my lips, I felt a little less heavy, as if the sentences were made of stone. The more I spoke, the more of the burden she carried. It was a good thing, too ... With all that was piled on my shoulders, I was started to feel a little like a crepe, which everyone knows is *flatter* than a pancake.

"Okay," Liv said. "Just so you know, so far, there hasn't been anything remotely close to being as bad a murder."

"I'm not finished yet." I drew a deep breath, let it out, then swallowed hard. "I found out Raine is planning a huge party. She's invited everybody who's anybody on the island ... all the big dogs." I paused, trying to fortify myself. "At this party, she'll be announcing that Black Pearl Bistro will soon be under new management."

Liv's blue eyes lit up like twin light bulbs. "No more Pearl? But that's great! What are you upset about? I should think you'd be throwing your own party."

I just stared at her wondering if she'd figure it out or if I'd have to explain it. I was pretty sure the wheels were moving ... slowly, but at least they were moving.

Liv's expression turned quizzical. "But why would Raine throw a party to announce new management at the restaurant?"

She was getting there. I started a mental countdown.

Five ... four ... three ... two ...

I paused to assess her progress. Nope, not yet.

... one and three quarters, one and a half ... one!

"Oh, my goodness!" Liv gasped.

Bingo! It was somewhat gratifying that Liv looked nearly as horrified as I felt.

"Raine is buying the Black Pearl?"

I nodded. "That's what she told Jeb."

"Could she be lying?"

"That's exactly what I asked him," I said, "But I'll tell you just what he told me: would she place that large of an order if it wasn't really happening? Raine might be a lot of things—many of them are words my mama would wash my mouth for if she didn't have Alzheimer's—but she's not a gambler."

"What are you going to do?" Liv asked.

I shook my head. "I don't know. I really don't know."

***

I still had time before I had to be at work, which was a good thing. I needed to get my head together. I was a basket case. Pearl would—no, no. I didn't want to think about what Pearl might do if I tried to come to work in this shape. Talking with Liv had helped a lot. She was a good friend, but it wasn't enough. I was heading to the only place I knew might really help.

I stepped from the chaos of the outside world into the empty sanctuary and felt instant peace. The building's thick walls and heavy wooden doors shut out everything that was happening on the other side of them. An escape.

The still air inside was scented with melted wax, lemon furniture polish, and the faint scent of roses wafting from last Sunday's flower arrangement in front of the podium. It felt hushed and sacred in here, as if the prayers of a thousand saints before me lingered still. Warm daylight poured through the rainbow-hued gothic windows on the eastern side, stretching colorful Bible illustrations and Christian symbolism from floor to ceiling, and splashing some of those colors over pews and carpet alike.

First Presbyterian Church was one of the oldest in Florida, established in 1858, before the Civil War, and built on land donated by David Yulee, who'd once been a member here. The building itself had withstood a lot, including several hurricanes and the occupation by Federal troops in the 1860s. Even the original bell had survived, though Union soldiers had threatened to melt it for its metal during the war. Miraculously, that plan had never materialized, and today, the same old bell still tolls each Sunday morning, calling worshippers to gather. *Bong. Bong. Bong.* I loved hearing the sound quivering the air.

The wooden pew creaked as I sat down. A complaint or a welcome? I chose the latter, because I had a desperate need to feel that way.

Choose joy … The phrase fluttered through my brain. Another bit of wisdom from my mother. Two words, but there was a lot of power wrapped in those nine letters. They'd been Mama's motto, something she'd adopted after reading a quote from some Franciscan friar back when she was a teen.

The gloom of the world is but a shadow. Behind it, yet within our reach, is joy. Take Joy!

My eyes popped open in surprise. The words had come back, unbidden; words I would've sworn I'd forgotten, but they were still there, so I meditated on them.

The gloom of the world … that was all of the gunk, the messy stuff, things like Alzheimer's and having an enemy for a boss … even murders. All of them were shadows. Nothing solid. Basically air. A shadow can't hurt me. Like the shadow puppets of my childhood, they might look ferocious, but they were all bark, and no bite.

These shadows were all that stood in front of joy, like a wall that was open on both ends. Something easily walked around. Joy was within my reach. All I had to do was go around the shadow-wall and take it from God's outstretched hand. The gift was there for the taking. The only thing that held me back was my attitude. I had to *choose* joy, and choose *not* to focus on the shadows.

"I choose joy." I spoke the words out loud, and a weight lifted from my shoulders.

I bowed my head and breathed in sanctity, embracing the peace that poured over me like the warm colored light pouring from the window, painting my hands, and arms, and legs, with molten rainbows. Symbols of God's promises.

"Thank you," I whispered, knowing it was heard. It was time for me to go work, but now I was ready.

CHAPTER TWENTY

He crept to a stop in the shadows with his headlights off. Quickly putting the car into park, he killed the engine and took his foot off the brake. He didn't want anyone seeing those red lights. He smiled at the scene to his right. A streetlight painted the area perfectly, just as planned. After what happened last night, he had to be sure.

"Our stage is set," he murmured to the back of his car. "I'll be able to see perfectly this time."

There was no answer. He frowned and bit his lip. He might've gone a little heavy with the drug this time. This girl weighed a good bit less than the previous one—another lesson he'd learned from last night—so she'd probably needed a smaller dose. He hoped he hadn't given her too much.

He got out and listened, closing his eyes in order to concentrate more. A rumble of thunder, followed by the whistle of a distance train. Nothing else. He opened the car's back latch and smiled into the darkness. "Everyone's tucked safely in bed, but you, my sweet."

Grabbing her arm, he slung her over his shoulders and hurried through the arbor draped with its tartan plaid, then wove through the bevy of small round tables and chairs scattered around the flagstones to the perfect spot he'd discovered for this verse of the song. After carefully leaning the girl against the bottom of the large bronze statue, he stepped back, gloating and almost giddy over his choice. This was the best one yet. He couldn't have done any better. The scene almost glowed in the light.

"Good, your eyes are open." He knelt down in front of her and smiled. "With the perfect stage and the spotlight, I'd have hated for you to miss the show," he whispered as he fluffed and adjusted her hair. "I know you're wondering why, so I guess I need to try to explain."

"You're the fourth verse. I wouldn't have made it without the song. It's the only good thing in my sucky childhood. It gave me strength while it fed my hate. So it's fitting, don't you think? Using that song? One girl for each verse? Each one looking like her? She needs to know what's coming. She needs to live with fear like I did for so long. Some people don't have anyone to be with them during hard times, no one to stand beside them when the whole world is against them. People who turn their back on someone like that have to be punished. You understand, don't you?"

Tears welled up in her eyes, spilling down her motionless cheeks and leaving wet trails that shimmered in the streetlight. "Shhh ..." he soothed. "You'll streak your mascara. We want you to look your best for the grand finale." He tilted her chin up slightly, wiping the tears away with his thumbs and his smile was sweet. "I'm ready. Are you?"

His gloved hands found their familiar place around her neck as he began to softly croon, "Hush, little baby. Don't say a word. Mama's going to buy you a mockingbird ..."

There was an art to this act, a symphony of perfection. Timing was everything. He squeezed gently with the first verse, slow and easy.

He increased pressure as he began the second verse. "And if that mockingbird don't sing, Mama's going to buy you a diamond ring." In his excitement he had to remind himself to keep calm. Concentrate ... concentrate.

He swung into the third verse. "And if that diamond ring turns brass, Mama's going to buy you a looking glass." Fear shone from the girl's eyes as her face darkened. The sight made his heart race, and he squeezed harder, tempering the force with effort. The timing had to be perfect. They were almost there. Careful ... not quite yet.

"And if that looking glass gets broke, Mama's going to buy you a billy goat."

Now! His fingers spasmed. He squeezed them together as tightly as he could. Her eyes bulged and her tongue protruded through blue lips as her frantic pulse slowed ... slower ... then stopped.

His hands dropped limply to either side of his knees. He was panting, out of breath, his heart thundered in his chest. He got to his feet and stared down at the vignette he'd created, full of endorphins and feeling completely euphoric. Perfect.

With reluctance to leave his beautiful work of art, he finally turned away, took two steps toward his car, then froze.

The whir of tires against pavement sounded loud in the still night air, the rattle of a metal basket echoed down the street.

No! This couldn't be happening. Not again.

He slipped quickly into the shadow of the building and waited, barely breathing.

A blur zipped by on the street, much too quickly to register any details. His rubber-soled shoes made no sound as he hurried to the arbor, careful to stay hidden within the shield of vines, but close enough to the road that he had a perfect line of sight. His stomach knotted as he peered through thin green leaves. It was the cyclist from last night, the one with the Rasta cap. There couldn't be another one like him in this town.

A flash of fury burned away the last remnants of his "high" and that made him even angrier. He felt robbed, his joy stolen before he'd really had a chance to luxuriate in it. His mind spun with rage and fear. What did this mean? Two girls are killed in two totally different places two nights in a row, and the same guy rides by at almost the exact time of their deaths? Once was bad enough, but twice? The odds of that happening were too astronomical to even consider.

He burned with the desire for revenge, to destroy this person who'd stolen his joy, not once, but *twice*.

Careful ... nothing good to come of reckless anger. Impulsive action was how people got caught. He needed a plan, something that would point the finger of suspicion at someone else, and it needed to be tonight.

He smiled suddenly to himself. He knew just what to do.

CHAPTER TWENTY-ONE

Ford

I fumbled for my phone. I had no idea how long it had been ringing, but it'd been long enough that my subconscious mind had managed to fit the sound nicely into the dream I was having. For the life of me, now in my semi-wakeful state, with the stupid phone still blaring in my ear, I couldn't think of how it fit together, but in the dream, it'd worked just fine.

I opened one eye, noticed the room was still dark and closed it again as my hand finally located my phone. I pressed talk, and held it to my ear. "'Lo."

"Ford?"

Both eyes sprang open and I rolled into a sitting position on the edge of the bed. I glanced at the clock.

2:24.

"Lacey?"

"There's been another murder. At Vivian's ... the little sandwich shop on Ash Street."

"Got it." I was already on my feet, pulling on the pair of jeans I'd stepped out of the night before, the same pair I'd pulled on yesterday morning about this time. I needed to do some laundry.

I pulled on my T-shirt, grabbed my wallet, but the silence on the other end made me pause before I stuffed it in my back pocket. "Hey, are you okay?"

"Um, yeah. I guess, though I could do with a little more sleep."

"Yeah. Ain't that the truth," I replied with feeling.

At her continued silence, my voice softened. "Look, Lacey, we're gonna catch this guy. I promise."

She sighed, then asked, "Why don't these girls fight?"

"What?"

"In my dreams. I never see them fight. They don't even move. I'm wondering why?"

"They can't." I hadn't told her this part, so it was news to her. "He's druggin' them."

"Oh." She went quiet, working this over in her mind.

I finally broke the long silence. "Try to go back to sleep, sweetheart."

Sweetheart?! I instantly clamped my lips together, but it was too late. The word had already escaped and there was no taking it back. A perfect case of shutting the barn door after the horses had already gotten out.

A soft *beep, beep, beep* indicated the call had ended. I tossed my phone on the bed, and I used the heel of my hand to pound my forehead. "Gah! Jamison, you're such an idiot!"

I rolled my head backward and seared the ceiling with an angry glare. If I'd had super powers I'd have burned a hole in the roof. After a moment, I heaved a sigh, leaned across the bed, and grabbed my phone. I had work to do. Any psychoanalyzing of my situation would have to wait.

I went through the same routine trying to rouse Craig as I had yesterday: ringing through to voice mail, hanging up, ringing through again. Finally, and without any patience for a preamble, I blurted, "Sir, we have another body."

***

I parked my car a block away and walked to the crime scene. I didn't want to park in front in case there might be evidence to find: a cigarette butt, tire tracks, a discarded wad of gum, *anything*. I was getting desperate. Four dead girls, and no closer to catching the killer than when I'd started. With only seven verses of the song, I only had three more chances. Lacey would be the last one. I knew that as well as I knew the sun rose in the east and set in the west. I had nothing to go on but gut instinct, but my years in law enforcement had taught me to trust my gut. I'd bet my life on it. Lacey would be this guy's grand finale.

We were barely keeping up, no sooner positively identifying one victim before we had another to figure out. I'd just gotten the name of victim three late last night. Charlene Tindale. Her kids were okay. They were with the grandma. Ages two and four. Poor kids. They were too young to have to deal with this kind of baggage.

With flashlight in hand, and wearing another pair of latex gloves, I took one step through the arbor and halted, my heart jumping up, lodging in my throat. The slender dark-haired girl was propped up against a large bronze statue of a goat: the legendary Vivian, prize-winning milker whose ample udders supplied all the organic goat cheese used in this little sandwich shop.

With a sick feeling in the pit of my stomach, I stared at the statue, mentally kicking myself for my ineptitude. Why hadn't I figured this one out? I mean how many goats were there in Fernandina? It was painfully obvious. I was pathetic! I should turn in my badge and go work at Walmart as a greeter or something. I probably had more future in that than in law enforcement at this stage.

I knew I was avoiding looking at the girl, not just because it made me feel like such a failure, but because this one looked even more like Lacey than the others. Her face was even shaped the same, her curly hair more auburn than brown. And even worse … this one looked young. Twenty or less. A wave of nausea washed over me, and I had to turn away. I couldn't look anymore.

The sound of what I was sure was the chief's truck roared closer. I needed to get my act together.

I stepped out into the road in front of the building, waving my flashlight when I saw his headlights coming toward me. I hoped to keep him from disturbing possible evidence. He wouldn't be happy that he'd have to walk farther than the few feet from the curb, but he needed some exercise.

The big truck screeched to a stop mere inches in front of me. It was obvious he didn't want to stop and would've probably just as soon run me down as look at me. It took all the courage I could muster not to dive for the sidewalk.

My legs were a little shaky, but I tried my best to appear macho when I approached the driver side. He lowered the window and hissed, "What do you think you're doing, Jamison? Get out of the way so I can park."

"We need to tape this area off, do a sweep for evidence. Might even be able to lift some tire tread prints or something. You can park where I did, down there," I waved toward the next block. "Or you can park across the street."

He glared at me. Probably reconsidering the idea of running me over. One of his eyebrows stirred. His face didn't change in any appreciable way other than his clenched teeth working furiously to grind the enamel off all chewing surfaces, but I knew he'd grasped the situation, and he knew I was right. Without a word, his window went up. His truck surged backward a hundred feet or so, then chirped forward again at an angle, right tires up on the sidewalk.

Slamming his door so hard it should've broken the glass, he stormed around to the truck's rear and wrenched down the tailgate, then tossed an orange cone at me. "Help me set these up so we can get tape around them before the others start arriving."

***

Though the sky was getting lighter, yesterday's sailor's warning would probably keep us from seeing much sun today. Hurricane Audrey was still a Category 2 and had Florida in her sights. Meteorologists were earning their paychecks, having to do more than wave a pointer in front of a television green screen to keep the public abreast of the latest up-dates, but even they were struggling. This storm seemed intent on keep-ing everyone guessing.

Under the gloomy sky, large spotlights were fastened to metal stands and were saturating the outside eating area of Vivian's with harsh, unfor-giving light.

Police vans were parked along the yellow tape barriers in an effort to keep both local and national camera lenses and nosy reporters out. The press was almost rabid, practically yapping and snarling, jockeying for position at the front edge of the mass. A few of the more reckless ones had tried to get around the barricade, only to be escorted out by a thick necked Robo-cop whose job was the police version of a bouncer.

I watched the media circus through tired eyes. By now, every network large and small knew that the murders were those of a serial killer. Craig had finally relented and used the word, but somehow, so far, we'd been able to keep the link between the murders and the lullaby under wraps. It probably wouldn't stay that way for long, though. Some wise guy or gal would put two and two together and figure it out. Either that, or someone close to the case would let something slip. I was actually surprised it hadn't happened yet.

Ahh. About time. Chief Craig and the coroner had finally finished their powwow. I wove through the all the uniforms with Craig in my sights. I needed to talk to him, and it wasn't going to be pretty—not that it ever was.

"Chief," I called when I saw him moving away from me. "Hold up, will you?"

He glowered the instant he saw who had called his name, but at least he stayed put. I sidestepped a guy who was dusting for fingerprints, finally getting near enough that I wouldn't have to yell. "Could I talk with you about something, sir?" I asked in a low voice. "Somewhere we can't be overheard."

He looked equal parts wary and curious. I knew it could go either way, but when I motioned for him to follow me, curiosity won out.

I thought my car would be far enough away from the hive of activity that we wouldn't be followed or overheard. At least that was my hope. What I was about to say probably wasn't going to go over too well, and Craig tended to get his inside and outside voices mixed up.

"What's this all about, Jamison?" he asked once he'd squeezed into in my car.

What the heck. Jump right in. "I think we should report about the dating website."

He narrowed his eyes. "What about it?"

Don't play dumb with me, you jerk. I could think those words, but I dared not say out loud. I needed to play "nice," if I could. "I think we should let the public know that the killer is using the Perfect Match dating website to target a certain type of woman," I answered, spelling it out.

A vein in Craig's forehead bulged. "Are you out of your mind?" his voice boomed inside the confines of my car. I wondered if hearing loss on the job was covered by workman's comp.

I tried to keep my voice Zen-like, as non-antagonistic as possible. "I think the public deserves a warning. If we let women know how they're being targeted, at least they'll be able to make an informed decision if they opt to go out with this guy. If we don't tell them—"

"It means we're playing our cards close to our chest like we're supposed to," he interrupted. "We don't show the bad guys our hand. We don't tell them everything we know. That doesn't even make sense. What did they teach you that at that fancy school, boy?"

I ignored the jab, but my voice ratcheted up, in spite of still trying to keep it in Zen-mode. "If we were actually making progress—getting any closer to finding this guy—I'd agree with you. But we're not. We know his game. We know the words of the song. We know the type of women he's looking for. But what good has that done us? Any? At all? How 'bout we ask one of these four victims. What do you think they'd say? Oh, that's right. We *can't* ask them. They're all *dead*!" Okay … all this Zen stuff was overrated. I clamped my lips together, breathing hard, and tried to calm down.

Craig brooded, stroking his goatee, his brow furrowed with deep grooves. "I want to put someone under cover," he finally said. "I got a girl officer, brand new. I think she's a fit for what he's looking for."

"You want to use a rookie as bait? With this creep?" I eyed him with renewed disgust. He was unbelievable. "And what if he doesn't pick her? What if he picks someone besides her … three more times? There are thousands of women on that site who fit his profile. Believe me … I've looked."

"Let's just give it try," Craig coaxed. "Just once. If he doesn't pick her for the next verse, we'll let the public know and try to get this guy some other way."

It was my turn to brood. I wanted to get this guy … *so* bad. Not just because I didn't want there to be any more victims. I also wanted the target removed from Lacey's back. What the chief was suggesting was a game of roulette with dangerously high odds of losing.

I drew a deep breath and pressed my lips into a straight line. "Once," I finally said. "We'll try it your way once. After that, I'm pulling rank." I gave him an icy stare, then added, "Better go let your bait know."

Craig eyes shot fire at me before opening the door and heaving himself to his feet.

I watched him go, debating on whether I'd done the right thing or not. One thing I did know. If this thing went south like I was afraid it would, I didn't want the job of explaining it to the next set of grieving parents.

***

By 7 a.m. I was barely functioning. I could count the hours of sleep I'd had the last two nights on one hand and I was ready for bed. I was also hungry, and since I didn't think I could stay awake long enough to make myself some breakfast if I went straight to my apartment, I decided to stop for a bacon, egg, and cheese biscuit and a coffee-to-go at a shop downtown before heading back. I could eat it on the way so I'd be ready to collapse in bed as soon as I got home. Maybe I could last long enough to brush my teeth—they were feeling a little furry by this time—but I wasn't making any promises.

While waiting on my order, my sleep-deprived eyes stared groggily through the window. Several runners whizzed by and I knew I should feel guilty or jealous or something about them running and not me, but I was too darn tired to figure out which one.

With paper bag in one hand and a large coffee in the other, I pushed the door open with my elbow and stepped out, right into the path of Raine Fairbanks who was sporting the least amount of Lycra running gear she could get away with in public without being arrested.

"Oops! I'm so sor— Ford? Oh, my gosh!" she panted. "I didn't know you were in town. It's so good to see you."

I barely kept from growling at her. She'd almost made me drop my coffee, which would've been a killing offense at this point. No one would've faulted me, either. It was only because both of my hands were full that I didn't reach for my gun.

I stared at her dispassionately. Still not hard on the eyes. She looked great ... always had. But Raine was like a snake ... a poisonous one: beautiful to look at, but lethal. It was best to admire her from a distance, something I'd tried to practice ever since high school, when she'd first starting making passes at me. Problem with Raine, though? She seemed to have some sort of sixth sense where I was concerned; like she was a pigeon equipped with a homing device and I was "home." Maybe a better comparison would be to call her a nuclear missile and I was the target. If she hit me, everything would go up in a mushroom cloud.

So her saying she "didn't know I was in town" was ludicrous. A bold-faced lie. I knew it, and she knew I knew it. I'd be willing to bet she knew the second I'd entered the city limits. Shoot! I wouldn't be surprised if she knew I was coming before I did.

"Yeah," I finally replied, forcing a smile. "They called me in to work on the serial killings."

Her blue eyes grew round as marbles. "Oh, isn't that just awful?" she gushed. Over-the-top theatrics. "All those poor girls. Tsk, tsk ..."

I didn't say anything to that, just waited, hoping she'd get back to her run—*willing* her to do so; silently urging, *Go, go, go*—but knowing it wasn't going to happen. barring a natural disaster—and the hurricane was still too far way to work—I'd have to say and/or do something rude to get her to leave me alone. She'd get mad, take it out on someone and the circle of life would continue. I'd been out of this hellish loop for five years and could honestly say I didn't miss this part of it.

"Where are you parked?" she asked brightly, trying to tuck her hand into crook of my elbow. "I'll walk you to your car."

Her brazenness floored me, and I just stood there—struck silent—wondering at her nerve.

It was at that precise moment that Lacey rounded the corner in front of us, stopping so suddenly, she nearly lost her balance. I instinctively reached to grab her arm, dropping the bag containing my biscuit in the process. Her face lit with a sudden spark when our eyes met, but doused immediately when she saw whom I was with. Her entire body tensed. I felt it in her arm, which had turned to stone. Her mouth opened, but no words came out. Her eyes absorbed the scene, hardening when Raine pulled closer to me, molding herself to my side. I stared down in horror to see a sly, cat-who-ate-the-canary smile light Raine's face.

I tried to disengage my arm from her clutches, but she clung to me like a squid on a clam. I could almost feel her suckered underbelly clinging for dear life. I was still trying to scrape her off when Lacey swung around and left.

Once Lacey was gone, Raine released me. I shoved her away in disgust, my eyes raking the length of her. I was so angry, my vision seemed tinted red. The desire to throw her in front of a moving car was strong, but I resisted the urge, bent over, grabbed the bag containing the remains of my now-flattened biscuit, and headed for my car.

Alone.

CHAPTER TWENTY-TWO

Lacey

It felt like the hooves of a thousand horses were galloping in my chest. I couldn't get enough air. My lungs were ill-equipped to work on half-rations, crying for more. I gasped and choked, trying to run, but mostly stumbling. Unable to see much through tear-blurred eyes, I gave them a furious swipe, angry at their betrayal in producing tears at this moment.

Hearing that deep, maple-sugar baritone utter the word, "sweetheart" on the phone this morning had struck through years of anger, chiseling it away into crumbles. My middle school "crush" came back in its new and improved grown-up form, made stronger by the compounded interest of lost years. That single word seemed to reach inside me and linger in impossible-to-reach places, music to my ears and balm to my soul. Almost making me forget the horror of why I called him in the first place. But that "music" had turned to the screaming of a grunge rock band, and the "balm" felt like battery acid the instant I'd turned that corner and run headlong into Ford, with Raine clinging to him like an overly endowed tick. That image was burned onto my retinas.

It was time to face some cold, hard facts. Ford's utterance of that world meant nothing to him, so I needed to get over it. This murder case would be drawing to a close soon. After that, he'd be going back to Tallahassee, back to his life there. I needed to pack up any hopes and dreams I might have, seal them up, nice and tight so nothing could leak out, then mail them to someplace cold and icy like Siberia. Stuffing them into the back of a closet so I could sneak them out and dance with them once in a while just wasn't going to work. Moving forward was the only way I was going to survive.

So, how was I supposed to do that?

"If I had that answer, I could rule the world," I choked out, wiping away another rebel tear.

The peace from yesterday's visit to the church sanctuary seemed a million miles away. Too far to reach at the moment. Maybe later. Right now, I needed to go home and spend some time with my mom before work. We hadn't had much of that since Monday when I'd taken her to the beach, when she'd seemed almost her old self for a little while. The time was coming, and it might not be that far away, when she became too much for Bonnie and me to handle by ourselves and I'd have to put her in a memory care facility, but until then, I needed to take advantage of every second I could while they were still there to take.

***

There was a small front-end loader moving dirt around on the lot next door to me when I arrived back at my house. The breeze off the ocean strewed the scent of diesel in the air. I stood and watched the worker as he moved back and forth, digging the mounded areas, dumping his bucket in the lower parts and then smoothing it down. Kind of reminded me of frosting an uneven cake.

The house that used to be there was long gone. It had burned to the ground about ten years ago when I was thirteen. They said it was bad wiring or something, but there'd been whispers of arson. They'd bulldozed the house site sometime after that.

The woman who'd lived there had disappeared without a trace, leaving behind her son, Coop. Yes, the same Coop I'd publicly humiliated at the diner all those years ago, though I was ashamed to admit it. Coop was his nickname. I never knew his real name. After his mother disappeared, he'd been sent to live with a relative … his grandmother, I think.

I couldn't remember which had happened first, the fire or his mom's disappearance. I only knew they'd happened about the same time, and that there'd been an investigation because both things had happened so close together. I'd overheard my parents talking about it one night after

I was supposed to be in bed. They never discussed it when they thought I could hear.

They were of the opinion that the police hadn't tried too hard to find her after her disappearance. Then there'd been some murmuring about a "revolving door" in relation to the jail, which I took to mean she was in and out of it a lot. The whole thing was kept hush-hush, so I assumed it was something they didn't think my tender thirteen-year-old ears needed to hear. But by listening carefully at strategic times, I gathered they weren't all that sorry she was gone. I'd forgotten about it until now.

I wondered if someone had bought the property. I'd grown accustomed to having the empty lot beside my house and had no desire for someone to come in and crowd some gargantuan showpiece right next to me, painted orange sherbert, Pepto Bismol pink, or some other horrible color one often saw along the coast. I liked the little bit of "wildness" that came from the lot's sea-grass covered dunes, and would miss it if it disappeared.

After a final look, I started up the stairs, and was surprised to meet Travis coming down. He gave me a smile that was something you'd see in a teeth-whitening ad and boomed, "Well, well, well. Look who's here. Figured you'd be in town by now."

"I've been and come back. Liv's store is closed on Thursdays and I've already placed my order with Jeb."

"Who's Jeb?"

I leaned in closer like I was about to whisper in his ear. "He's who I order my seafood from, but don't tell anyone."

"Hmm …" One eyebrow rose and his eyes got a devilish gleam. "I like a girl with secrets."

I couldn't help but laugh. I had to admit that his flirtation did a lot to soothe my wounded ego.

"So …" I eyed his sports coat, the brief case he was carrying. "Where are you off to?"

"I have appointments in and around Jacksonville all day, but I'll be back tonight." He eyed me hopefully, eyes traveling from my face and slowly down. "Maybe we could get a dinner or a drink later." His eyes seemed to smolder at me.

Gulp. Whoa! Was he hitting on me? What just happened? Time to back up a little. I tilted my head and plastered on my best "I'm-sorry" face. "My only days off are Mondays. Every other night I work 'til at least midnight. Sometimes even later," I added, thinking of Raine and what would always be known as the "calamari incident."

"Well, I guess I'll have to wait until Monday, then, won't I?"

His answer sounded decidedly suggestive, but before I could reply, I heard a car turn into the driveway, and I knew who it was without having to look.

Ford.

A wave of pain washed over me. The memory of how I'd last seen him, with Raine clinging to his side like a coat of paint, was too fresh.

With a burst of speed, his car was under the house, pulling into his spot within seconds. A few ground-eating strides later, he was at the foot of the staircase, starting up, then feigning surprise at see us standing there. "Oh, I'm sorry. Didn't see you guys." His mouth wore a pleasant smile, but his eyes simmered, just under the boiling point.

Something inside me snapped. Why was *he* angry? I'd just been witness to Raine draped all over him like laundry on a drying rack, but he was mad that I was *talking* to another man? Hunh! We'd see about that!

I turned back to Travis, making sure nothing was blocking Ford's view of my hand resting lightly on the other man's broad chest, or the deep and meaningful gaze I was lavishing on him. "Yes," I gave him my best smile. "I'm looking forward to Monday."

I knew it was childish, and I was playing with fire—in more ways than one—but I couldn't help throwing a "so there!" look back at Ford before continuing up the stairs. Just inside the doorway, I turned and our eyes met once more, then I closed the door with a deliberate *click*.

***

I spent the rest of the morning with Mama.

We colored for a while in the coloring book Bonnie had recently bought her, sitting side by side at the kitchen table, mostly staying in the lines, but she lost interest before finishing her picture. She seemed perfectly content to watch me, though, so I colored the whole thing, then scratched the date at the top corner of both pictures.

"Why'd you do that?" she asked.

"So when I look back at this later, I can remember the date."

"What?"

"I want to be able to remember the date, Mama," I leaned toward her ear and repeated loudly.

"Oh."

I watched her fidget, pleating the fabric of her sweater over and over, and I struggled for a topic of conversation. "Bonnie bought some cookies, Mom. Would you like some?"

She brightened. "Cookies?"

Funny how I didn't have to repeat *that* word louder. Her appetite may have dwindled on a lot of things, but she still had a sweet tooth. I chuckled and patted her hand. "I'll be right back."

I returned with two glasses of milk and the bag of chocolate chip cookies. "I brought us milk to go with them," I announced loud enough for her to hear.

"Go with what?"

"The cookies."

"Cookies?" She looked around, excited, as though that was the first she'd heard of them. "Where are they?"

"Right here," I answered, setting them down in front of her and opening the bag.

She looked puzzled. "How do I get them out?"

"Just reach in and get one."

"Help me. I don't know how," she replied in a small, childish voice.

My heart sank. She didn't even know how to get a cookie out of an open bag. My own desire for the sweet treat had evaporated, but I pulled out a couple for her, setting them beside her glass of milk. She munched until hers were gone, then gulped half her milk.

I laughed when she set her glass down. "You have a milk mustache."

"Where?" She looked around in confusion.

"Right here under your nose." I took a napkin and dabbed it away. "Where mustaches usually are."

She smiled at me when I'd finished. "What's your name?"

I was stunned. This was the first time she'd actually asked me who I was. I'd been suspecting she didn't know me lately, but there was a big difference between *suspecting* it and *knowing* it. I swallowed the lump in my throat and croaked. "I'm Lacey, Mom. I'm your daughter."

"Pretty name for a pretty girl." She squeezed my hand, smiling again.

I blinked back tears.

Then she started humming. Not a recognizable tune, but bits and snatches of different ones mashed together into her own "arrangement." Then, amazingly, she repeated it exactly the same as the first time. She hummed that mutated composition over and over and over again like she was providing accompaniment to a symphony in her head. How she did it? I had no clue.

After about the twentieth time, she stopped suddenly and leaned toward me, whispering hoarsely. "Who is that man?" she asked, pointing.

Bonnie winked at me from the living room where she sat knitting. "That's Bonnie, Mom. And she's a woman."

"Is it okay for him to be here?"

I laughed and patted her shoulder. "She lives here. With us."

She shook her head. "I don't want a strange man in here. It's not safe."

"Bonnie's a woman, Mom." I knew there were rules in dealing with someone with Alzheimer's. One was never to say, "You remember when …" and then fill in the blank with whatever you wanted them to remember. All that did was upset them. Because of course, they *couldn't* remember.

Another "rule" was never to argue with them, and I knew that's what I was doing. I could feel Bonnie's warning look from her place on the couch. I was taking a chance, but I wanted to reassure my mother we didn't have a strange man living with us.

After a moment, Mom said, "He looks familiar." Then she started humming again. The same tune.

Wow ... just, wow. I thought, leaning back in my chair, exhausted from riding the mental and emotional roller coaster. I watched her pleat her sweater in time with the music in her head. At least she was talking in whole sentences today, rather than her word salad, which was becoming more and more common. I guessed this was better, but I wasn't quite sure.

***

I was in my car, on my way back into town to work, when I had an epiphany. The fact that it was so obvious made me feel like an utter fool. The fact that Ford hadn't bothered sharing it with me, when I was certain he knew, and *had* known for a while, made me furious.

The murderer was using the lullaby for his game plan. He was killing each girl in a setting that went along with each verse. How could I have not seen it?

I almost pulled over to the side of the road so I could beat my head against the steering wheel, but I was running late, and I didn't have time. That didn't stop be from mentally flogging myself, though. *Stupid, stupid, stupid ...*

Ford had known this and hadn't told me. Just like he hadn't told me about the murderer drugging his victims. I narrowed my eyes, glaring through the windshield. Just what else hadn't he bothered to tell me? I gave a grim smile. *That* would be exactly what I'd ask the very next time I saw him.

I went through the first verse in my mind. *Hush, little baby. Don't say a word. Mama's going to buy you a mockingbird.*

They found the first girl on the porch swing. Beside her was a pillow with the outline of a mockingbird stamped on it.

Next verse. Blah, blah-blah, blah, blah ... I hummed through to ... *diamond ring.*

They found girl number two on the Yulee bench with a fake diamond ring.

I skipped through to the end of the third verse ... *looking glass.*

Number three was found in the gallery courtyard, leaning against the wall that was plastered with bits of glass, pottery, and *mirrors.*

I fast-forwarded through the fourth verse to the end ... *a billy goat.*"

The last victim was leaned up against a bronze statue of Vivian, the goat.

It all fit. Every verse. Every victim.

I stared through the windshield in a sort of daze, trying to take it all in. Wait a minute. What did the fifth verse say? I couldn't do anything for those four dead girls, but maybe I could keep any more from being killed.

"And if that billy goat don't pull, Mama's going to buy you a cart and bull." I sang it aloud, in hopes that doing so might make a clue obvious.

It didn't.

Cart and bull? There were no carts or bulls in Fernandina Beach. Well, maybe a cart, but certainly not a bull! Not in town anyway. Maybe out in the country . . .

Okay, I needed to think outside the box. That was what the killer was doing. That was why they couldn't seem to catch him. So, where was there a bull in this town?

Mmm ... maybe it was a *picture* of a bull. Wait, wait ... there was one in that little Mexican restaurant a block off the beach, one of those black velvet ones with the garish colors. I guessed I remembered it so well because I always thought it was kind of gory for a restaurant. A bull with a bunch of spears sticking out of its back charging a matador. I mean ... people *ate* in that place. There was an awful lot of red on that velvet. Could that be the bull? Maybe ... but what about the cart? I scoffed and shook my head impatiently. No, no ... that couldn't be it. He killed the girls at night. He wouldn't be able to get in there. I needed to think of something else.

I'd made it to town. So I found a parking spot, pulled in, and just sat there. After several minutes of unproductive thinking, I gave up. Unless there was some obscure picture or engraving at one of the antique shops in town, the only other bull I could think of was the one on the Merrell Lynch logo, and I was pretty sure that wasn't it.

It was no use. I couldn't think like a killer because I wasn't one.

I sighed and unbuckled my seatbelt. Pearl was waiting and I couldn't be late.

TWENTY-THREE

Ford

'd somehow gotten a couple of hours of sleep in spite of my thoughts being stuck in "repeat mode," allowing me to relive that scene on the stairs with Lacey and Sterling a few hundred times before my brain simply refused to function anymore and I'd crashed. I'd still have been sleeping if Chief Craig hadn't called.

I was leaning against my car, trying to think of anything else besides how much I couldn't stand Sterling. I started by studying my surroundings. I was parked at the end of a dirt driveway under the sweeping arms of a live oak tree that was at least a hundred years old. Thick limbs, each one at least three feet in circumference, spread from a massive trunk. It would take three tall men, arms stretched out, fingers barely touching, to measure around it. Small ferns carpeted the upper part of each limb, like wavy green leeches, getting their sustenance from the tree. Spanish moss draped from the branches like dirty rags. Though the temperature wasn't high—mid-to-upper seventies—the air was still and heavy. Hurricane Audrey was creeping closer to the coast, bringing her moisture with her.

Two men were at work, digging a hole in Jeb Billings' yard. Craig had gotten an anonymous tip that afternoon. The call had gone to voicemail so they had a recording of a whispery voice giving a set of longitude and latitude coordinates, which had led us to Jeb's yard. The words "under the keystones" were also part of the tip. We hadn't understood that part until we got there. In the corner of his yard, we'd found a pile of what looked like rocks at first glance, but we'd discovered they were really window keystones, discards from downtown Fernandina Beach building projects from the 1800s. They were wedge-shaped concrete chunks, bearing a decorative cross-like design. Each one was chipped and weathered, some of them broken. They looked like a useless pile of debris to me, but this property had been in the Billings family forever, so maybe one of his ancestors had gathered the stones for some project. Who knew? Craig's men had moved the keystones out of the way, marked the intersection of the coordinates they'd gotten from the tip, and started digging. They'd been at it about twenty minutes or so.

The tip itself was from an untraceable number, which I thought was a little fishy, but the chief wasn't about to ignore it. I guess I didn't blame him, but I knew this was a waste of time. Jeb and I hadn't been close, but I'd known Jeb Billings since grade school, and while I'd be the first to agree he was a bit odd, the only thing he'd ever killed was sea critters, and everybody here knew it. Public outcry was trumping common sense. Mob mentality had taken over. People were scared ... with good reason. They wanted results and expected law enforcement to deliver it. At this point, I think Craig was willing to do almost anything. I only hoped, for Jeb's sake, that the press didn't get wind of this. They'd have him tried and condemned before an arrest warrant could be issued. The news would be smeared all over every media outlet. It would probably ruin him.

There was a sudden stir of activity by the hole, men milling around like angry bees on a hive. I heard a shout, "Chief, you're gonna want to see this, sir."

I pushed off from the side of my car and started meandering that way, not in any hurry at all. They probably just found Jeb's stash of weed.

I frowned and picked up my pace. The chatter was getting louder ... more excited. Craig starting barking orders, men rushed around, two of them raced past me the opposite direction. Someone located a hand shovel and tossed it to one of the men in the hole.

I pushed my way through the crowd gathered around the five-by-eight-foot pit that was now around three feet deep, and peered in. One of the officers was using a large, soft-bristled brush to sweep dirt away from the slightly jumbled, but unmistakable, bones of a hand. The other man was using a hand shovel to dig carefully around what could only be a skull.

I shook my head in utter disbelief, blinking my eyes several times to make sure that I was really seeing what I thought I was seeing.

Chief Craig stepped up beside me. He looked as stunned as I felt, but there was also relief. "Well, Jamison. Looks like we found our killer."

***

Officers were waiting at the dock, ready to arrest Jeb when he returned from a day of fishing.

Nothing like unwinding from a hard day's work … in jail. The forensics team worked feverishly on the site, digging and brushing away soil until they had the entire skeleton uncovered. It was a woman, that much they knew. They also knew she'd been murdered—her neck was broken—and that this murder had occurred much earlier than the other four victims. The bones were stained from the silty black dirt, but there were no bits of flesh or muscle left, no tendons holding the skeleton together. There was also the unexplained issue of the skeleton's layout seeming somewhat "jumbled." That was the word they kept using. Jumbled. Shifting did occur as the tendons decomposed, they said, and gravity could account for some of the movement, but this seemed more than usual. It would take more study. After taking enough photos to stack to the moon and back, they loaded everything up and hauled it off to the lab. They'd be working through the night, but not me. I was headed back to the apartment. I wanted to get a head start on sleeping. I didn't believe they'd arrested the right man and it was entirely possible that my night would be cut short by another call from Lacey.

***

The call never happened, and I wasn't sure what that meant.

The next morning, I stopped outside Craig's office, rapping on the open door to get his attention. "You got a minute?" I asked when he looked up.

He nodded, rubbing tense shoulders and rotating his head. "Yeah. What you got?"

I handed him a file. "A positive ID on victim four: Kathy Dreisbach, 20. She was from St. Mary's."

His brow furrowed as he studied the file. "First one from Georgia. Has her family been notified?"

I nodded. "The father is the one who identified her."

He winced and sighed, still scanning, "Heck of a thing for a parent to have to do."

I just stood there, waiting.

He finally glanced up. "You got something else on your mind, Jamison."

"Yeah. Mind if I sit down?"

"Help yourself." He gestured at the chair across from him.

"Okay," I started once I was settled. "I found out that Dreisbach also had a Perfect Match account."

"Not sure how that's relevant, now that we have the suspect behind bars, son."

"Just hear me out, sir."

Craig glanced at his watch and made a "get-on-with-it" motion with his hand.

"Right. Well, the first three girls had two or three common contacts, but with victim number four there's just one in common. Username is *whoareyou*. He doesn't have a photo on his profile page, but he did include some info about himself. Sir, that info doesn't sound anything like Jeb Billings."

Craig scowled. "For goodness sakes, Jamison. You know as well as I do, that anybody can put anything they want on those sites—and they do. That proves nothing, and you know it."

I knew he'd respond like that. He wasn't interested in finding out if he had the right man. As far as he was concerned, his job was done. He had his suspect locked up safely behind bars, which was all fine and good … until another victim showed up, which was what I was afraid was going to happen. I ignored the fact that there hadn't been a murder last night and that Jeb Billings was in jail. I didn't believe they were related.

"Look," I said, trying again. "All I'm sayin' is, can we check it out? Common sense says this *whoareyou* is our guy. He's the only one common with all four girls. If we get his picture, and it's Jeb, then fine. Case closed. But let's find the picture. Let's make sure. Especially ..." I raised my voice when he picked up a pen and started scribbling on a notepad. What I was about to say was important, and I wanted eye contact when I told him.

His expression was bored when he finally looked up. "What?"

"Sir, Jeb Billings doesn't have a computer. Not even with his business. Keeps all of his records on paper. Everyone I've talked to has told me the same thing. Jeb thinks computers are just a way for Russia to spy on us. He avoids them like the plague. Yes, it's possible he could use a computer at the library, but judgin' from what I've just told you, do you think that's likely?"

He just stared at me, no flicker of any kind of emotion on his face or in his eyes. I sighed and got up, started to leave. Then I stopped, turned at the door. "One last thing, and I'll get out of your hair—uh, sorry." I winced at my unintended pun. The corner of his mouth twitched, but he didn't say anything. "What are you gonna to do when another victim shows up?"

***

I got word that forensics had matched the bones' DNA with that of Joelle Cooper, one of Fernandina Beach's "undesirables." Joelle had been a frequent "guest" in the city jail, arrested for anything from assault, to DUI, to prostitution, but most of the charges were drug-related. She was into the hard stuff: meth, cocaine, heroin. She was also Coop's mother.

Then ten years ago, she'd disappeared. That part I remembered. I'd been in high school then—sixteen, if I remember correctly—and there'd been a lot of speculation. It was hard to blame city officials too much for the laxness in their investigation. Joelle had been a headache that affected the entire city, and her beachfront cottage—right next to the Campbell's place—was a blight on the coastline. It affected tourism, Fernandina's bread and butter. Though they'd never admit it, I believed they were happy not to have to deal with her anymore. But with her disappearance, they were faced with another problem: what to do with Coop.

A few phone calls by an enterprising city councilman had taken care of it. Joelle's wealthy mother zoomed in to claim the beach property. She reimbursed the city for any delinquent back-taxes her daughter might have incurred, and then whisked Coop away on her private jet to Miami. Everyone had breathed a sigh of relief.

Within days, the decrepit beach house had burned to the ground. The fire was deemed "faulty wiring" in an arson investigation. The rich grandmother had the house's remaining shell bulldozed down, and thus marked the end of the Joelle Cooper embarrassment.

I propped my chin in my hand and stared at the computer screen. So what had become of Coop? The records didn't include his given name, and there was no forwarding address, at least not that I'd seen so far. I was glad he'd been allowed to start a new life in Miami. I hoped he'd put his life here behind him. There'd been rumors about what had happened to him while under his drug-addicted mother's care. Things I didn't like to think about.

My mind went back to the skeleton ... Joelle. She wasn't one of the lullaby murders. It had happened too long ago. So why the tip? And who would know about it?

An idea flashed through my head and I sat forward quickly. My heart rate sped up, and thoughts were coming at me hard and fast.

We'd been given exact coordinates for finding her. All we had to do was plug those numbers into a GPS and it'd taken us straight there. The only person who would know the whereabouts with that much precision would be the person who had buried her.

And why would someone give a tip to find the body of a victim from a ten-year-old murder victim in the middle of the lullaby murder investigation unless you hoped to link them? Joelle's neck was broken while the lullaby victims had all been strangled, but they all involved the *neck*. Could the same person have killed them all? Jeb had been arrested for the lullaby murders because Joelle's body was found on his property using coordinates given by the killer. Jeb couldn't have called that tip in for several reasons. One … he was fishing yesterday. He used a radio, not a cell phone on his boat. He didn't own a cell phone. Another Russian spy thing, same as the computer.

Two … ditto for being able to supply GPS coordinates. All technology was taboo to him.

And three … though not a "techie," he was a pretty smart guy. He'd started a business from scratch and had grown it into a successful enterprise. He wasn't dumb enough to rat himself out.

Ha! I gave a triumphant little laugh when I thought of something else. Ten years ago, Jeb would've been thirteen, same age as Lacey. They were in the same class. Back then he'd had the scrawniest, bird-like physique imaginable, sickly and asthmatic. It was all he could do to be the water-boy for the football team. He could no more have broken Joelle's neck than sprout wings and fly. Even if you figured in anger and adrenaline, and even if she'd been passed out cold. He wouldn't have had the strength.

I jumped to my feet, unable to sit still anymore, and began pacing. Jeb was innocent. I was sure of it. All someone had to do was work through it logically. Problem was, I doubted Craig was thinking logically at the moment. I would need to give him the killer on a platter … with a parsley-sprig garnish. I couldn't think here, though. I needed fresh air even if it was as humid as a wet sock outside. I needed endorphins to get my brain synapses firing full throttle. I needed to run.

***

I propped my foot on the boardwalk railing, stretching out my leg muscles before taking off. I eyed the dunes to the left. The spot where Joelle's cottage had been. There was a front-end loader parked beside a trailer. Someone had done some grading yesterday, a little nearer the road. It was easy to see where they'd worked and where they hadn't. Were they done? I'd assumed someone was getting the lot ready to built, but they'd need more grading than that.

I eyed the narrow strip of beach trying to decide where to run. The tide was extra high. Hurricane Audrey's doings. Angry gray waves crashed and thundered, churning up mounds of pale sea foam, waist-high in places. The wind sent clumps of it scuttling down the shore like ghosts. Though the storm was estimated to be another two to three days away, outer bands of clouds were already reaching out greedy fingers. Maybe I'd better run along the sidewalk.

The sprinkling started at almost the same time I began my run. Didn't bother me. I'd run in worse.

Once I got my stride, I let my thoughts go where they would. Of course they went straight to Lacey. She hadn't called during the night and I found myself missing her voice. Not that I wanted there to be another murder. I didn't. I just wanted to talk to her. There was a lot we needed to talk about. How there was *absolutely* not anything going on between me and Raine, how there *better* not be anything going on between her and Sterling, about what was different about her mother, about how Pearl's got changed to the Black Pearl, about how she became a chef, about how she'd gone from "that crazy Campbell girl" to "sweetheart" in a matter of days. Lots of things. The "talk" was coming. I'd make sure of it, but maybe it wasn't time yet.

No call last night meant no new bodies. Craig would say that was because the killer was in jail, but I disagreed. The points I'd come up with earlier were valid and made sense.

The rain was getting harder. I glanced up. A thunderstorm was building, written in invisible ink across the sky. Come on, endorphins, get to work! I was afraid my run was going to be cut short.

Okay, if Jeb wasn't the killer—and I was sure he wasn't—who was? So far we had five victims: Joelle, ten years ago, and four recent girls. While the lullaby murders were planned, calm and meticulous, done by someone with a degree of self-control, Joelle's murder involved so much rage that the killer had broken her neck. On the surface, it looked like there must be different killers, but what I kept coming back to was they all involved the neck.

Could it be the same person? Hmm. Possible. The broken neck could very well be the result of a crime of passion, committed by someone rash and impetuous—*younger?*—while the strangulations denoted a more calculating, logical mind ... someone older. Maybe ten years older?

Of course, Joelle's death could've been nothing more than a drug deal gone wrong, someone who felt they'd gotten the short end of the deal in the sex-for-drugs exchange.

But the evidence didn't back that up. The sheer rage evident in Joelle's remains spoke of intense anger ... even hatred.

Who could have hated her that much? To hate someone, you usually had to know them, or at least something about them. Joelle hadn't been married and, as a rule, any male friends had probably only stuck around for an hour ... or less.

I read somewhere that love and hate are two sides of the same coin; that they're both deep emotions that occur in the same area of the brain. Whoever wrote it claimed it was very easy to bounce between the two because the line was so thin between them. So say, if someone you loved hurt you badly enough, it would be easy for that hurt to turn to hatred. Interesting concept.

In Joelle's case the only known person who was close to her was her son. Had she hurt him? *Maybe.* If the rumors I'd heard were true, the answer was *Yes.* No question that it could have turned his love for her into hate, but in order to rule him out, I would need to track him down. Find out where he was now. Which would mean I'd need his given name. The only thing I'd ever heard anybody call him was Coop. That wasn't enough to go on. I'd need more than that.

As if to punctuate that thought, a bolt of lightning cut the clouds in half, slicing open the bottom to dump out a wall of water. Thick, white sheets of rain soaked me to the skin in an instant. Rain I could run in, but not lightning. With no shelter nearby, I spun around and began sprinting back toward the apartment as fast as my legs would carry me. Lightning cracked and popped all around me. I pictured tomorrow's headline: "Runner struck by lightning." The thought made me push a little harder.

I was soon pounding up the first, then the second set of stairs. Rainwater streamed from all parts of my anatomy, mixing with sweat and creating puddles at my feet. I shoved my key in the lock and practically fell through the door. Cool air from inside the apartment hit my drenched clothes, making me shiver. Time for a hot shower.

The soles of my running shoes squeaked against the floor, my feet squelching around in soggy, water-logged socks. I made my way straight to the bathroom, leaving a drippy trail behind me.

CHAPTER TWENTY-FOUR

Lacey

"You haven't said anything about your mom lately," Mia commented while she peeled and deveined the evening's shrimp. "How is she doing?"

"Ugh," I groaned and shook my head, grating some Parmesan into the pot of grits I was fixing to go with the shrimp dish I'd planned for tonight. "I can practically see her decline day by day. We had cookies yesterday." I looked around to make sure no one was near enough to hear and whispered, "Store-bought. Can you believe that? Don't tell anybody. It's embarrassing enough just having them in the house. But"—I shrugged—"she likes them better than homemade, so that's what we get." I gave the pot a good stir and continued, "Anyway, I opened the bag up and set it on the table so she could serve herself ... get how many she wanted." I stopped to look Mia directly in the eyes. "She couldn't figure out how to get the cookies out."

Mia's inhaled a sharp breath. "Oh no! That's no good."

Removing the pot from the heat, I set it on the warmer and glanced over at what she was doing. "Is that bowl of shrimp ready to go?"

"Oh, yeah. Here."

"Mmm. Handsome-looking guys, aren't you?" I crooned while pouring them into a large skillet that held melted butter, sprinkling them with salt and pepper before adding minced garlic and cayenne. "Then this morning," I went on, "I have her some M&M's, the peanut kind. Because, again, that's her favorite. And I put some out in a bowl because, as I learned yesterday with the cookies, she can't get them out of the bag, but she just looked at them. 'What's that,' she asks. 'They're M&M's,

Mama.' 'What am I supposed to do with them?' 'You *eat* them. Here ... watch me.' I demonstrated it for her, and she *still* just sat there ... so long that I didn't think she was going to eat any, but after a while, she picked some up and put them in her mouth. Keep in mind she's not *chewing* them. She's just sitting there, with a mouth full of candy. Finally, she looks at me, and says, as best she can around the M&M's, 'They're not doing anything.' By that time, the color is coming off the M&M's and multi-colored drool is seeping out of the corners of her mouth because she hasn't swallowed. And I'm trying to keep my cool. 'You have to *chew* them, Mama.' Which finally she did, and once she started chewing, it's like she remembered how good they tasted, and ate the rest of the bowlful." I sighed and continued, "The whole thing scared me a little, because I know, eventually, that part of her brain might go, and if it does, she won't be able to eat or drink by mouth anymore. They'll have to put in a feeding tube."

"Oh, Lacey. I know it doesn't help much, but I'm so sorry," she gave me a sad half-smile.

"Yeah. Well, thanks."

I tossed the shrimp around in the pan another minute, making sure they were pink and coated well with the buttery sauce before setting it down. I dipped out two portions of grits on waiting plates and topped them with the shrimp and roughly chopped parsley. "These are ready to go."

"I don't know how you do it, girl."

I snorted, "This is easy."

"No, I'm not talking about the shrimp and grits. I can't stop thinking about the situation with your mother. How long are you going to try to keep her at home? She's pretty young. She could live for several more years."

"I know. Believe me, I've thought of that. Bonnie—that's the nurse who's living with us—anyway, she says the early-onset version of this disease, which is what Mama has, goes faster, so they don't suffer as long. We haven't talked about when to move her, but I guess we need to have that conversation, sooner rather than later."

***

"Psst."

I looked up from drizzling mole sauce over fish tacos and met the eyes of my favorite server, Sarah, at the kitchen door. My eyebrows rose in question and she motioned me over. Uh-oh.

"Is there a problem?" I asked when I'd hurried over to her.

"I hate to bother you, but I thought I should give you a heads-up. Raine is here."

"What do you mean 'here'? Dining here? Or ... something else?"

None of us talked about it. Not to each other, anyway. And Pearl hadn't mentioned it at all. Not even any dropped hints. It was as if we'd each taken a personal oath not to bring it up. But gossip traveled at the speed of sound in downtown Fernandina. It was a pretty small place. Everybody in the kitchen had heard the rumor of the possible new owner.

"She's dining." Her expression was miserable, and my stomach started churning. Since she'd been part of the last Raine disaster, she was just as wary of the woman as I was.

"Is she alone?"

Her brows shot up into her bangs, and she gave an incredulous laugh. "Raine?"

"Right," I nodded. "Stupid question. Who's she with?" The mental snapshot of her and Ford being all cozy outside the coffee chop flashed through my mind for the umpteenth time and caused me to wince. "Anybody you know?"

She shook her head. "I can't really tell. They're at one of the outside tables. Under the awning at the end."

I turned toward Mia. "Watch things for me, will you? I'll be right back."

I didn't wait for her response. I was too busy hurrying after Sarah.

The smell of damp earth from the afternoon's thunderstorm hit my nose the instant I stepped outside. Water still dripped lazily from the edge of the awning. A light breeze riffled through the tops of the trees that surrounded the restaurant's alfresco dining area. The air had a tropical feel to it, heavy with humidity, as if another storm could happen at any time. The rain had stopped for now, though.

Standing in the shadows, trying to stay as invisible as possible in case Pearl happened to stroll past, I stood on tiptoes in order to get a better look at the table to which Sarah had directed my attention. I could see Raine clearly. She was wearing a V-necked little black dress—emphasis on "little"—that showed off her assets to their full advantage. Her hair was pulled up into a loose Gibson Girl sort of bun on top, with tendrils hanging down in artful wisps. Diamonds sparkled from her ears and a single thick strand of silver circled her neck. She looked stunning, with flickering candlelight from the tabletop spreading a complimentary golden glow over her skin, but I was more interested in the man whose back faced me. From this angle, though, with the sparkly lights wrapping the trees behind Raine's seat, he was just a silhouette. All I could see was his outline, but that was all I needed to see. I was pretty sure who it was.

I turned away quickly and hurried back to the kitchen.

You're so dumb, I mentally flogged myself. *Why couldn't you just go on hating him? It worked fine like that ... so much easier. But noooo ... you have to go and do something stupid, like fall in love with him. Do. Not. Cry. Don't.*

The first thing I did when I got back to my station was grab an onion and start chopping furiously. It would give me a momentary reprieve, an explanation for the tears streaming down my face. The kitchen grew uncharacteristically quiet while I did this, sounding more like a library instead of its usual noisy hubbub. Mia gave me a quick look, then bent to the task of flaking more perch for the fish tacos.

And with tears rolling down my cheeks, I imagined the smiling, handsome face of the man seated across the table from my enemy; the streaked blond hair and the sea-green eyes of the man who held my heart in his hands.

***

I somehow made it through the rest of the night without encountering Pearl's ire, unsure how I managed to avoid it. I certainly didn't have my mind in the game. It was a wonder I didn't burn the kitchen down. I was glad Mia was watching out for me. I'd have to thank her properly tomorrow.

I groaned when I got home and saw my mother's lights were still on. Great. Those lights were an unwanted topping on the horrible sundae that had been my day. I thought briefly about turning around and leaving, driving around aimlessly for an hour or so and then coming back. I sighed. No. Might as well face it. Running from it wouldn't make it go away.

Bonnie met me at the door. "I'm sorry," she apologized. "I know this is the last thing you want when you come home late, but I couldn't get her settled down. She kept saying, 'where is she?' I'd ask her, 'who?' and she'd garble out some gibberish I couldn't understand. I made up answers, but they obviously weren't answers to what she was asking. It just made her more mad."

I smiled tiredly. "It's okay. I'll go see if I can calm her down. Reading usually does it."

"I tried that, but she snatched the book and threw it across the room."

"Wow," my eyes widened. "She *is* in a snit, isn't she?"

"Little bit."

"Okay," I said, trying to stand a little straighter, squaring my shoulders. "Here goes nothing. Wish me luck."

"Good luck."

I opened her door timidly. After hearing what Bonnie had said about Mama throwing the book, I was fearful of a similar missile flying at my head. I saw her sitting in her bed with her arms crossed. In one of her hands she held the colorful necklace I'd given her last Christmas. She was scowling and I approached her carefully, as if she were perched on top of a land mine.

"Mama?"

She cut her eyes sideways at me, acknowledging my presence, but the scowl remained on her face. "Who are you?"

Oh, I did *not* need this right now. "I'm Lacey. Your daughter."

"My daughter? Haven't seen my daughter."

"Yes, you have, Mama. I'm right here."

"My daughter hasn't come to see me in a long time."

Don't argue, I reminded myself. *Go along with her.* "Well, then she should be ashamed of herself, shouldn't she? A good daughter visits her mama."

The scowl disappeared and she uncrossed her arms. Immediately, she started fingering the colorful charms on the necklace in her hand, sliding them around, one-by-one, like rosary beads. The colors were one reason I got it for her. She'd always liked bright, vibrant colors, but they had seemed even more important to her in the last several months. The other reason I chose this gift was that the charms were replicas of books ... children's classics, like *Goodnight Moon, The Little Engine That Could, Charlotte's Web, The Poky Little Puppy,* and others. Altogether there were about twenty of them. When I'd seen it, I knew I had to get it for her. It was the perfect accessory for the "Reading Lady."

I gestured at it. "I like your necklace. They look like books I remember you reading to me when I was little."

She looked down at it. "Yes," she said. "That's what I used to do with them. Then I decided I would put them on a necklace and wear it." She picked up a photograph from her nightstand and handed it to me. "Will you read to me?"

I smiled and took the picture from her, fighting tears. It was a photo of her and Daddy, back before she'd been diagnosed with Alzheimer's. Happy smiles—almost laughter—shone from each of their faces. "Oh, good. This is one of my favorites," I choked out around the lump in my throat. "Scoot over so I can sit down beside you."

She moved over just far enough for me to rest exactly half of my rear on her bed, and I began. "This is the story of a wonderful man and his wife who loved each other very much ..."

CHAPTER TWENTY-FIVE

He shifted the girl on his shoulder, taking a moment to catch his breath in the darkest shadows under the sagging limbs of an oak tree. Though far from overweight, his burden was tall, with long graceful limbs, which made her heavier than expected.

"I hope you'll like the spot I picked for you," he murmured. "It took a lot of work to find it. Well, that and a good imagination, as well as some luck." He chuckled softly at the thought. Oh, to be a fly on the wall when they found her in the morning, he thought, wishing he'd have rigged a motion-activated video camera to preserve the moment. He'd give anything to be able to see their faces. But setting up something like that attracted attention, and attention was something he couldn't afford until after this was done.

He wiped a drip of water from his forehead, glancing upward. Left-over rain still clung to the thick leaves overhead, occasionally dribbling reminders from the afternoon's storm, while the smell in the air held promises of more to come.

He was almost there. He could see the light colored gash at the side of the tree where a limb had been. That marked the spot where he'd get in. There was a break in the heavy iron fencing there that the limb had created when it had fallen, and the city hadn't repaired yet.

That gash had been how he'd found this place. He'd been on the hunt for this verse's perfect setting, and had actually started to worry that he'd be forced to improvise with something less than perfect, because nothing he'd seen yet had been right. Then he saw the gash in the tree where the limb had been, looking as if a giant hand had ripped it out. It must've been enormous, weighing a ton or more. The remaining limbs were equally huge, spreading a green canopy equivalent in size to that of a mansion.

The bent and mangled section of fencing wasn't the only destruction the falling limb had caused. Several toppled gravestones were also victims. Another one had been cracked in half, the two pieces propped crookedly against each other. He was marveling at the results of nature's power when his eyes paused on a larger monument a few feet to the left of the tree.

The plot was surrounded by a smaller, more ornate iron fence, about three feet high. It had its own gate with a slightly Celtic flavor. Knots and curlicues were woven together with vines and leaves, and in the center was an oval that bore the figure of a woman, kneeling, with her face in her hands, like she was crying. He'd never seen anything like it. It was beautiful and sad at the same time, rusted with age.

But the best part was the marble headstone. It stood five feet tall, lavish and ornamental. A bas-relief lily, a cross, and several fern fronds decorated the surface. Below the birth and death dates was a banner that read, "Darling." Two long slabs of marble extended perpendicularly from the bottom of the marker and were attached to a smaller, less ornate footstone. The whole thing resembled a narrow bedframe without a mattress and box spring.

Then his eyes moved upward, and the name at the top of the headstone sent his heart pounding like a kettledrum.

Carter Andrew Bullington.

He'd blinked several times to make sure he was seeing straight, but it was there, alright. The first letters of each of the three names had seemed to almost glow. *Cart and Bull.* Fate had led him to the perfect spot.

He hurried the last few feet to the break in the tall fence and eased through, careful not to catch his pants on the iron's sharp edges. He stepped over the shorter fence and was just starting to shrug the woman off his shoulder when she lunged violently in his arms and gave a loud moan.

He grunted in surprise. The unexpectedness of the action nearly made him drop her, but he managed to recover and hurriedly set her down. Her bottom had barely touched the ground, when she gave another awkward lunge, this time forward, catching him off-guard and making him lose his balance. He fell backwards, hitting his head on the footstone hard enough that black spots danced in front of his eyes.

He shook the spots away, and touched the back of his head where the air was making it sting. His eyes narrowed and a flash of fury burned through his veins.

He scrambled toward her and she moaned again, loud and incoherent. In the light from the street, he could see determination in her eyes that gleamed feral, like a cat's. The second he moved, she began waving her arms and legs wildly, with no real control. One foot caught him in the crotch, not a solid hit, but hard enough that he clutched himself and almost cried out. An animal growl came from his throat and he sprang forward. Her flying elbow caught him in the jaw, jarring his teeth together, and another loud, unearthly moan rolled from her depths.

He had to stop her. Someone would hear. Avoiding her wildly waving hands as best he could, he reached blindly, feeling along the ground for something, *anything* to stop the noise. His hand closed around a chunk of stone and he brought it down on her head with a *thud*.

Instant stillness.

Dropping his weapon, he sat back on his heels, gasping for breath. The rush of rage dissipated as quickly as it had come and left him feeling empty. The young woman slouched in front of him. The headstone rose behind her, Carter Andrew Bullington still at its top, the word, "Darling" arcing right over her head. Her long arms and legs sprawled, unmoving. Her mouth hung open. Her wild eyes were now closed. Blood streamed down her forehead, beside her right eye, down her cheek, puddling between her breasts.

How had his flawless plan gone so wrong?

He'd miscalculated the drug dosage again … by a lot, it seemed. He hadn't given her nearly enough, and she'd been able to rally and fight through it. She hadn't scratched him—thank god—but she'd given him a wallop on the side of his face. He opened and shut his mouth, working his jaw, making sure she hadn't broken or dislocated it. No, it was good. He'd probably end up with a bruise, but the way he wore his beard should camouflage that.

He frowned at the blood coursing down her cheek. It spoiled the presentation he'd planned so carefully. Disappointment left him feeling drained.

He sighed, leaned forward, and dipped his gloved finger in the blood on her chest, then traced it on the headstone, head cocked to one side, concentrating. When he was done, he sat back and admired his work, nodding his head in satisfaction. Leaning forward again, he placed his hands around her neck. This wasn't how he'd meant for it to be, but the fifth verse had to be sung.

"Hush, little baby. Don't say a wor—"

He broke off when a screech of tires rang through the air, sounding much too close. Across the cemetery, a block away, headlights swung across the treetops in an arc.

He scrambled to his feet, eyes wide with panic. He had to get of here … now! He turned and stumbled over the short fence, scrambling on all fours until he was able to get his feet back under him. He raced to the outside fence and hurtled through. There was sudden rending tear, and he winced, squeezing his eyes tightly together and hissing an expletive through clenched teeth. There was no time to check the damage.

He was in his car in an instant. The engine roared to life and he squealed away from the curb, roaring down dark, residential streets, ignoring stop signs along the quiet road, turning right, then left, then right again. His eyes flicked from the street in front of him, to his rear-view mirror—back and forth, over and over—searching for a set of headlights. He turned left again, just as an emergency vehicle streaked by, going the opposite direction the next block over. He bit his lip at the close call, tasting blood.

He pounded his gloved fist against the steering wheel in helpless rage, gulping air, almost hyperventilating. Fury and fear fought for first place in his head. How could this have happened? How could his perfect plan have gone so horribly wrong? At least she was dead; not the way it was supposed to happen, but dead, nonetheless. She had to be. No one could live through a hit like that. He could still hear the *thunk* of the rock hitting her skull, the impact shuddering up his arm. If it hadn't killed her instantly, she wouldn't last for long and she certainly wouldn't be talking.

Get off the road! The urge screamed through his brain. *Whip into a parking lot, a back road—even someone's driveway. Turn off the engine. Hide.* The impulse was strong, but he knew that the more time that went by, the more cops there would be out looking for vehicles that didn't belong where they were. The safest place was home, with his car parked right where it was supposed to be. That's where he had to go.

He only had to make one other evasive maneuver before making it back to his apartment, and he sighed with relief when he slowed to turn in.

The sigh caught in his throat. Lights! Why were lights on? It was supposed to be dark.

He killed his headlights before making the turn and crept up the driveway at a snail's pace. The pounding surf and the steady wind masked any noise his car made, but he kept his eyes trained on the lighted windows, watching for shadows that would indicate someone passing by, maybe looking out.

He slipped off his shoes at the foot of the stairs, tiptoeing up with the slowness of melting ice, his ears straining for any unexpected sound. There was his door. A few more steps and he'd be inside.

There. He had made it.

He sagged against the wooden surface once it was closed and drew a deep, calming breath, letting it out slowly.

His shoes thudded to the floor, and he walked sock-footed over to the makeshift bar that was actually a desk, pouring himself a measure of whiskey, tossing it back, neat. The amber liquid slid down his throat, sending a rush of mellow fire into his chest.

He needed to figure out what had happened, to go through each step of the night, debrief his mind, and plan his next move. He couldn't stop now. His mission was almost complete. He pressed the cool glass to his forehead as if trying to press his thoughts into order, then he grabbed the bottle and headed to his bedroom.

CHAPTER TWENTY-SIX

Ford

I leaned back in my chair, rubbed my tired eyes, and groaned. *What a day.*

I'd come back to the police station after my disastrously short run so I could have access to their files. I had wanted to follow up on the whereabouts of Joelle's son, Coop, but I hadn't had much luck.

It hadn't taken me long to find an address for the grandmother, Josephine Cooper. She was the wealthy widow of Stanley Cooper, a Miami-based luxury yacht broker. After his death, she'd surprised everyone by taking over the business and doubling profits, making her a millionaire several times over. Hard to hide something like that. From what I'd read about her—which was plenty, due to a bigoted narrow-mindedness that landed her in editorial pieces on a regular basis—I believed I knew why Joelle had fled from Miami. It couldn't have been fun growing up having Josephine for a mother.

The Miami address was a dead-end, though. Josephine had died a couple of years ago, leaving everything to Coop, but he'd disappeared. And I hadn't been able to track him down. Maybe I'd have better luck tomorrow, but for now ... I was outta here.

I shut down the computer, glanced at the time, and grimaced. A little after two. I really needed to get my days and nights back on more normal footing. Shoving files into my bag, I slung it over my shoulder and was heading down the hallway when my phone rang. I answered without looking at who it was. I knew.

"Lacey, what is it?" I asked, already running down the hall, bursting through the doors and racing to my car.

"The cemetery!" she gasped. "St. Peter's cemetery. It's Raine! He has Raine! Hurry!"

***

Where in the world do I start? I groaned when I made the last turn and my headlights panned across the large city block. The place was huge … and dark. A search might take hours and from what Lacey had told me, I didn't have that long.

I slid to a diagonal stop across three spaces, wrenched the door open, and jumped out, wondering again where to start. Before I took the first step, an engine roared to life, tires squealed … sounds that rang through the still night air. My head jerked to the right, eyes narrowed. A set of headlights swung wildly on the opposite side of the block and disappeared.

Was that him? Leaving just now? I slid back into my seat and shoved the key in the ignition, blood pumping fast. *Follow him, follow him …* my heart pounded out the syllables. *Follow him.*

Just before yanking the car into gear, I paused. No. I needed backup. There was no way I could pick up this guy's trail. He had a head start. By the time I got around to the other side of the cemetery, he could've taken any number of turns. I'd lost him before even starting and if I tried to tail him in spite of those odds, another girl might die. Lacey said he hadn't strangled Raine … that she might still be alive. We might have a way to ID this guy.

I hesitated a second longer, then pushed the desire to follow him aside and reluctantly turned the car off. Before exiting, I paused to radio in the information about the suspect's car, then grabbed my flashlight and took off in the direction I'd heard him leave, praying I wasn't too late.

Lacey told me she thought Raine was near a fence, no, *two* fences, one tall and one short. And that there was a gate … and a tree, with a large gash where a limb had come down. I swept the light around me. Trees were scattered all over the place. It would take too long to check them all. But a tall black iron fence ran all the way around the perimeter. I'd start there, work my way around.

It was a good thing I had a flashlight. Trying to run through a cemetery at night without a one would've been suicidal. If there'd been a moon, it might've helped some, but thick clouds kept any celestial light hidden. It was tricky even with a light, requiring a lot of zig-zagging back and forth, and being on constant lookout for smaller markers that made perfect tripping hazards. The place was a maze, especially when I didn't have an exact location. How was I supposed to find this girl?

The bright beam of my flashlight bathed everything it touched in a bright halogen glow, which was good, but a mixed blessing. The light created deep shadows behind each stone ... shadows large enough large enough to hide a body. It required checking behind each one, eating up valuable time. I chafed at the delay. Craig and his men should start arriving soon. I'd called him right after I got off the phone with Lacey. I wished they'd hurry up. We could cover more ground with more people looking.

I heard a roar of an approaching engine and gave a grim smile. Speak of the devil. Craig had arrived. I heard his truck door slam and I stopped and waved my light to get his attention. "Start around the fence-line the other direction. I'll keep going this way," I shouted. "She's supposed to be near the fence."

Craig didn't reply, but I saw the glow from his flashlight head off in the other direction. I continued my search.

Several feet later, up ahead of me, I could see a massive, live oak tree blocking my path. It grew right up to the fence, leaving a narrow opening between them that I wasn't sure I could squeeze through. Gah! Looked like I was going to have to back up and go around it. I turned, but when my light swung around, I caught a flash of something that didn't fit, a lighter patch that seemed out of place. I spun back around, skimming my light backwards and forwards, up and down, hoping I'd see whatever it was that caught my eye.

About twenty feet up, a large gash, probably three by four feet, glowed in my light. That was it! That's what Lacey said to look for. I raced toward the small gap between the fence and the tree and was about to slip through when I saw the next thing I was supposed to look for: a missing section of the outer fence. When the great limb had fallen, it'd flattened a panel. I could see the bent and broken the metal, the sharp edges that Lacey'd warned me about.

While I was still squeezing through it, I saw the second, shorter fence, then the rusty gate.

"Over here!" I yelled to Craig, over the pounding of my heart.

Raine looked dead. Her skin glowed an unhealthy pasty color in the beam from my flashlight. Blood streaked down her forehead, dripped from her brow onto her cheek, pooling across her chest, running down between her breasts. I couldn't tell whether she was breathing as I stepped over the short rusty fence that surrounded the grave plot she sat in, but I was afraid we were too late. That was a lot of blood.

I knelt and pressed my fingers to the side of her neck, checking for a pulse, but feeling nothing. "C'mon, girl. You can't be dead!" I hissed through my teeth. I moved my fingers down a little and pressed again, harder this time.

I felt the faintest movement, hardly even noticeable, but it was a pulse. She was still with us … barely. "I got a pulse!" I yelled to Craig, who was huffing my direction. "She's still alive! Call an ambulance!"

Craig staggered the last few steps, hand pressed to his side, and gasping like an emphysema patient, fumbling in his pocket for his phone, dialing. "We need an ambulance," he wheezed. "St. Peter's cemetery. What?" The single-syllable word sounded like a lion's roar. "You don't get paid to be a comedian, son," he snapped. "I need an ambulance, and I need it now. This girl's not going to make it if they don't get here, like yesterday!"

"You got a handkerchief or somethin'?" I asked when he'd hung up. I had my hand pressed against her head, trying to stem the flow of blood. She couldn't have much more to lose.

He dug in his pocket, pulled one out and gave it to me. "Here."

I wadded it up, pressing it firmly against the gash. "C'mon, Raine. Hang in there, girl."

A strangled, choking sound came from Craig's direction.

"What?" I asked, glancing back at him. He'd gone a little pale and his eyes bugged out. He pointed with his chin and I looked up at the gravestone in front of me.

Carter Andrew Bullington.

The first letters of each word were traced in blood, making them impossible to miss.

"Cart and bull," I whispered, hardly able to believe my eyes. "Why is she still alive?"

***

"Well? Don't you have a phone call to make?" I asked Craig later in the ER waiting room as I flipped through a months old copy of *Southern Homes and Gardens.* My question was just a formality. Of course Jeb would be released. He wasn't the killer.

When he didn't answer, my eyes shot toward him, noting his confused expression. "To the station?" I prompted.

Still nothing. I shook my head, amazed. Was he really that dense or was it an act? "To release Jeb Billings. You got the wrong guy."

The air hummed with a guilty silence … well, as silent as a hospital waiting room could be. Craig studied his shoes as if they held the secret to world peace. He refused to make eye contact with me, but his face had gone that all-too-familiar shade of hot pink.

I closed the magazine with calm deliberateness, setting it carefully on top of the others as if a sudden motion might make it explode, all while reminding myself that punching Chief Craig in the face was not an option. Though it might make me feel better, it would mean a lot of extra paperwork, and the momentary pleasure just wasn't worth it. "It happened again," I pointed out. "*While* Jeb was locked up. Admit it. You've got the wrong guy."

Craig opened his mouth to reply, but snapped it shut when he noticed the curious eyes of others in the ER waiting room. He tilted his head toward the door. "Mind if we chat about this outside?"

He was right. This wasn't something that should be discussed with an audience. We pushed our way through the two sets of double doors, out into the gray light of early morning. The air was so heavy with moisture it was difficult to breathe. I could almost taste the salt in the breeze. As soon as we were a safe distance away, I swung around to face him. "Well?"

"Billings had a skeleton buried in his yard. I'd hardly call that innocent."

"Uh … don't you think *that* was a little suspicious? The whispery voiced recordin' … the longitude and latitude coordinates? I think the killer was settin' Jeb up, drawin' attention away from himself by paintin' a bulls-eye on an innocent man's back."

"It's still under investigation. Until we know more, he stays locked up. This attempt tonight could've been a completely unrelated attack … not even part of the lullaby murders."

My eyes bugged out. "What? Are you out of your mind?"

He shrugged that off. "She doesn't fit the MO. Until we investigate further, he stays where he is."

"Doesn't fit the MO?" I echoed, incredulous. "You're the one who noticed the tombstone. Pretty obvious, don't you think … even without the letters outlined in blood. But the killer erased any doubt with that stunt. He actually spelled it out for you: cart and bull. It's part of the song. Jeb's *not* our guy."

Craig's bottom jaw set in a stubborn line. "It might be a copycat."

"How can it be a copycat if no one knows about the song? We've taken great pains to make sure that bit of information didn't get out."

He shook his head, ignoring my question. "She wasn't strangled. The others were. End of story."

"You unbelievable piece of—" I broke off and pressed my lips together, capturing the unsaid word. My face twisted at its bitterness. "So what? We sit on our hands and wait for the *real* killer to strike again so you'll be convinced? Is that what you're sayin'?"

If possible, Craig's face turned an even deeper shade of pink—bordering on fuchsia—and his eyes narrowed into dangerous slits. "We wait for Ms. Fairbanks to regain consciousness so we can question her."

"She's in a coma, for heaven's sake. They had to drill a hole in her skull to relieve pressure on her balloonin' brain, not to mention the fact that she almost bled out. She might not wake up! And if she does, it'll probably be a while. Time enough for the *real* killer to strike again. And before he does—strike again, that is—we need to let people know about that datin' site"

He shook his head. "We will, but not yet."

I thought the top of my head might explode. "Are you freakin' kiddin' me?"

"This wasn't a lullaby murder; it didn't count. You allowed me one more."

Words failed me. All I could do was gape at him ... and glare. I let that glare do my talking.

He returned my glare with one of his own. It was obvious he wasn't going to change his mind.

I shook my head in disgust. "You think the good folks of Fernandina Beach are going to thank you for lockin' up the wrong man? For givin' them a false sense of security? You got another think comin', pal." Then I pivoted and stalked away.

***

I was too wired to think about sleeping, and I knew Lacey would have questions if I went back to the apartment; questions I didn't have answers for yet. Add in the fact that I was livid over Craig's idiocy, his blatant refusal to face facts, and I wasn't in good shape. All together, I knew it was no use thinking about bed for a while. I'd have to calm down first.

I headed back to the station. Something had been niggling at me ever since finding out the skeleton in Jeb's yard belonged to Joelle. So far, I'd been unable to grasp whatever it was, but maybe doing some more research would bring it to the surface. I believed Coop was the key. I just didn't know how he fit yet.

I sniffed appreciatively when I walked into the building. Coffee, thank God! Some kind soul had brewed a fresh pot. I veered to the break room before hurrying to my makeshift office. Settling at the conference table, I booted up the computer and proceeded to dig my way back down through multiple layers of sub-files to where the old Joelle Cooper file had been buried. I picked up my styrofoam cup for another sip, clicked a bit deeper, and jumped, spilling hot coffee all down the front of my shirt. I'd found a photo of Coop. No, actually two of them ... one younger, one older.

Not wanting to step away from the computer screen, even to grab a paper towel, I plucked my shirt away from my chest so it wouldn't burn and studied the pictures. The first looked like a school picture of Coop at about seven years old. Haunted, wide-set eyes—so light blue as to appear colorless—stared from a narrow face. He had a sprinkling of golden freckles across a nose that was too long for his face. Rodent-brown hair, badly in need of a brush, topped his head. His expression was wistful and indescribably sad. The name under the photo was: Cooper, Davey T.

In the second one—another school photo—he looked fifteen or sixteen. About the age he'd been when his mother disappeared. The sad, haunted expression was gone, replaced with anger and defiance ... a hardened jawline, a set mouth. His mousy hair had darkened; his long nose was even longer and now had a hook.

Davey? I shook my head. No, that didn't ring a bell. This was the boy I remembered from school and the only thing I'd ever heard him called was Coop. I leaned back in my chair, comparing the photos.

Let's say the rumors I'd heard back in high school were true. Joelle had allowed certain of her boyfriends who were so inclined, free rein to torture her son, just for kicks. The younger photo would support that. There was a world of misery trapped in those strange blue eyes; deep sorrow, such as what might come from knowing your own mother was letting the unthinkable happen to support her drug habit. I didn't blame the creeps for refusing Joelle's needle-ridden carcass as payment, but the thought of one of them hurting this little boy turned my stomach.

The teenage photo of Coop supported that theory, too. He'd filled out, bulging muscles and thick neck of an athlete. I seemed to recall him being on the wrestling team. The sadness was gone, replaced with barely-hidden rage. I could see it smoldering in his eyes. It wouldn't take much to fan those coals into a roaring flame.

A theory was developing in my head like a Polaroid snapshot, the shadows and edges just beginning to show up against the white background. I needed to find this guy. Only he could answer some of my questions. I had a name now—a real one, not a nickname. That should help me in a search. But Coop had inherited a bunch of money from his grandmother and money was pretty useful if one really wanted to disappear. If the rabbit didn't want to be found, it would be difficult to pull him out of the hat.

Ding.

I looked up, almost expecting to see the proverbial light bulb hovering over my head in a cartoon bubble.

I sat forward so quickly the chair squeaked in protest, and snatched up my phone, scanning through the recent calls, punching the one I wanted, waiting impatiently for the ring.

"*Yell*-ow!"

I rolled my eyes at the familiar greeting. "Hey … do you have one of those programs that will enhance a kid's photo so you can see what he'll look like as an adult?"

"You mean an age-progression app?"

"Right. You got one of those?"

"Yeah, why?"

"So if I email you a photo of a teenager, you could add, say … ten or so years?"

"You bet."

"Okay. That way we won't be flying completely blind. It'll give us a better idea of who we're lookin' for. Emailin' it now." I quickly attached the file and hit, *Send.*

"I'll get right on it."

"Great. Thanks."

CHAPTER TWENTY-SEVEN

Lacey

I awakened to pounding on my bedroom door. The act of knocking was more a warning than asking permission, though, because Bonnie barged right in before I could push the hair out of my face and roll over, much less bid her enter.

"Lacey." Her voice was high and tense. "Your mother is gone."

"Gone?" The word sounded foreign to my sleep-dulled ears. I needed an interpreter, or maybe this was a dream. Thinking of the word *dream* brought instant visions of last night's nightmare, but then I saw Bonnie's stricken expression, and my heart rate spiked to the stroke level. I scrambled into an upright position, and all thoughts of Raine and what might or might not have happened to her evaporated. "W-what do you mean, gone?" I stammered.

"What do you think it means?" she snapped, clearly frightened. "When I went to check on her this morning, she wasn't in her room."

I jumped to my feet and rushed to the bathroom to grab a scrunchie for my chaotic hair. I couldn't think with it clouding all around my head. "She's not in the house anywhere? Hiding, maybe?" I asked as I finger-combed the mass into a hasty ponytail while hurrying back out.

"No, I did a quick search of the house—even the closets—before waking you up."

"Okay." My thoughts were racing. "Call the police, then hop in your car and start driving around looking for her. She can't have gotten far. I'll take the beach."

"The tide is really high—" Bonnie broke off, and winced.

Her unsaid words only made my heart rate increase. There wasn't a lot of beach left due to the hurricane lurking a hundred miles offshore. "Just go," I ordered.

While she dashed for her phone, I slipped on a pair of shoes then grabbed my own phone. As I raced down the hallway, I could hear her voice saying, "Yes, hello. We have an emergency ..." I skidded to a stop at the front door, wrenched it open, and gasped. My heart jumped so hard at the unexpected presence of someone standing in the doorway that it lodged itself in the vicinity of my throat and stayed there.

Travis.

He stood there for a long, shocked minute, looking as startled at my sudden appearance as I was with his. Then his face broke into a huge grin. "I found something I think you might be looking for." He stepped aside with a flourish ... and there was Mama.

Relief made my knees nearly give way. "Oh, God! Mama! Where have you—" I broke off and called into the house, "Bonnie ... It's okay. I found her. She's here."

Bonnie rushed around the corner, phone still pressed to her ear. She closed her eyes and drew a deep breath to calm herself before speaking again into her phone. "False alarm. We found her. No ... that's right. She's okay. No, you don't need to send anybody. Thank you." She ended the call and when she held her hand out to Mama, I could see it trembling. "Well, Mrs. Campbell, you certainly gave everyone a scare this morning. Let's go get you some breakfast."

Before Mama shuffled off, she looked up at Travis. "Bye, David."

"No, Mama. It's Trav—" I broke off and shook my head helplessly, muttering, "Psh! Why do I even try?" I turned to Travis with an apologetic smile. "Sorry about that. My mother has Alzheimer's, and once she makes her mind up about something, it's nearly impossible to change it."

"No problem." He watched her disappear around the corner before turning his attention back to me. "So, does she do that a lot? Wander off, I mean?" he added at my questioning look.

"Uh, no. This is the first time, but from everything I've read and people I've talked to, it's a pretty common occurrence among those with this disease. So …" I forced a brighter smile. "… thank you for being at the right place at the right time for this inaugural event. You've kept it from being much scarier than it could've been. How can I ever thank you?"

"Mmm." His brows waggled up and down and his eyes held a wicked twinkle. "A beautiful woman who is beholden to me. What can the payment be?" He rubbed his hands together in anticipation.

With the shadow of a beard darkening the lower half of his face, he looked decidedly roguish. If he'd had a moustache, he'd probably be twirling it around his finger like the bad guy in one of those old-timey black-and-white movies. I couldn't help but laugh at his theatrics. "Well?"

"A date," he decided. "I know you have to work in the evenings, so it can be lunch. We'll do a picnic."

"A picnic?" I grimaced and gestured to the sky behind him. "Uh … have you looked outside lately? There's sort of a hurricane trying to move in. I keep listening for the sirens to let us know to evacuate. They haven't yet, but it's not what you'd call great picnicking weather."

"Well, then, we'll have it indoors. I know just the place. I'm on my way to Jacksonville for the day. Won't be back here until late tonight. So, noon, tomorrow? I can meet you here."

"An indoor picnic?" I questioned doubtfully, then shrugged and smiled. "Okay then. It's a date."

***

Mama was staring out the window and eating dry Cheerios from a bowl when I joined her and Bonnie in the kitchen. I followed her gaze. The tops of palm trees whipped and whirled around in the strong wind; beyond them, the angry ocean rolled and boiled, pounding and crashing against the large granite boulders that formed a barrier between the now non-existent beach and the dunes in front of the house. I looked back at the cereal and then at Bonnie, questioning with my eyes.

The nurse explained, "She doesn't like the way milk makes it look."

"Riii-ght." I nodded, as I stuck a slice of bread in the toaster, then poured myself a glass of orange juice, setting it on the table. I leaned against the counter, waiting for my toast, and eyed Bonnie glumly. "I guess I should've changed the locks like you suggested weeks ago, huh?"

"We can't cry over spilt milk," she shrugged. "The wandering has started. We deal with it now. Keyed deadbolts are a must. That needs to happen first. We have to have a way to lock the door where she can't open it. Windows, too, while we're at it. It'll probably make her mad, but that's how it has to be. Especially living this near the water . . ."

Her warning made me swallow hard. Trying to keep Mama from hurting herself was a full-time job—worse than living with a toddler, since you can teach a toddler and they eventually learn. That doesn't work with Alzheimer's patients. We'd already put safety latches on cabinet doors, eliminated area rugs because they might be tripping hazards, moved all fragile valuables to secure locations, covered all the sharp corners on the furniture and counters with foam and duct tape, taken down all mirrors except the ones in my bathroom and Bonnie's room so Mama wouldn't get confused and agitated, and gotten rid of the glass topped coffee table in the living room in order to avoid that potential calamity. The recliner too … it terrified her when she sat in what appeared to be a chair only to suddenly find herself on her back. It was exhausting trying to stay a step ahead of her.

"What's that?" Mama interrupted, pointing at the glass I'd just put on the table.

"It's orange juice, Mama."

"What am I supposed to do with that?"

"You drink it. It can help wash down those dry Cheerios."

"Cheerios? Oh, yes. I like them, but not right now. I have something stuck in my pockets."

"Pockets? You mean, your teeth? Your throat? Here, drink some juice." I pushed my glass toward her, then reached in the cabinet for another one, pouring a second serving.

She took a few obedient sips, and stared out the window again. "Look at the people."

"Mama, there aren't any people out there." I asked.

"Yes, there are. See them? Shaking their heads. Mad about the wind."

"Oh," I replied, figuring it out. "The palm trees. There's a storm coming, Mama. A hurricane. This one is named Audrey. The last bad one we had was Matthew a couple of years ago."

"I don't think I lived here then."

"Yes, you did, Mama. Remember, we had to leave because of the storm surge. We drove up to Atlanta to see your sister for a couple of days."

"Who was visiting?"

"*We* were. With your sister, Danielle. Aunt Dannie? You remember Dannie?"

I shot a helpless look at Bonnie, whose eyes met mine with sympathy.

"Remember the rules, Lacey," she murmured a reminder.

Right. The rules. No arguing with her. No insisting she remember something she clearly didn't. I sighed. "Sorry. I guess I'll never learn." I turned back to my mother. "Eat your Cheerios, Mama."

"What are Cheerios?"

I closed my eyes and bit my lip, praying for peace.

***

Since my number one source of seafood was still in jail, I had to line up another avenue for tonight's menu, and it took more time than I thought it would. I'd just pulled into the parking lot when God unzipped the bottom of the moisture-laden clouds and they began dumping their contents in a Niagara Falls-like deluge. I could barely distinguish the outline of the buildings across the street, so seeing Liv's shop, a block away, was out of the question. Lightning forked across the sky; the cannon-fire of thunder boomed on its heels.

Ugh! I gazed miserably through the windshield. Of all the days to forget my umbrella. Tilting my gaze upward, I grimaced. I doubted I could wait this one out. It looked like it was settling in for the long haul. No way around it. I was going to get wet.

"Hurricane schmuricane!" I muttered, along with some more colorful ideas of what said hurricane could do with all this rain. I stepped out of my car directly into an ankle-deep puddle, and groaned. I was soaked in an instant, but tucked my chin and sprinted down the sidewalk toward Liv's, splashing water in all directions. I knew she would have towels and I hoped she'd have a spare umbrella I could borrow. Although, as soaked as I already was, by the time I got there, using an umbrella was probably a moot point.

Head still down, I barreled around the corner, and—*wham!*—I collided with someone hurrying, almost as fast, the opposite direction.

Oomph! The air that used to be inside my body was knocked to the four winds. I staggered sideways, trying to drag oxygen into lungs that screamed for air.

"Lace!" A strong hand grabbed my shoulder to steady me, pulling me under the shelter of a large umbrella. "Good grief! Are you okay?"

I knew that voice. Blinking water, I pushed back the curls that were plastered to my forehead and met Ford's anxious eyes. "Sorry," I tried to laugh, but it came out a wheeze. I hadn't regained my ability to breathe properly, yet. "I didn't see you."

"Oh yeah?" He grinned, rubbing his side. "You mean you haven't changed professions? I thought maybe you'd switched and were now a linebacker. That was quite a hit. I think you might've cracked a rib."

I narrowed my eyes at him while water puddled at my feet. Great. I looked like a drowned poodle, and he looked like he was on break from a GQ photo shoot. Not only that, he *smelled* amazing. It wasn't fair.

I started to return his smile, but the effort was interrupted by a memory from last night's nightmare: Raine, pale and death-like, blood streaming from her head and pooling on her chest. "Raine!" I gasped. "Did you … ?"

"Find her in time?" His grin faded and he stared off down the street. "Yeah. Barely. She's in the hospital … in a coma. She never regained consciousness and we don't know if she will." He shook his head; his expression clearly bewildered. "I can't figure out why he didn't kill her like the rest of his victims."

"Because she fought him," I answered without hesitation.

His eyes shot back to mine. "What do you mean?"

I shrugged. "Just that. She fought him. I saw it in my dream. Her arms and legs started flailing around, like an out-of-control windmill. It surprised him. I don't think he does well with surprise."

"But how could she fight?" he asked. "That's why he uses Rohypnol … so they *can't*."

"Ah, yes … Rohypnol. The drug you forgot to tell me about." I narrowed my eyes at him before continuing. "And him using the lullaby as a 'playbook.' Maybe these are minor details to you, but they're pretty darn important to me. Listen up!" I poked him in the chest, harder than necessary, but I wanted to make sure he was paying attention, and I had some anger that needed to be released. "This pattern you've developed of 'forgetting' to tell me stuff is going to stop. Right here … right now. Got it?" I poked his chest again and he nodded. "Good. Now, is there anything else that you might've left out?"

"Well . . ."

My eyes widened. "There is! Oh, do pray tell."

I watched without remorse as he squirmed, my arms folded across my chest like a shelf.

"I, uh, only just figured it out for sure myself. I wanted to be certain before tellin' anyone. Haven't even told the chief yet."

I rolled my eyes. "Yeah, yeah. Go on."

"Okay, the time between when you have your dream and when the murders actually occur is decreasin' with each subsequent murder."

My mouth dropped open. "How …" I finally spoke after several seconds of gaping at him. "How can you possibly know that?"

"Simple math," he shrugged. "I take the TOD from the coroner—that's *time of death*—"

"I *know* what TOD is. I watch TV."

"Right." He nodded once before continuing. "Anyway, I subtract the time of your dream—as closely as we can estimate—from the TOD and get the difference. The first murder happened forty minutes after your first dream. The second one was thirty-five minutes; the third was thirty, fourth, twenty-five. The fifth one was supposed to be Raine, but she didn't die so we don't have a TOD. It's a pretty safe assumption so say it would've been twenty minutes. So, if the pattern continues, you should dream the next one fifteen minutes before it actually happens."

Silence stretched like a long piece of elastic as I digested this. "Okay, then. Is that everything? Not holding back any other information?"

"Nope."

"I doubt that, but we'll let it go for now." I fidgeted a second before asking my next question. "Does he know?"

"Who?"

"The killer." At his questioning look, I added, "Does he know she's not dead?"

He grimly shook his head. "No. I'm sure he thought he'd killed her."

"So ... What if he tries to finish the job? Sneak into her hospital room and, I don't know ... inject something into an IV or something?"

"I wish he would."

"*What?*" My jaw dropped.

"Don't look at me like that! I only meant, we'd catch him if he tried it. We have a guard posted right outside her door."

I drew in a deep breath, let it out slowly. "Okay. So ... back to the Rohypnol issue. Maybe he miscalculated the dose she needed. I don't know, but she was able to fight it off somehow. She even got in a few good licks. Made him hit his head."

He stiffened, instantly in cop-mode. "On what?"

"There was a footstone—"

Before I finished speaking, he already had his phone out, pressing numbers. Putting it to his ear, his eyes fastened on mine. "Yeah. Are you still at the crime scene? Good. Check the footstone. The perp hit his head on it. Maybe we'll get his DNA. What?" His eyes flashed sea-green fire. "I *know* it's rainin', Al Roker. Work fast." His angry finger punched his phone's screen to end the call. "Unbelievable!" he muttered heatedly. "Apparently Larry and Moe called in sick and I'm stuck with Curly."

I gave an uncomfortable laugh and shifted. I tried to break away from his stare, but couldn't. The circle of dry space we were sharing under his umbrella suddenly felt too small. I felt a rush of heat creep up my neck and redden my face. I was caught; the hypnotized prey of a cobra, unable to wrench my gaze away. I watched his pupils dilate, his lips parting slightly, and the space between us seemed to shrink. My heart started to pound. I was afraid he'd see steam rising from my soggy clothing. I ran nervous fingers through my tangled hair, trying to regain some semblance of order, while, at the same time, trying to calm my racing pulse.

Without warning, another of last night's memories flashed through my mind: Raine ... laughing seductively at him from across the table. The vision was like a bucket of ice dumped on my head, dousing the flame of desire licking along my nerve endings. It stabbed deep, drew blood. I lashed out in retaliation. "So ... how does it feel being the last person to see Raine before she was almost murdered?"

He drew back as if struck, his pupils shrinking to normal size. "What?"

I couldn't seem to stop myself. "Has Chief Craig questioned you yet? No? Well, maybe he should."

"What are you talking about?"

I ignored his question, intent on my attack. "And while I'm on the subject, did you have to choose the restaurant where I work for your date? There are plenty of others in town."

"Date? What date?"

"Don't play dumb. I saw you." His look of utter confusion only fueled my anger. "Last night?" I prompted. "The bistro's outdoor seating? Table for two? Candlelight? Little black dress? Ringing any bells?"

He drew a deep breath as if trying to calm himself before speaking. "You seem to be under the very mistaken impression that I had a date with Raine last night. I'm not sure why you'd think it, but I can assure you that wasn't the case. I was at the police station all evenin', tryin' to track down Joelle Cooper's son. In fact, I was actually just leavin' there when you called me with your latest nightmare, and there are witnesses to prove it," he snapped.

His words rang with truth, and I couldn't help feeling relieved by them. "But if it wasn't you then—" I broke off, eyes widening. I knew exactly who'd sat across the table from Raine last night. The same person who thought I'd be having a picnic with him tomorrow. Well, we'd see about that!

"Excuse me for one minute, please. I have a quick phone call to make," I said, already fishing in my purse for my phone. I dialed quickly, and when the other end picked up, I held up my index finger to Ford, to let him know it would only take a second. His mouth opened as if to speak, then his jaw snapped shut, and he motioned magnanimously for me to go ahead.

"Hello?"

"Hi. It's Lacey." Before he could reply, I went on, "Just wanted to let you know, the picnic isn't going to happen tomorrow."

There was a beat or two of silence, then, "Okaaay. Mind if I ask why?"

"Something's come up. I would say, 'some other time,' but that would be a lie. Got to run, now. Bye."

After ending the call, I paused to press a few more buttons in order to block any future calls he might try to make, then glanced up to meet the question clearly visible on Ford's face. "Don't ask."

He turned his head toward the road where cars crept by with their windshield wipers slashing wildly, trying to clear the window enough for their drivers to see, then turned back to me, one brow raised, a smirk playing hide-and-seek around his mouth. "Picnic?"

"I said don't ask," I ground out through clenched teeth. The streetlight turned red, and the crossing sign started flashing 'walk.' Before he could open his mouth again, I drew a deep breath, braced myself, then ducked and made a run for it.

"Lacey!" His voice sounded exasperated and I knew things weren't finished between us, but I didn't stop until I reached Liv's shop.

***

"Here you go," Liv draped a towel over my shivering shoulders and pressed another one into my hands for me to dry my hair. "I wish I had some clothes to loan you, but the only thing I have here is another pink tutu." She made a face. "Not your average kitchen apparel, and I'm sure Pearl wouldn't approve."

I laughed over my shivering. "Yeah. I can just picture it ... me, decked out with wings and halo—while running through tonight's menu. That would go over like a balloon at a porcupine convention."

"At least you'd be dry."

I waved her concern away and gave my head a vigorous rub before replying, "Don't worry. I have a pair of jeans and a T-shirt in my locker. My chef's coat will cover it up." I stopped and sighed, shoulders slumped in despair.

"Okay," Liv interrupted my melancholy mood. "Are you going to tell me or am I going to have to start guessing?"

I blew a curl out of my face and swung my eyes up to meet hers. "I'm having guy problems."

"Is it the *you-need-help-disposing-of-a-body* kind of problem? Or the *you-like-him-but-he's-being-a-jerk* kind?"

Her answer made me giggle. "I'm glad you're my friend."

"I'm glad I'm your friend, too," she grinned. "Now, which is it?"

"You have something I could use to detangle this mop?" I asked, pointing to my head. We both knew I was deflecting her question, buying some time.

Liv pulled open the bottom drawer of her desk and retrieved a brush, handing it to me. "So?"

"It's Ford ... and Travis."

"Wow!" Her blue eyes went round as saucers. "*Two* guys?'"

"Yeah." My voice sounded as dismal and bleak as a fog bank.

"In some universes, that would be a good thing."

I snorted. "Not this one."

"So, tell me."

"Well, to put it in a nutshell: I have feelings for Ford, but I thought he was interested in Raine, so I told Travis I'd go on a picnic with him, but then I found out it was Travis—not Ford—who was on a date with Raine, and now she's in a coma and—"

"Whoa, whoa, whoa ... back up!" She held up a hand to stop me midstream. "Raine's in a coma? You need to fill in a few more blanks. I'm missing some pretty crucial pieces of this puzzle."

I brushed my hair quietly for a few strokes before answering, "The murderer tried to kill someone again last night."

Liv gasped, "Oh, no!" Then she paused and looked confused. "What does this have to do with Ford, Travis and Raine? And what do you mean, he *tried?*"

I opted to ignore her first question for now. Giving Liv too many moving parts didn't usually work. We'd chase the other rabbit later. "I mean he didn't succeed this time. She's still alive. She's in the hospital … in a coma."

"Coma? But you just said *Raine* was in a coma."

I waited for her to put it together. It didn't take as long as I had thought it might.

Her eyes widened and her mouth dropped open. "He tried to kill Raine?"

I nodded.

"Is she going to be alright?"

"It's too early to know yet, but the police hope she'll be able to tell them who the killer is when she wakes up." *If she wakes up*, I added silently.

Liv's face wore an expression I couldn't make out. "What's that look all about?"

"I was just wondering if all this might change Raine's plans."

"Plans? What plans?"

She didn't answer, and she wouldn't meet my eyes, either. Instead, she focused intently on the star end of her wand. I studied her with a frown. I usually had no problem reading her, but this time I was baffled. Then my jaw dropped. "You mean her plans to buy the restaurant, don't you? How could you think about that at a time like this?"

"You mean, you haven't?"

"Believe it or not, no!"

Her blue eyes were suddenly filled with guilt. "I was just wondering. You know … idle curiosity? What?" she asked when I continued my accusatory stare. "It's not like I was *hoping* anything bad would happen to her."

"You mean worse than being in a coma? Worse than almost being killed?" I didn't know what surprised me more, the fact that Liv had thought of that or the fact that I hadn't. I finally reached over to pat her on her arm. "Look, Raine is a jerk of the highest order and her main goal in life is to make mine miserable, but she doesn't deserve this. No one does."

"I know. I'm sorry. She's got to wake up. They have to catch this guy."

"Yes," I agreed solemnly. "They do."

CHAPTER TWENTY-EIGHT

He pulled his car into the alley, creeping along in the dark until he was tucked into the shadows between the two buildings. His eyes darted in all directions, all senses on high alert. The steady rain was a handicap, masking noises he needed to be able to hear, but he couldn't wait for a more opportune time. It had to be tonight, because the grand finale would be tomorrow, maybe not exactly as he'd planned, but it would work out. He'd make sure of it.

He wasn't comfortable with the spot he'd chosen. It was risky—more so than usual—even with three of the nearest streetlights not working. He'd taken care of them a little earlier with a steady hand and a silencer, but even so, it felt too exposed. Maybe he was just rattled from the night before. That was probably it. Totally understandable. All his carefully-laid plans blown to smithereens when the girl had started fighting off the drug. Well, she was dead and that wouldn't happen tonight. He'd had to get creative with this one, adding a hefty dose of the drug to the salsa when he'd noticed her avoiding her drink. He wouldn't be able to stare into the girl's eyes while singing the song, but he couldn't afford another mistake. Not here.

Once he was sure there was no sign of movement outside, he carefully opened the door, pushed it to, then hurried around to the back of his car. Before opening the hatch, he paused, ears straining, trying again to discern any noise over the rain.

Nothing. Good.

He swung the door upward and reached inside, grasping an arm in one hand and a leg in another, dragging her out and slinging her over his shoulder.

Another pause to listen.

Still nothing.

He crept to the corner of the building, peeking first to the right, then to the left, repeating the motions. The only movements he saw were caused by the wind and rain.

Hurrying as fast as his burden allowed him, he knelt in front of the little blue chair, dropping the girl into it. He quickly positioned her, not taking his usual care with the presentation. His mistakes of the previous night made him jumpy and unsure. All he wanted was to get the job done and escape.

It was so dark under the awning, he couldn't see whether the girl's eyes were open or not, but with the amount of drug he'd given her, it was safe to assume they weren't. It didn't matter this time.

"Hush, little baby. Don't say a word," he whispered, placing his hands around her neck. "Mama's going to buy you a mockingbird."

He paused and swallowed nervously, glancing over his shoulder before turning his attention back to his victim. "And if that mockingbird don't sing, Mama's going to buy you a diamond ring."

He began squeezing her neck, not bothering with timing like he usually did. "And if that diamond ring gets broke, Mama's going to buy you a billy goat."

Another nervous glance over his shoulder, then back. "And if that billy goat don't pull, Mama's going to buy you a cart and bull."

As he sang those last three words, scenes from the previous night's fiasco rip through his head, adrenaline shot through his veins. His fingers too convulsed with a rage so violent he felt the crush of her larynx under his thumbs, heard the snap of her neck, but he kept squeezing, gritting through his teeth, "And if that cart and bull turn over, Mama's going to buy you a dog named Rover."

Time stood still as his emotions spun out of control. It wasn't until his hands started cramping that he regained awareness of his surroundings and realized he was still gripping the girl's neck. With excruciating deliberation he managed to release his death grip, one stiff finger at a time. After completing this painstaking process, he collapsed backwards. His knees went up, elbows propped on them, and his hands tangled in his hair as he gasped for breath.

Without warning, there was a whir and rattle of a bicycle as it whizzed past him on the sidewalk, mere inches away. He'd never even heard it coming. The pounding rain had masked its approach. Astonishment rendered him immobile for a long second before he scrambled to his feet, peered out from the darkened alcove where he was hidden. He narrowed his eyes when he saw the now familiar Rasta cap bobbing up and down in the yellow glow of the streetlights the next block down.

His mind churned as his heart raced. If he'd had any doubts about this guy being a problem, he didn't now. He'd been an idiot to not take care of it after the second time. His plan of pinning the blame on someone else had worked like a charm and bought him some time, but that short reprieve was over. This was the third time. Three times made a pattern, and a pattern was something he couldn't afford. Three different girls ... three different places . . .

"Three strikes. You're out," he growled under his breath.

CHAPTER TWENTY-NINE

Ford

I raked angry fingers through my hair, then remembered the cup of coffee I still carried, gulping down a big swallow and almost spewing it out. Ugh! Disgusted, I turned and pressed the offensive cup into the startled hands a junior officer who scurried by. "Here," I snapped. "Find a trash can, will you?" I ignored the look he gave me, turning back to the garishly lit scene in front of me.

Another murder. I'd thought the killer might lay low a couple of days, let the dust settle a bit after his mistake the previous night, but the fact that he hadn't was right in front of me, in living—make that *dead*—color.

It was all here, just like Lacey had told me when I got her frantic call after her latest nightmare. The bulldog painting, with its bright colors washed out in the spotlights; the book with a dog on the cover, sitting plain as day on a stand in the window. I read the title and shook my head. *A Dog Named, Rover.* If I'd had any doubts about this being a lullaby killing—which I *hadn't*—seeing that title obliterated them.

Something moved in the corner of my eye; the store's sign, hanging out over the sidewalk. Gusts of wind kept it swinging wildly, back and forth. Large, colorful mosaic letters spelled out the name of the shop: Dog Days—a gift shop dedicated to all things canine. Lacey had only seen flashes of the "D" and the "Y" in her dream. The rest of her clues were just as random as usual, not enough to pinpoint where to start, especially in the dark with a storm moving in. I thought we'd caught a break when she mentioned the book, assumed it meant the town's bookstore. I'd headed there first, hoping to arrive within the fifteen-minute span between dream and murder. There'd been nothing there, of course. That would've been too easy. Nothing was ever easy or expected with this guy.

I'd almost missed the body here, in the shop's shadowy alcove; had actually stumbled over it right before the store's owner arrived to do some early bookkeeping.

My eyes drifted to the chair . . .

I'd thought the girl was sitting on the ground when I'd first seen her—long limbs crossed, Indian-style, propped against the wall. Then I realized she was sitting in a chair ... a squatty one, with stubby little legs that were only six inches or so high. It made her look like a dark-haired mystic, hovering slightly above ground. The killer had dumped her into it. That's the only term I knew to use. The combination of momentum and gravity was the only way I could explain how her hips had gotten wedged between the chair's arms. I winced at the way they dug deep into the flesh of the girl's hips and thighs, almost glad she couldn't feel the pain and pressure of it. We'd have to break it off of her. There was no other way to remove it.

Over the sound of the rain, I heard the approach of footsteps behind me, followed by a guttural groan. I knew it was Craig without turning. "Still believe you got your man in jail?" I was picking a fight, using my words as weapons.

Silence.

What? No blustering? No cocky explanation about how he shouldn't be held accountable for another girl's death? Nothing? I turned slightly, glancing over my shoulder, wondering if I'd been wrong about who was back there.

No. It was Chief Craig, all right. He stood there, white-faced, jaw muscles working, brooding eyes staring at our newest victim, his shoulders drooping with defeat. I waited for him to speak.

When the silence continued, I realized I'd be the one who would have to break it. "Forensics just finished gettin' the lights set up. They're ready to start takin' pictures. We'll have to break that chair off her—no other way to remove it—but they wanted to get the 'before' shots first. Heard someone say she's local, but when I asked one of your guys, he gave me a weird look and almost ran away." I studied the man's pasty face as I waited for a response. Still nothing. "You got any idea who she is?"

His Adam's apple bobbed up and down with a swallow. He nodded once, opened his mouth to speak. Nothing came out. After clearing his throat, he tried again. "Jill …" he rasped. "Uh … Gillian Owens." His bleak eyes flickered up to meet mine, then down again. "*Officer* Gillian Owens. My …" His voice cracked, but he forced himself to continue. "… my bait."

"Your bait?" I closed my eyes and rubbed my forehead, feeling the first pangs of a headache. "This is your rookie officer? How in the world did he get the drug in her? You told her he used the drinks, right?"

He nodded miserably. "Yeah … I told her."

I bit back the words, *I told you so.* As much as this guy pissed me off, I just couldn't do it. Guilt had to be eating him alive right now. He'd just lost an officer. That was bad enough. What made it worse was that it was his fault. He and I both knew it. That would never change and there was no way he would ever forget it. Reminding him of it at this point would just be cruel.

"You want me to call her parents?" I asked, in spite of the words I'd said to him when he'd first mentioned his plan.

He winced and pressed his lips together in a grim line. He remembered them too. Shaking his head, he answered in a voice so low, I almost didn't hear him. "No. I'll do it. It's my job."

I watched him pull his phone from his pocket as he turned and walked away with slow, deliberate steps.

***

I hung around at the crime scene until I could hardly stand up. I kept zoning out … sort of falling asleep with my eyes open, which wasn't surprising. Seemed like a month since I'd had an uninterrupted night's sleep. Something like this was bound to happen. Right now, I had that sluggish, underwater feeling, where everything was moving at a sort of half-speed. I was beyond the point where a brisk face-rub would help, but I tried it anyway.

Nope. No jolt of energy. Barring sleep, the only thing that might help was coffee … copious amounts of coffee. Intravenous intake would get it in my bloodstream the quickest, but since that wasn't likely to happen, I'd choose the next best thing: an extra-large cup, brewed strong, with easy access to free refills. The coffee shop was only a couple of doors down. I wouldn't even need my umbrella; the awnings between here and there should keep me mostly dry. They had a "robust" blend that might work if I could get them to add a couple of shots of espresso.

I drank the first cup fast; even added cream—which I hated—in order to cool it down so I wouldn't scald my mouth. The second cup—black, this time—was getting rid of the underwater feeling, helping me "surface," and think more clearly.

Hardly anyone was in the shop, so I nabbed a small booth in the corner and phoned the hospital, hoping for a positive update on Raine.

No change.

"C'mon, girl," I muttered to myself as I ended the call and shoved my phone back in my pocket. "You have to wake up."

She was the only one who knew what this guy looked like, the only one of the victims who'd survived an attack, and so the only one who might be able to help us stop him. If he stuck with his lullaby theme—and there was no reason to believe he wouldn't—the horse-and-cart victim would be his last ... his grand finale.

"... if that dog named Rover don't bark, Mama's goin' to buy you a horse and cart." I sang the verse softly to myself, and a feeling of dread seeped into my bones. If my theory was correct, there'd be no Lacey-lookalikes this time. No ... it would be Lacey, herself.

My stomach clenched at the thought and I yanked my phone back out of my pocket, my finger poised to press her number.

No. This wasn't news I could tell her over the phone, for two reasons. One, she'd think I was overreacting and wouldn't believe me, not that I'd blame her. Gut feelings are hard to explain.

And secondly, I needed to be near her when she found out. That way, if she didn't believe me, I'd be close enough to grab her if she tried to run. She needed to hide somewhere safe until we found this guy. Shoot, I'd lock her in a jail cell if I had to.

Find her. My brain barked the order. *Find her now!*

Grabbing my coffee with one hand, I rammed my phone back into my pocket with the other, and slid out of the booth. In three strides I swung the shop's door open, intent on getting to Lacey as quickly as possible.

I stopped dead in my tracks once I stepped through the door, wondering where to start. Would she still be at home? Or was she already out lining up the seafood she'd need for tonight's menu?

Just before stepping out from under the awning, I heard something that made me pause. What was that? Music? A radio? No, not a radio ... someone singing. I closed my eyes so I could concentrate better, straining to hear over the rain.

Notes of a song ebbed and flowed between the torrents of rain, weaving in and out, until I could finally make out the melody.

"... and if that looking-glass gets broke ... "

My head jerked to the left and I peered through the rain. The singing grew louder as it got closer.

"... Mama's gonna buy you a billy goat. And if that billy goat don't pull ..."

Obie rode his bicycle down the sidewalk on the other side of the street, wire basket full of pineapples. He seemed oblivious to the pounding rain. A train horn sounded in the distance. It only caused him to increase his volume.

"... Mama's gonna buy you a cart and bull . . ."

Why was he singing that song? My mouth went dry, my thoughts tumbled over themselves as my brain tried to come up with an answer. Obie rode all over town, day and night. Had he seen something? Something that triggered that song? Could he have a clue? If so, why hadn't he contacted me? Had he lost my card?

Another blare of the train's horn, louder this time.

The old man's volume rose likewise, "... and if that cart and bull turn over ..."

"Hey, Obie!" I shouted, waving my hand to get his attention.

His head turned my direction, and he grinned at me through the rain.

"C'mere." I motioned to my side of the street. "I need to talk to you."

I saw him give an exuberant nod, then without hesitation, or looking for traffic, he bumped over the curb and started across the road, continuing his song. "... Mama's gonna buy you a dog—"

Two things happened at once: the train's horn blasted another warning, and a car engine roared to life nearby. I could see Obie's mouth moving, but the noise was so loud I couldn't hear him. A sudden flash of movement caught in my periphery, and I watched in horror as an older model, white Cadillac streaked by in front of me.

The impact, when it hit the bicycle, sent Obie and his pineapples hurtling through the air. The former landed in a soggy, unmoving heap while his cargo bounced and rolled off in multiple directions.

A silent second stretched long.

Then someone screamed, and several people splashed out into the street toward the fallen man. I was already moving toward the white sedan, my hand reaching for my shoulder holster, my eyes intent on the car. The driver should be getting out any minute ... any ... minute ...

The engine roared again and before I could react, it sped off. Gun in hand, I sprinted after the car, squinting against the rain that tried to blind me. Another car screeched out of a parking space and squealed after the retreating sedan. The Cadillac hurtled on, ignoring the stop light at the next intersection, narrowly missing a collision. It was heading straight toward the railroad tracks with the pursuing car closing the gap.

The red railroad crossing lights started flashing, and the bars began lowering. Perfect timing. The driver was trapped with nowhere to go. When I saw brake lights, my adrenaline surged, and I sped up. I wanted to be there with my gun in case the creep tried to make a run for it.

Then the glow from the brake lights disappeared, and the engine roared for the third time. The train's horn blasted on and on. With disbelieving eyes, I watched the Cadillac surge forward, crash through the safety bars, and lurch over the tracks, nearly going airborne. The chase-car screeched to a halt just as the train blurred past us, preventing any other visual. I brought up the rear, breathing hard. In a daze, I slowly re-holstered my gun, feeling the ground tremble under my feet, while train car after train car rushed past. What in the world had just happened?

***

The EMT workers were lifting Obie onto a gurney when I joined the huddle of bodies sheltered under the awning closest to the scene of the hit and run. My heart sank when I saw them pull a blanket up over his face.

"He's dead," Chief Craig's informed me unnecessarily. "Blunt force trauma. From what witnesses told me, he probably died instantly."

I didn't reply, just watched them load the gurney into the back of the ambulance. Once they slammed the doors, I turned to Craig, using my sleeve to wipe the water out of my face. It did little good. My sleeve was even wetter. "Anybody get a look at the driver?"

"Couple of people said it was an old woman; one said white hair; one said white scarf. It was raining too hard to see anything else. One guy noticed the plates. Dealer tag. Big red letters. As much detail as he could give me, though."

"That's it? Red letters? Got any ideas?"

He shrugged. "Red's a popular color with car dealerships."

The ambulance pulled away, ominously quiet … no siren, no flashing lights. I sighed. "Well, get one of your guys busy researchin' which dealers have big red letters on their temporary tags." I gave him a direct look. "This was connected to the lullaby murders."

His look was dubious. "How do you figure?"

"Obie was singin' before he was hit."

Craig rolled his eyes. "That doesn't mean anything. He was always singing."

"It was the lullaby."

That shut him up. He narrowed his eyes, staring at the spot where the ambulance had just been, his expression speculative.

I continued, "I called him over as soon as I heard him. I wanted to ask him about it. He was crossin' the road to see me when he was hit."

"Could just be a coincidence," he ventured.

I could tell by the way he said it, he didn't believe what he was saying. I didn't respond to his comment. It didn't deserve a response. "Obie's place overlooked the courtyard beside the art gallery," I reminded him. "I think he saw something that night. He rides—" I stopped, grimaced and corrected myself. "He *rode* all over the place on that bike of his, all hours of the day and night. He might've seen one of the other murders, too. The killer would've seen him as a loose end ... somethin' that needed to be tied up." I gestured toward the middle of the street. "Guess he tied it."

I was surprised that Craig didn't immediately shoot down my idea. Maybe he was still shaken up over the death of his officer, or maybe he agreed with me. Either way, the fact that he was quiet told me he was thinking about it. After another beat or two of silence, he pushed his bulk away from the wall he'd been leaning against. "Welp," he grunted. "Guess I need to get someone started on that dealership tag search."

"Right," I nodded. "Keep me posted."

He lifted his hand in assent, then ducked his head and trotted over to his truck.

CHAPTER THIRTY

The car rocked and bucked over the deeply rutted road. He bounced and jarred up and down, side-to-side, pinging around like a pinball. Silty water splashed high on the side windows. He didn't dare slow down. Getting stuck in the mud wasn't an option. He had a schedule to keep.

The strong smell of kerosene hung in the car's interior like a suffocating curtain, choking him. Nauseating, but necessary, and something he wouldn't have to deal with much longer.

Everything had taken longer than he'd anticipated. First? The car. He knew he wouldn't be able to use his own, since that would defeat his goal of anonymity. He had to steal one, but that wasn't the hard part. No, it was the hotwiring, not that he couldn't do it. He had the skill. It was something he'd learned it from a past acquaintance, but it had been a while since he'd done it, and he'd underestimated how long it would take. It was harder than it looked in the movies.

Then he'd had to follow the bicyclist around for well over an hour, careful to stay far enough back to not draw attention to himself, but close enough to stay alert for the right moment to make his move. This part of his plan had been a bit wrinkly in spots, not completely ironed out, but he was certain the plan would come together when the time was right. It wasn't until he first heard the train's whistle that he knew what he had to do. But how could he get to this guy when he kept riding on the sidewalk like an idiot. Get off the sidewalk!

Then, the unbelievable happened. That cop hollered at the man, motioned him over. It was the cue he'd been waiting for. He'd pressed his foot to the floor, heard the train's whistle blare and prayed that his luck would hold.

It had, but he was running late. He had other, *very* important things to do and a tight schedule in which to do them.

Daring to take one hand off the wheel, he clawed furiously at his head. This wig was making his head itch like a beast. Could he take it off now? Why not? There was no one fool enough to be out here in this storm. Snatching it off, he flung it into the passenger seat, scratched quickly, then resumed his death grip on the steering wheel.

Ahh ... better.

He gave a quick glance at the cheap white hair that lay tousled on the seat beside him and smirked. It had been uncomfortable—and hopefully didn't have fleas or lice living in it—but the disguise had worked. He was sure no one had recognized him.

Adrenaline still spiked his blood, causing his heart to thunder in his chest. He tried deep breathing in an effort to calm down, knowing the human body wasn't equipped to handle that fight-or-flight chemical for prolonged lengths of time, but soon gagged and gave up. An adrenaline high didn't mix well with heavy doses of kerosene fumes. The combination made him dizzy and sent ripples of nausea through his stomach.

How much farther? He didn't remember having to drive this far before, or the road being this bad. Of course, it had been raining non-stop, and that was bound to make things worse, but nothing looked familiar now. Was this even the right road?

Road! He scoffed at the inaccuracy of that term. More like a pair of ruts through the woods.

Panic began welling up inside him, increasing the feeling of nausea. Just as he started scouting for a way to turn around, he caught a glimpse of a clearing up ahead. Was that it? Oh, please let that be where he'd left his car. A few more jousts and vaults, and there it was, right where he'd left it. When the panic drained away, it took some of the adrenaline with it, leaving him feeling much like a deflated balloon. He only needed a few more minutes, but he'd better hurry.

Pulling into park, he turned off the ignition, then reached into the floorboard for the kerosene jugs. He opened all four doors, as well as the trunk and the hood, dousing everything with a liberal stream of accelerant before tossing the empty jugs into the trunk. Then, reaching into his pocket, he retrieved a lighter and leaned into the car to touch the flame to the seat, dropping the lighter once it ignited.

The flame spread quickly, hungry tongues greedily licking at the kerosene, feeding the glow until it became a raging ball of fire. He turned and splashed his way over to his car, watching from a safe distance, feeling the heat on his face. Then his eyes followed the plume of smoke billowing upward, very visible against the sky. It was time to leave. Even weather conditions like this wouldn't keep the curious away for long.

He gave the roaring fire one final glance, then got into his vehicle and began the wallowing journey back the way he had come.

CHAPTER THIRTY-ONE

Ford

I'd just inserted my car key into the ignition when my phone rang. "Jamison," I answered.

"Detective?" an efficient voice queried. "This is Lynette Greenley. I'm a nurse at Baptist Medical. I'm sorry to call you so early, but I understand you wanted to be kept apprised on the status of one of our patients … a Raine Fairbanks?"

"Yes." I felt myself cringe a little, bracing for her next words. The way everything else was going this morning, she was probably calling me to let me know Raine was dead.

"The patient is starting to show signs of regaining consciousness."

"Oh." Her unexpected words made my mind go blank for a second or two. Then it started racing. I needed to find Lacey and put her somewhere safe until this was over. But I also needed to talk to Raine to see if she had any information that could help me find this guy. I wavered between the two needs, unsure of what to do.

"Detective? Are you still there?"

"Yes." I shook the indecision away. The sooner I found this guy, the sooner Lacey would be safe. Raine was the key. "I'm sorry … yes, I'm here. That's great news. I'm on my way. I need to ask her a few questions."

"I'm not sure how much she'll be able to communicate," she informed me with a frosty tone of disapproval. "She's still in ICU and in serious condition. I can let you see her for five minutes—maybe less if she shows any signs of agitation or distress. We'll just have to see how it goes."

In other words, I thought. *You upset my patient and I'll show you the door.* "I understand." I spoke calmly, trying to placate her. "I'll be there as soon as I can."

***

I hurried down the fluorescent-lit hallway. The rhythmic tap of my shoes sounded loud and urgent against the gleaming linoleum. I paused outside the double-doors that separated the ICU unit from the rest of the hospital and pressed an intercom button.

"May I help you?" A disembodied voice warbled over the speaker.

"Detective Jamison here to see Raine Fairbanks."

There was a loud buzz and the doors swung open.

I approached a pear-shaped woman wearing hot pink scrubs that were a couple of sizes too small. Her fingers fairly flew across the keyboard as she typed information into a small laptop sitting atop a rolling cart just outside of one of the rooms. I glanced at the badge hanging from the lanyard around her neck. "Ah, Nurse Greenley," I gave her a disarming smile when she looked up at me. "Just the person I was looking for." I pulled out my badge, holding it so she could inspect it. "Ford Jamison. We just spoke on the phone?"

She studied it like a Russian customs agent, glancing up at my face and back at the badge several times before finally handing it back to me.

"Follow me, please."

The soles of her New Balance sneakers squeaked as she made a one-eighty turn and bustled a few more feet, turning left into a darkened room. She motioned for me to enter, whispering a warning. "Remember what I said, Detective. Five minutes … or less." She arched her eyebrow at me to emphasize her last two words, then turned with another rubber-soled squeak, leaving me alone with Raine.

I approached the bed with tentative steps. She looked like death warmed over, her skin practically the same color as the turban of white gauze wrapped around her head. Bruises provided her only color. Plastic tubing snaked from the IV stand that stood to the left, attached to the bottoms of multiple bags of clear liquids. One of the bags was busy replenishing one of the many pints of blood she'd lost. More tubing piped oxygen into her nose, another collected urine. A machine beeped in a steady rhythm. A screen to the right provided a visual for heart rate, blood pressure, pulse, and other numbers I didn't recognize.

"Raine?" I said in a voice just above a whisper. "It's Ford."

Her eyelid flickered, opened slowly. Did she recognize me? I couldn't tell for sure.

"Can you talk?" I asked.

There was a barely imperceptible shake of her head. I gave her a reassuring smile.

"That's okay. I think you can still help. I'm going to ask you a couple of questions. I need you to blink once for 'yes;' twice for 'no.' Okay?"

One blink.

"Good. Now, do you remember what happened to you?"

Her blink was accompanied by a jump in some of the numbers on the screen, the beeping got a bit faster.

"Shhh … It's okay," I soothed, listening for the squeaky shoes of Nurse Greenley. "You're safe. I just need your help so somethin' like this doesn't happen to another girl. Can you do that?"

A long pause, then one blink.

I took a deep breath. "Okay, here we go. Did you see who did this to you?"

One blink.

"You did? That's real good. Could you identify him?"

Again, one blink.

I stepped closer, swallowed hard. "Was it a stranger, Raine?"

She blinked once … then a second time. The numbers on the screen jumped some more, as the beeping increased in tempo.

Not a stranger! Her heart wasn't the only one beating fast. I knew I had to hurry. Gestapo Greenley would be forcing me out of here any second now. "You knew him? You know his name?"

Her eyes filled with tears, an endless pause, then … one blink. Her numbers rocketed, the beeping went crazy.

I could hear the rapid squeak of shoes against linoleum. Frantic now, I fumbled in my pocket for a scrap of paper, pulling out the receipt for the cup of coffee I'd bought earlier this morning, but I couldn't find my pen. "Raine, this is really important. I need you to write it down for me so I—"

"Detective!" Nurse Greenley's voice snapped right behind me, making me jump.

Whirling to face her, I snapped right back, "I need a pen!"

Her mouth dropped open in shock, but that only lasted a second, then her eyes narrowed into an angry glare.

Uh-oh ... time to defuse this situation. I needed this woman's help. "I'm sorry," I said, desperately trying to smooth her ruffled feathers. "But this is a matter of life and death ... and that's not just a figure of speech. I'm tryin' to keep this ..." I gestured at the battered figure in the bed. "... from happenin' to another girl. I need your pen."

"Detective ..." Her voice was deadly calm, but I could tell it was costing her to keep it that way. "I realize you're not a doctor, but it doesn't take a medical degree to read these machines. I warned you about upsetting this patient."

"Just one second ... " I was begging, but I didn't care at this point. "Or less than a minute. I just need to borrow your pen so she could write down a name."

Her stance was unbending. "Are you going to leave voluntarily, or do I need to call security to escort you out?"

I bit back my opinion of autocratic know-it-all nurses and stalked to the door, mouthing the words, "Whose side are you on?"

"The *patient's* side," she answered in a snippy voice.

Good thing she was behind me so she didn't see the way I rolled my eyes. I thought I'd spoken the words inaudibly, but it must've come out louder than I realized. Then again, she was so close behind me she was practically walking *in* my shoes, so I guess I shouldn't be surprised she heard me.

A few steps before I reached the double-doors, I decided to give it one more try. I turned and faced her, blurting, "I need you to do me a favor."

She gave me a *you've-got-to-be-kidding-me* look, which I ignored. "When she calms down, could you *pleee-ase* try to get her to write down the guy's name who did this to her?"

At first she just glared at me, her mouth pursed tightly. It looked like someone had run a drawstring around its edges. I sent her a hopeful smile and her expression seemed to thaw a half a degree, so I waited.

Finally, she leaned forward and pressed the button that automatically swung the doors open. When I didn't immediately take a step, her hand motioned for me to get moving.

Once through them, I turned to stare at her with brooding eyes. It felt as if a deep chasm separated us. Just before the doors closed, I heard her say, "We'll see."

CHAPTER THIRTY-TWO

Lacey

I was building a house, standing at the top of a high ladder. The air was filled with the sound of pounding and wind and rain that went on and on. Why was I doing carpentry work in with a hurricane approaching from offshore?

"Lacey!"

Bonnie's strident voice joined the pounding. She was at the building site? Why? She was a nurse, not a carpenter. But then ... neither was I.

"Lacey!"

Now, the ladder had started shaking. I dropped my hammer, but it became a book. I caught a glimpse of the title before it fell into space: *Arabian Nights*. I clutched the rung in front of me, but the shaking continued ... rocking me so hard, I lost my balance and was falling, falling ...

"Lacey! Wake up!" Bonnie's voice was insistent. Her hand clamped my arm like an iron band, dragging me out of my dream. "It's your mother. She's gone again."

My brain struggled with the meaning of the words. They didn't make sense. I rolled over, trying to shrug off the threads of the dream that were quickly disappearing. "Gone?" I asked, my voice sounding as groggy as I felt.

Then that word sunk in. *Gone!*

I sat up so quickly the room seemed to tilt. I could hear the rain pounding on the roof, the combined roar of wind and surf. The sound spurred me out of the bed. "No!" I exclaimed and snatched a pair of jeans from a drawer, yanking them on quickly. "Not again!" I lifted frightened eyes to Bonnie's. "How long do you think she's been gone?"

The stricken nurse shook her head and stood by my bed, nervously twisting a ring, round and round on her finger. "I don't know. I checked on her about three this morning when I got up to use the bathroom. She was still in bed then, so ... sometime after that."

I glanced at the clock and groaned. A few minutes after seven. Four hours ... Mama might have a four-hour head start on us.

"Call the police." My voice cracked on the final word, and Bonnie hurried to the phone. "I need to find a shirt." I spoke the words aloud. The directive seemed to help focus me. Pulling open another drawer, I grabbed a T-shirt and hurried to the bathroom.

Shirt in place, I bundled my hair into a messy heap on top of my head and pulled on a ball-cap, while my mind lashed me with accusations. This was all my fault. I was supposed to have picked up the new locks yesterday. Why hadn't I gotten them? I should've made time. We wouldn't be in this predicament if I had. Mama wouldn't be out there, somewhere, in this terrible storm. Cold and wet and frightened. *Lost.* My fault ... my fault—"

Rrriing.

I stepped out of the bathroom and swiveled my head toward the sound, staring at it blankly. Why was my phone ringing at this time of the morning? Who would be calling me now?

It's about Mama. The thought jerked me out of my semi-hypnotic state and sent my heart to hammering. I scrambled over the tangle of covers, to the other side of the bed to reach my phone. "Hello?" I blurted without looking at the number.

"Lacey?"

Travis? I drew back in surprise when I recognized the voice. *But I'd blocked him.* I pulled the phone from my ear and stared at the words, "unknown caller," glowing across the screen. It was him, but a different number.

Before I could work it out in my head, he jumped right in, "I found your mom. I wanted to let you know she's safe."

All thoughts scattered and I sagged with relief, pressing the phone closer to my ear. My other hand gripped the edge of my dresser with white-knuckled desperation. "Oh," I breathed. "Oh, thank God. I'll be right up to get her."

"Lacey, wait!"

His raised voice stopped me from ending the call. I put the phone back to my ear. "What?"

"I'm not in the apartment."

"Not in the—" I broke off, frowning in confusion. "Where are you?"

"Over at the Harbor Marina."

"Harbor Marina?" I felt like an idiot parroting everything he said, but his words weren't making sense. "What are you doing there? And how did my mother get that far?"

"I decided to bring my boat up on my last trip to Jacksonville. I thought since I'm living here, I might as well have it close enough to enjoy whenever the mood strikes."

I almost blurted, "That's nuts!" but held my tongue. I didn't have time to get into a discussion of why he hadn't found a safe place to dry dock it until the storm was past. I had more important things to worry about. "Can you bring my mother back out here, or do you want me to come get her?"

"She's very agitated. I think she'd do better if you came to get her."

My eyes went to the window. The wind had the rain coming down in sheets at an almost forty-five degree angle. I pressed my lips into a straight line and took a deep breath. "Right. Which boat slip is yours?"

"One-oh-seven."

His voice sounded strange ... almost excited. I pushed the thought away, repeating, "One-oh-seven. Okay. I'm on my way."

"Oh, and Lacey?"

"Yeah?"

"Look for the name *Arabian Nights*. It's on the hull."

CHAPTER THIRTY-THREE

Ford

My repeated forays through the morning's drenching rain had my car windows so steamy, it looked like teenagers had been using it for some serious necking. I had zero visibility.

I tried wiping them with the scrap of a napkin I found stuffed in the console's cup holder.

Great. Now I had ketchup smeared in the steam.

I heaved an impatient sigh. It was either wait for my defroster to work its magic, or risk finding myself in a ditch or wrapped around a telephone pole. I'd have to go with option one. It would allow me to get to Lacey faster. Chafing at the delay, I flicked the switch over to full blast and flopped my head back against the seat. *Hurry ... hurry ...*

I sniffed and wrinkled my nose. Ugh. Smelled like *eau de wet dog* in here; something sure to impress Lacey. What I needed was some Febreeze and some dry clothes to change into. Unfortunately, I had neither.

I jumped when my phone rang, and I fumbled to retrieve it from my pocket; I glanced at the screen. *Ah ... the computer nerd.* "What you got, Myron?"

"I used the age progression program on that photo you gave me. Just sent it to you. Did you get it?"

"Hold on. Let me boot up my laptop. I should have Wi-Fi here. One ... second ... Okay. Yep. There it is ... one email with one attachment. Thanks."

"No, prob. Glad to help. Let me know if you need anything else."

"You bet."

I clicked on the attachment and my impatience surged when I read the probable load-time. *Two minutes?* It was either a big file or slow Internet ... maybe both.

My phone rang again. *What now?*

"Jamison," I barked. The hand on the clock-face was at about half, but it was moving quicker than expected. My eyes were glued to the screen, urging it to move faster.

"Detective? This is Lynette Greenley again."

I sat up straight, pressed the phone to my ear. "Nurse Greenley ... I didn't think I'd be hearing back from you ... at least not so soon," I tacked on the end to make it sound a little nicer.

There. The timer was done. The photo was loading onto my screen—line by line—starting at the bottom and moving up.

"Well, I thought about what you said about keeping the guy from doing the same thing to another woman, and ... well, this is not something I'd normally do, but . . ."

"Yes?" I prompted, striving for calm, but mentally screaming, *Spit it out!*

A narrow chin was appearing on the screen, sullen mouth and jawline . . .

"I did what you said ... asked Ms. Fairbanks to write down the name of the man who did this to her."

"And did she?" I asked, my attention divided. I was trying not to be distracted by the emerging photo on my laptop.

Long, thin nose, slightly hooked, high cheekbones. The age progression had Coop's hair darker as an adult, his wide set, pale, pale blue eyes, set back under dark brows ...

"Well, she wrote two things, actually ... a name, and something else."

"Is it legible?" I asked while studying the now-complete photo.

Something clicked in my mind. It felt like a punch in the gut. With sick certainty, I knew the name she would say. "Can you read it?" My voice sounded hoarse. Cold dread crept up my spine.

"It says ... Travis, I think."

Travis ... My mind raced.

Hair? A box of Miss Clairol would take care of that in minutes.

Eyes? Immediate fix with contacts.

Nose and chin? His inheritance from his grandmother would give him easy access to a skilled plastic surgeon's knife.

Davey T. Cooper. The "T" stood for Travis.

David ... Another punch in the gut. Lacey's mom had called him David. She'd *known*.

"Detective? Are you there?"

"Yes," I managed to choke out. I cleared my throat, tried again, "What else?"

"I'm sorry?"

"The other thing she wrote," I snapped, tired of messing with her. I needed to go! I had to find Lacey!

"Yes," her voice stiffened, sounding more like the nurse I'd met earlier. I pictured her face hardening, her shoulders drawing back at my tone "It says, 'marina.' I'm sure *you* can make sense of that."

I ignored the snide emphasis. "I hope so," I said, ending the call without thanking her. There was no time for niceties. My racing heart was trying to keep up with my brain. Marina ... The Harbor Marina? That's where all the wealthy people kept their yachts. Coop had inherited his grandmother's company, so he was sure to have a yacht of his own. Had he been bragging about it to Raine during their dinner date? He must've. Why else would the word "marina" come up? I needed to know—right now—if he had a boat docked at the marina, and I knew exactly who could help me.

I yanked my car into gear and wheeled out of my parking space while re-dialing Myron.

"*Yell*-ow."

I didn't even roll my eyes this time. "It's me," I said without preamble as I pulled out onto the road. "I need you to get into whatever record is necessary for you to find out if David Cooper or Travis Sterling owns a yacht."

He didn't answer. Maybe my tone spoke of urgency. All I heard was the tapping of computer keys for an interminably long time.

"Mmm … nothing for David Cooper. Trying Sterling now …"

Another nerve-wracking wait.

"Yes. Wow! Sweet! You should see this thing."

I ground my teeth. "The name. I need the name?"

"Right. Uh … yeah, here it is—*Arabian Nights*."

"Okay." *Arabian Nights? Horse-cart?* There were Arabian horses, so there might be a link there, but there wasn't time to work it out right now. I took a quick breath, then ordered, "Hack into the Harbor Marina's records to see if *Arabian Nights* is docked there."

"Not sure if I'm—"

"Just do it!"

More tapping at a keyboard. More waiting . . .

"It's there, all right. Slip number 107."

"One-oh-seven. Got it."

Ending the call, I pressed another button and waited. I began speaking as soon as I heard a click at the other end. "I need as many men as you can get at Harbor Marina. Slip 107."

"What's this all about?" Chief Craig asked.

Beep.

Another call trying to interrupt. I ignored it. This couldn't wait.

"I know who our lullaby killer is. Travis Sterling. Real estate developer. You've probably seen him around town. He's actually David Cooper … Joelle Cooper's son. You remember the rich grandmother who adopted him? Well, apparently he used some of his inheritance to change both his looks and identity after she passed."

"How do you know he's the killer?"

"I don't have time to get into it. You'll have to trust me on this. I'm on my way to the marina now. Just get there with some backup as fast as you can."

"Right—"

I ended the call before he could say anything else. Glanced at the missed call and my heart almost stopped.

Lacey.

She'd left a voicemail. I gave the button a savage punch, then pressed my phone against my ear so hard it hurt.

No! I hit redial, and waited, one nervous finger tapping on the steering wheel like I was subconsciously sending Morse code. *C'mon, Lacey! Pick up. Pick. Up.*

Each time it rang, my heart jumped a little higher in my throat. By the fourth one, it was lodged right over my larynx, so when I heard the beep, all I could choke out was, "Lace? Call me."

I tossed my phone over to the passenger seat and pressed my foot to the floor.

CHAPTER THIRTY-FOUR

He stood in the doorway, swaying with the movement of the boat, staring at Lacey's mother, asleep in the center of the king-size bed, and smiled at the serendipity of it all.

That wasn't the case yesterday, when Lacey had called to cancel their picnic date. No, not serendipitous at all. The *opposite* of that. All he could see, at that moment, was an implosion of all his plans. Lacey was ruining his grand finale, and he was furious.

After he'd calmed down some—thought things through—he'd come up with another plan … better than the first. Lacey's mother had started it all; it was only right that she be part of the finish.

Memories swooped through his mind like bats … memories that would never completely go away. Childhood nights, when he'd huddled on his lumpy mattress, yanking a flimsy, too-small blanket over his shoulders to then expose his feet. He remembered the smells: stale urine, fear-laced sweat, and the reek of cigarette smoke so strong that he was sure he'd get lung cancer from simply breathing. He remembered making a deal with God, promising never to do anything bad again if He'd just make him invisible.

The ritual had started by accident. He'd been hiding under his bed, his window open to allow the ocean breeze to blow the smells away. Suddenly, he heard music … a soft voice, lilting an old lullaby. He could hear love pouring through the words. "Hush, little baby. Don't say a word. Mama's going to buy you a mockingbird …"

He listened, mesmerized. For the few minutes it took to go through the multiple stanzas, it allowed him an escape from his hellish life. It ended all too soon, but at least it was something.

The next night was the same.

And the next ... and the next. Each night provided one bright spot in his gray existence.

He smiled again at the sleeping form in the bed. Such a good mother ... kind, and loving, protective ... the way a mother was *supposed* to be. He should've had a mother like that. Had it been his fault? Something he'd done?

No way. A child couldn't do anything bad enough to deserve what she'd done to him. It wasn't fair ... any of it. Not fair that Lacey had a good mother and he hadn't. Especially when she didn't appreciate her. And she was bad. Look what she'd done to him back in high school.

He'd taken care of part of the problem years ago; it was time to finish the job. He turned away from the bed and staggered down the hallway, grabbing for the wainscoting when the wind and waves rocked the boat, making it bump and tug at the ropes that held it secured to the dock.

He stumbled over to the bar and poured himself a single whiskey, neat. It would help him wait for Lacey to get here. Eying the amber liquid carefully, he doubled it, then lifted the glass of liquid courage in a mocking toast to the massive oil painting hanging over the bar. "Here's to the end of the lullaby."

Lurching and swaying, he zigzagged his way over to an oversized easy chair and collapsed. He took another swallow, flung his head back against the cushion, and allowed his mind to retrace the last few hours.

After he'd left the last girl in front of that shop, he'd headed back to the apartment, his mind in a turmoil wondering how he could get Lacey out to his boat without the excuse of a picnic. Somehow, he'd known her lights would be on again, When he saw lights blazing from her windows, he repeated the silent approach he'd used the night of the "Raine debacle," which was what he called the previous night.

It was while he was creeping up the stairs that the idea hit him: Mrs. Campbell. She'd make perfect bait ... one Lacey couldn't refuse. He already knew wandering was an issue with her Alzheimer's. He could use that to his advantage and no one would suspect a thing.

Perfect, he congratulated himself.

Yes, perfect, but how? The likelihood of Mrs. Campbell deciding to wander outside in the middle of the night with a hurricane approaching wasn't one he could pin his hopes to, so he'd have to come up with another way to get her.

He'd waited until the lights finally went out before he made his move. Already having successfully experimented with a credit card on his apartment door lock, he'd crossed his fingers, and hoped Lacey's door was similarly equipped. It'd been a series of gambles; the lock was only one of them. The deadbolt was another. If it'd been engaged, there'd have been no hope of getting in. Then there was the matter of getting the right room. The morning he'd signed the lease agreement, he'd seen Mrs. Campbell exit a room on the right at the end of the hallway. He'd assumed she'd been coming out of her room, but he also knew the cliché of what happened when one assumed. Finally, there was the issue of noise. The operation had to be silent. If she'd started making a fuss, the whole thing would've blown up in his face.

He downed another swallow of whiskey, closing his eyes, enjoying the slow burn of it sliding down his throat, settling in his stomach. Yes, his lucky stars must've been lined up perfectly. Mrs. Campbell had taken the hand he'd held out to her, smiled sleepily as he draped a hooded raincoat over her shoulders, and slipped noiselessly down the hallway with him. From entrance to exit, the whole operation had taken less than five minutes.

All that changed the moment he got her aboard. He'd left his flare gun out, intending to reload it after his recent trip up from Jacksonville. The bright orange case was out on the bed and had caught her eye. She'd snatched it up, hugged it to her chest, and would not give it back, no matter what he'd tried. He'd finally given up. It wasn't loaded, so what harm could it do? She'd calmed down after that, and gone straight back to sleep, still hugging that stupid case.

He lifted his glass to take another swallow at the same time a gust of wind sent the boat slamming against the pier. Whiskey sloshed violently against the side of the glass, splashing some of it straight up into his face.

A drop hit him squarely in the eye and he yelped at the sudden scald of alcohol. Rubbing at the burn only seemed to make it worse.

Water … he needed to rinse his eye with water.

In an instant, he was at the sink, cursing with every breath while cupping his hands, filling them with splash after splash of water.

He lifted his dripping face at the sudden thump on the deck above him. His eyes followed the invisible trail of footsteps thudding over his head. Then they stopped, and after a moment's hesitation, he heard a knock at the door.

Lacey.

Heart pounding, he grabbed a towel and dried his face, rubbing at the water splotches on his shirt and muttering more black curses. It wasn't supposed to be like this. He'd looked forward to the surge of anticipation, the thrill of excitement building as he walked to the door. Not this.

No time to change. No time to check the mirror.

He staggered over to the door, trying to gather his wits.

This was it … showtime.

CHAPTER THIRTY-FIVE

Lacey

I knew something wasn't right the instant Travis swung open the door. Normally dressed to the nines, with every hair in place, he looked unkempt, water-blotched, hair mussed like he'd forgotten to brush it. But there was something else … something …

"Lacey …" He stepped back and extended his arm with a flourish, beckoning me in. "Welcome to my humble abode, my home away from home. I give you—drum roll, please—*Arabian Nights.*"

His actions seemed theatrical, too expansive, and confused me until a fog of whiskey fumes wafted into my face. I wrinkled my nose at the smell. Well, that explained it.

"'Humble' is hardly the correct adjective to use to describe this place," I replied dryly, hurrying into the cabin, flinging the hood of my raincoat back, sending a spray of raindrops across the floor. "But you're crazy for being out here in this storm. Where's my mother?" I demanded. My eyes swept the room. There was no one else present, and the feeling of "not right" grew stronger.

I was swinging around to face him when I stopped mid-swing. An oil painting of ridiculous proportions hung over the bar. Its massive frame was probably six inches wide, giving added dimension that it certainly didn't need. Colors slashed across the canvas, like a painted argument. I could feel the artist's fury reaching out, shrieking at me. It reminded me a little of one of my father's paintings, with its thick streaks and blobs of anger, but Dad's style hadn't been impressionistic like this one.

I stared at it; somehow knowing it was important for me to see whatever was hidden in that painting, willing myself to break the code. Something teased at my vision, trying to come into focus, like those Magic Eye pictures that were so popular a few years back. Maybe if I tried squinting . . .

There! Daubs of color began to coalesce, forming solid masses. It looked like a . . . a coliseum? Yes, that was it. I could see rising bleachers in the background filled with crowds of people, their faces indistinct, cheering—or maybe screaming. And there, some kind of soldier . . . no, a Roman gladiator. I could tell by his helmet. He was standing in a chariot, his hands gripping the reins, desperately trying to control a . . .

I swallowed hard and my eyes dropped to the small brass plaque attached to the bottom center of the frame. My stomach clenched when I read what it said.

"Arabian Nights," Travis spoke the words aloud, echoing the words I'd just read. "I named my boat after that painting. It's perfect, don't you think?"

My heart was thudding painfully against my ribs while my brain raced. The Arabian horse and chariot . . . horse and cart . . . from the last verse of the lullaby. *No!* My mind rebelled at what my eyes saw. This isn't how it's supposed to happen. I always dreamed it first—

Wait. I *had* dreamed . . . or at least started to. Bonnie had woken me up before I finished it. *Arabian Nights* . . . the book in my dream.

I turned slowly toward him. His face was flushed, almost feverish. And his eyes . . . his eyes . . .

I gasped and took an involuntary step backward.

One eye was the same sea green as the last time I'd seen him. The other, though bloodshot and irritated, was a totally different color: blue . . . pale, pale blue. Almost colorless. "Your eye . . ." I blurted.

"Oh," he shrugged. "An accidental splash of whiskey. It burned like the devil, but it'll be okay. Thanks for your concern."

I shook my head. "No, the color . . ."

"The color?" A confused crease showed up between his brows. He closed one eye, then the other and the crease smoothed away. "Hmm. It appears I've lost a contact. Looks like I flushed out more than the whiskey."

"But . . ."

He gave me a hard smile. "You don't recognize me do you?"

"I—"

"Of course you don't," he interrupted. "Why should you? I was only the poor schmuck you humiliated in front of everyone that night in the diner years ago; the same guy who was your next-door neighbor for years ... the unwanted offspring of Fernandina Beach's biggest problem." He pointed to his chest. "That would be me."

"Coop?" I asked with growing horror.

"Davey T. Cooper," his voice mocked and he began pacing, slowly, back and forth, his steps jerky and uneven with the constant bumping and swaying of the boat. "David ..." He cocked an eyebrow at me, smiled wryly. "Your mother recognized me, even with all the changes I'd made ... the hair, the eyes, the new nose and chin. I made them for you, by the way ... the changes," he added at my questioning look. "I saw how you were with that jock, so I made myself look like him."

David! Mama called him David, and I tried to correct her. She knew. I straightened my shoulders. "Where's my mother?" I repeated, feeling desperate.

"She sang to you," he said, ignoring my question. His smile turning into something from a nightmare.

"What?"

"Every night. I heard her. She sang you a lullaby, tucked you into bed, made sure you were safe. While my mother—" he broke off, shook his head. His laugh sounded hard ... brittle.

"Your mother disappeared," I finished his sentence, suddenly desperate to change the direction of this conversation. Was he getting closer to me? I took another step back. "She disappeared and your grandma came to get you. Took care of you. She *adopted* you."

"My mother 'disappeared,' as you so quaintly put it, into the dune right in front of our quaint little beach house," he snarled. "I only meant to choke her, but I guess my anger got the best of me. Ended up breaking her neck. After I buried her, I burned that miserable dump to the ground."

Any response I might've made froze in my throat. *It's him,* my mind screamed over and over. *It's him. It's him. It's him. He's the killer. This is a trap. He used Mama as bait, and I walked right into it. Ford ... I have to call Ford.* My hand patted my empty pocket, and my heart sank, taking my last hope with it. My phone was right where I'd left it ... in my purse, tucked under the seat in my car.

"It's because of the lullaby, you know." His voice now turned dreamy. "All of it ... everything I've done. Your mother's lullaby started it, and everything has been building up to this exact moment in time."

He *was* getting closer to me. The zigzagged line of his pacing had been moving him a little closer each time he turned. I tried to take another step back, but felt the bar pressing into my back. Nowhere to go. I was trapped, staring into his crazy, bi-colored eyes. I blinked away a blur of tears, sucking air in ragged gasps.

He stopped in front of me and his lips curved into a tender smile. His finger traced the side of my neck where my pulse was hammering away. "Let's finish the song, shall we?"

"No!" I slapped his hand away, turning to run. He made a grab for me, knocked my hat off, my hair tumbled down. Grabbing a fistful, he twisted his hand, jerking me around to face him once again. Nails bared, I raked his face, leaving deep gouges from the corner of his eye to his chin. His eyes blazed and his free hand gifted my cheek with a stinging slap.

The blow stunned me; tears blurred my vision. While I blinked, trying desperately to gather my wits, I felt his hands settle into place around my neck. I couldn't watch. The perverted excitement I saw in his face made me feel sick. Squeezing my eyes shut, I silently prayed, *Please, let someone take good care of Mama.*

"Where's my husband?" a belligerent voice demanded directly behind us.

My eyes popped open. Travis jumped like someone had jabbed him with a hatpin, whirling to face my mother, who stood in the doorway looking rumpled and confused, clutching a flare gun.

Taking advantage of the distraction, I searched for a weapon of my own, eyes lighting on the heavy crystal whiskey decanter. It would have to do. I snatched it up, lifted it over my head, and crashed it down on the back of Travis' head.

He staggered sideways, dropped to his knees, one hand to his head, the other clutching the bar.

I froze in place—bottle still gripped in my hand like a baseball bat—gaping at what I'd done. The stopper was missing, and pungent amber liquid glugged out, dripped off my elbow, and puddled beside my right foot.

Travis groaned and it broke the spell.

I dropped the bottle and lunged for my mother's arm. Snatching the flare gun from her hand, I shoved it into the back waistband of my jeans while dragging her toward the door as if all the demons of hell were after us. The floor of the boat bucked and jerked underfoot, feeling alive and anything but stable. My mother kept trying to turn around and gape at Travis, significantly slowing the swift getaway I was picturing in my head. "Mama!" I urged, frantically tugging her arm. "We have to get out of here. Come on!"

When we stepped through the doorway, I eyed the angry waves sloshing over the deck, the slanted sheets of rain, and wondered how we'd ever make it across. The boat was yanking this way and that like a wild animal, trying to break free from the ropes that secured it in place, banging against the dock's heavy pylons with teeth-jarring regularity. It seemed like a long, treacherous way to the ladder that led to safety. If I could get us over to the railing, it would at least give us something sturdy to hold onto as we inched our way to escape.

I'd taken two steps when Mama's hand was wrenched from my own. I whipped my head around in time to see Travis slinging my mother across the rain-slick deck. She landed hard, skidded to the railing.

"Mama!" I shrieked, trying to go to her, but Travis yanked her to her feet, then shoved her so hard, she sailed right over the railing while I just stood there, frozen in horror.

"NO!" The wind snatched the scream from my lips, whirling it out to sea.

Travis turned toward me wearing the smile of a madman. He took a step forward, then the boat jolted violently, ricocheting against the pier.

The impact sent him teetering at the edge, arms waving. He made a grab for the railing. Missed. Tumbled over.

I staggered to the railing, searching the roiling churn of water. There was Mama! She was alive. Her head was bobbing like a cork, arms thrashing in the froth, but still alive. I had to save her. Swallowing my fear, I whispered, "God, help me." And jumped.

Cold, stunning, burning ... like someone had dipped me in acid. The water still held winter's chill, in spite of what the calendar said. I broke the surface just long enough to drag in a breath before a wave crashed over me. I fought to the surface, again, kicking my shoes off, hoping that might help. The cold had me disoriented. I clawed my hair from my eyes, trying to see. I glimpsed a dark blob I thought was Mama's head to my left, and splashed clumsily toward it.

It was unbelievably cold. My skin was numb, fine motor skills already gone. Some part of me remembered that I only had about ten minutes before blood flow to any non-essential body parts would stop in order to keep my heart beating. I had to get out of this water.

A wave slammed into me, or at least I thought it was a wave, but a hand suddenly grabbed my elbow, fingers digging in. Pain shot up my arm. I knew the wave had a name. "Travis!" I spluttered, trying to turn and kick him. "No!"

"We have to finish the song!" he yelled in a voice that held a maniacal edge. "We have to finish the song!"

Another wave broke, pushing us both under and temporarily breaking his hold on me. When I came to the surface, I paddled frantically away from him, dragging in desperate gulps of air, bracing myself for the inevitability of my approaching death. If I didn't drown, Travis was going to kill me. My talk with Ford wasn't going to happen. He'd never know that I loved him. I'd never be able to tell him.

I knew Travis was gaining on me. I could feel him, even if I didn't hear or see him, but I couldn't let myself think of that. I had to find Mama. The cold was paralyzing. I'd never been the greatest of swimmers and the cold was stealing what little skill I had. It had to be affecting Mama too. She was older and she had Alzheimer's, for goodness sake. Did she even remember that she knew how to swim?

Thud.

It felt like I'd run into a brick wall. The impact nearly knocked me out. Wheezing and choking, I patted the flat surface, realizing it was the side of the boat, and looked up as the cold knifed deeper.

Arabian Nights. The black letters danced crazily on a white background.

I was so numb, I didn't feel the hands slip around my neck at first, not until they spun me around and started to tighten.

"Hush, little baby. Don't say a word …" Travis gasped and coughed out the words. Spitting out ocean water when a wave crashed over him. "Mama's gonna buy you a mockingbird."

No! My brained screamed the words my lips were unable to form. I gave a clumsy kick. His wince was the only thing that told me I made contact since my foot had long since lost feeling.

He renewed his grip on my neck, squeezing harder. "And if that mockingbird don't sing …"

I made a swipe at my back, clamoring for the flare gun, dragging it around in my deadened hand, pressing it against his chest.

He looked down and barked a laugh. "That won't help you. I never reloaded it the last time it was used."

My heart sank, taking my last hope with it. My numb finger convulsed on the trigger and I felt a jolt go up my arm. My eyes shot up to meet his.

His entire face was a mask of shock. One sea green eye, one almost colorless, both widened in surprise as the froth and foam of the water turned pink. Then red bloomed around us and he sank like a stone.

While my brain was trying to put everything together, a loud bang rang out behind me, louder than the roar of the wind and the crash of waves. Then I heard a shout. It was the voice of an angel.

"Lacey!"

Another wave broke over me. It took longer to surface this time, and my lungs were screaming before I finally broke through the roiling swells, coughing up a mouthful of seawater. I tried to push my hair out of my eyes again, but this time my hands were having trouble obeying my brain's commands.

A neon orange life ring dropped into the water in front of me. I stared at it dumbly. Some part of me knew I was supposed to do something with it—something important—but, for the life of me, I couldn't figure out what it was.

"Grab the ring, Lacey!" The furious angel-voice ordered. "C'mon … you can do it. Hook an arm through and hang on. I'll pull you in."

I knew what he was saying was supposed to be words … supposed to *mean* something, but nothing he said made sense. Was there such a thing as auditory dyslexia? If so, then I was suffering from it. The noise was nothing but letters of the alphabet whirling in a vortex of confusion. I gazed up with uncomprehending eyes at the livid angel.

"Lacey," he roared. "Grab. The. Ring!" The enraged bellow somehow pierced through the fog enshrouding my mind and I grabbed clumsily for the ring, looping one deadened arm through the center on the third try.

I'd barely clamped my other hand around my wrist before I was being towed through the punishing water, the life ring buoying me in the froth of churning coldness. All thoughts, but one kept disintegrating like bubbles as they surfaced: Don't let go.

I was heaved upward with stunning force as lightning forked sideways across the sky. In another second, I was scooped into hard arms and carried like a child into the warm cabin. Full-body shivers sent my teeth chattering so badly my skull vibrated. I was afraid my flesh was going to rattle right off my bones. Hurried hands stripped off my sodden clothes, but before my brain defrosted enough to tell me to be embarrassed, I was swaddled—like an oversized burrito—in a blanket, still shuddering violently.

I looked up at the angel who had rescued me. He had his phone pressed to his ear, and his mouth moved rapidly as he spoke, but the staccato barrage of words sounded like a foreign language. His sea-green eyes blazed at me, never leaving my face. He looked familiar. I was sure I should know him, but I couldn't seem to recall his name.

The call must've ended because, when I opened my eyes again, the phone was gone. He leaned toward me, speaking more gibberish. I think he said the word, *ambulance*, but I couldn't be sure.

Ford.

The name unfurled like a banner flung to the wind. I remembered, and felt the sting of sudden tears. "F-ford," I tried to speak, but my teeth still clacked together like castanets, my throat felt raw, burned by the ocean's salt.

"Shhh," he soothed, brushing a curl from my cheek. "Don't try to talk. Spend that energy on getting warm."

The bone-jarring shudders were slowly decreasing, both in numbers and severity, but with that came the prickling of cautious blood, attempting to circulate. Needles began stabbing feeling back into my hands and feet. I clenched my jaw, tried to keep from crying out, but as the blood flow in my extremities picked up, so did the pain. I was finally unable to keep from moaning out loud.

Ford looked relieved. "I know it hurts, sweetheart, but believe it or not, the pain is a good thing. It means you'll be able to keep your fingers and toes."

"N-not … h-helping," I croaked through clattering teeth, giving him a glare. Maybe he wasn't an angel after all.

There was a rattling noise overhead, several thumps, then a peremptory knock at the door a split second before it opened. Two men wearing raincoats and caps proclaiming them to be EMS workers carried a large wire basket between them. They hurried over to the couch where I lay, setting the basket on the floor, unbuckling the straps, removing a folded tarp.

In no time, I was loaded into the basket, draped in the tarp, and strapped in place. With a guy on each end, they carried me carefully up the stairs to the deck. The wind didn't seem to be blowing quite a strong now, nor was the rain as heavy, though the boat still tossed and bumped about on the waves.

The sounds on deck reminded me of something … something I could almost remember, but not quite.

The EMS fellows took slow, careful steps across the rocking surface of the deck. They'd draped the tarp over my head to keep rain out of my face, and with my head turned sideways, it allowed me a narrow band of vision under the edge of the plastic.

"Watch your step," I heard one of the emergency workers murmur. "Don't trip over them."

Them? I was jostled a little as they made the necessary adjustments to avoid whatever was in their way, and I wondered what the obstacle might be. Then I caught a glimpse of a bare foot with bright red toenails ... the same bold color I'd painted my mother's toenails a few days ago.

"Stop!" My scream was a raspy croak. "Stop, stop *stop!* Put me down!"

The basket was hastily lowered and Ford was there, lifting the tarp, holding it so the rain wouldn't hit me, but also blocking what I was trying to see.

"Unbuckle me. I need to sit up," I ordered, suddenly frantic, struggling against the straps.

He shook his head, not quite meeting my gaze, "I can't do that, Lace."

I stopped struggling and waited until he finally looked at me. "My mother?" I asked.

He swallowed hard, looking miserable, and I *knew*. I squeezed my eyes closed, but couldn't escape my last memory of Mama's dark head bobbing in the waves. Tears welled up, spilled down my cheeks, and I choked on a sob. "She's gone, isn't she?"

The hand that wasn't holding the tarp reached out to squeeze my shoulder through the blanket still wrapped around me, and nodded. "Sterling, too. He can never hurt anyone ever again."

"I shot him," I rasped. "How? He said it was empty. How did I shoot him with an empty flare gun?"

"Shhh. We'll figure it all out later." Ford glanced up to the EMS guys and gave them a curt nod. "Get her to the hospital. I'll be there as soon as I can finish up here."

CHAPTER THIRTY-SIX

Ford

It was midmorning before the automatic glass doors at the hospital swished open and I hurried through, anxious to see Lacey. It'd take entirely too much time for a second ambulance to arrive at the scene to pick up Chief Craig, who'd somehow been shot during the take-down. After that, I'd had to wait another eternity for the coroner's van to come pick up the bodies. I knew part of the blame could be placed on the weather. The outer bands of Hurricane Audrey had done a number on several roads between the flooding and downed trees, making logistics a nightmare, but I was pretty sure our van from Tallahassee could've gotten there sooner. Thankfully, the bulk of the storm had finally veered northeast and was heading back out to sea. We were past the worst of it. I'd finally made it to the hospital and was within eyeshot of Lacey's room, just down the hall.

"Jamison!" a voice called from the room I'd just passed.

I gritted my teeth, recognizing the voice. The desire to pretend I hadn't heard it was strong, but I gave a martyr's sigh and retraced my steps.

Chief Craig looked up expectantly from the chair where he sat, a plastic bag containing his belongings was on the floor by his feet, a cane leaned against the hospital bed. He shifted in his seat when he saw me, grimacing with pain as he did so. If I hadn't been so aggravated at the delay, that grimace might've made me smile. "They lettin' you out already?"

"Yeah," he grunted. "I talked them into discharging me. I'd rather recuperate in my own bed. The wife is finding a wheelchair so I can get out of here."

I pointed to the cane. "How long will you have to use that?"

"Depends on physical therapy," he shrugged. "Everyone keeps telling me it could've been worse. Any higher up, it could've got my kidney … or even my spine." He squirmed again. "I guess they're right, but a gunshot in the butt feels pretty bad to me, not to mention embarrassing," he added in a mutter, and his bald head turned hot pink.

I looked down at the floor, biting my lip and scrambling desperately to think of tragedies … Ebola, or starving kids in Africa … *anything* that might keep me from laughing out loud. Being shot in the line of duty was bad enough; that it was done by one of his own men made it worse; but that the shot was in his *butt,* was something you'd expect from Barney Fife on *The Andy Griffith Show.* I kept that observation to myself. I doubted Craig would appreciate its humor in his present situation.

"Jeb's out," Craig's brusque voice interrupted my musing. "Released this morning … with a clean record. I made sure of it."

I nodded without answering. This was the chief's way of admitting he was wrong. I wouldn't get more than that.

"Glad we got the guy, anyway," he continued.

I looked up at that, one eyebrow raised. "We?"

"Well …" he back-pedaled. "The case is closed. That's what's important. Good thing, too. Our coroner is working overtime. Five girls dead, plus Obie, Eve Campbell, Sterling … and that's not counting him almost killing Raine Fairbanks, and of course, Lacey." He cleared his throat and added, "I'm sorry about Lacey's mom."

"I am too," I answered gruffly. "But it could've been worse. Thank goodness for that 'empty' flare gun or we'd have had another body in the morgue right now. Don't exactly know how that worked, but I'm sure thankful for it."

"Yeah, well, I'm going to be wanting to talk with Lacey a bit more about that, but I guess I'll give her a day to recuperate. She might be crazy as a June bug, but shoot, I might be too, if I were in her shoes."

My head snapped up. "What do you mean by that?"

He shrugged again. "Well, you know … Alzheimer's is a heck of a way to go."

"Alzheimer's?"

His eyes sharpened. "You didn't know?"

"No, but that explains some things."

He studied me carefully for a minute before speaking, "So ... what's next for you?" he finally asked.

"You mean, besides the paperwork?"

He cocked his head, almost as if he were sizing me up. I'd seen that look before, and wondered what it meant this time.

"What if you stayed?" he finally asked.

"Stayed?"

"Yeah," Craig answered. "My wife never liked me being a cop, so as you can imagine, me getting shot has really shaken her up. Me too, if you want to know the truth about it, but ..." he leveled his gaze at me. "... you breathe a word of that to a soul, I'll call you a liar and deny it 'til the day I die." He reached for his cane, fiddling with the handle. "I've decided to take early retirement. I'd already been thinking about it before all this happened. Nothing like a bullet in the rear to give some incentive, though." He laughed without humor, then added, "All this could be yours if you're interested."

It took the words a minute or two to sink in. "Are ... are you offerin' me a job, sir?"

"It's what I said, isn't it? What do you need? An engraved invitation?"

I bit back a grin. "No sir. Just makin' sure I wasn't hearin' things." I spent a quiet moment thinking about the burn-out I'd been experiencing before this case; the desire for a quieter life ... settling down. Coming back home to Fernandina Beach could give me that. And then there was Lacey ...

"So?" he prompted. "Is that a yes or no?"

"Uh, do you need the answer immediately, or could I have some time to think? This is a pretty big decision."

He scowled. "I guess, but don't take all day."

***

It was all I could do not to break into a run as soon as I turned right out of Craig's doorway. My thoughts were focused on Lacey. I needed to find her ... *now*.

"I thought that was you," a familiar voice spoke behind me.

Gah! Are you freaking kidding me? What was *she* doing here? ICU was on the other side of the hospital! The urge to beat my head against the wall was strong, but I managed to check the impulse. After all, Raine had played a big part in saving Lacey. If it hadn't been for her writing down the words 'Travis' and 'marina,' I never would've gotten there in time, so I guess I owed her. I just hoped she wasn't going to demand a payment I wasn't willing to give. Bracing myself, I turned to face her

Her face was still very pale, but she was up, and using a walker. I relaxed a little when the male nurse, who seemed glued to her side, shot me a hostile look. The hand at the end of his muscular arm gripping the belt she wore around her waist was both protective and possessive, plainly telling me to "back off." Another of Raine's conquests. "When did you get out of ICU?" I asked her.

"After breakfast."

"Well, I have to say, you're lookin' much better than the last time I saw you."

I thought I heard the nurse growl at my words.

Raine sent the guy an indulgent smile. A pat on his thick chest muscles turned into a caress. "It's okay, Karl."

Nurse Karl tore his glare away from me and turned his attention to her. His face underwent a transformation into that of a lovesick puppy, practically drooling. She glanced my way, wearing an expectant smirk.

Checking to see if I was jealous? Not hardly.

Her blue eyes turned hard as sapphires when she didn't get the desired response. "So?" she snapped. "Did you get him?"

I nodded. "Thanks to you. I'd tell you all about it, but I'm on my way to talk to Lacey. She was his intended victim, by the way."

"Lacey?" she gasped, then gave an incredulous laugh. "I guess it *was* her, then." At my questioning look, she continued, "I thought I heard her voice in the room next door to mine earlier. So, when Karl got me up to walk, I checked, but the room was empty."

"Empty?" I echoed in disappointment. "They discharged her already?"

She shrugged. "Either that, or she checked herself out. On another note," her face and voice brightened. "I'm buying Pearl's."

"Pearls?" I gave a little shake of my head, confused by the leap between topics. "Um … that's nice. Thanks for sharin' your important jewelry decision with me."

"Not *pearls*." She rolled her eyes and laughed. "*Pearl's*. You know— Black Pearl. ' Where Lacey works?"

"Ah. Well, that makes more sense, though your segue way could used some work."

"When everything's final,"—her smile turned decidedly snide—"I'm planning a *huge* party. The whole island will be invited. You too, of course, if you're still here. Bring a friend. The more the merrier."

Her invitation turned Nurse Karl's glower into a "drop dead" glare. She gave him another indulgent smile, another pat on the arm which brought on another lovesick-puppy routine. "I think I've walked enough for now, Karl. Could you take me back to my room?"

He turned them around, only too glad to get Raine away from me. As they started their slow way back down the hallway, she tossed over her shoulder, "Oh, and tell Lacey I'm reeeal-ly looking forward to being her boss."

CHAPTER THIRTY-SEVEN

Lacey

I removed the next shirt from its hanger, pressing it to my nose, closing my eyes, inhaling the faint floral scent.

It smelled like Mama.

Blinking away tears, I folded it carefully, stacking it on top of the others in the cardboard box. When one box filled, I reached for another.

I'd finally convinced Liv to leave a few minutes ago. She'd picked me up from the hospital and brought me home since my car was still at the marina. She'd wanted to stay—insistent, really, but she had too many questions that I didn't want to face yet. She was probably mad at me, but I'd worry about that later.

"Lacey?" Bonnie asked from the doorway.

I wiped wetness from my cheeks and turned, beckoning her in. "I needed something to keep me busy, so I thought I'd go ahead and start packing up Mama's things," I explained.

"As a nurse, I need to tell you, I think you ought to be resting. Do I need to remind you that you nearly drowned this morning? Not to mention the hypothermia. Any person with an ounce of medical training would insist on bed rest." She laid her hand on my shoulder, squeezing lightly. "But as a friend, I understand. Can I help?"

Another wave of tears welled up in my eyes, blurring my vision. "Thanks, Bonnie. Yes … please." I pushed an empty box toward her.

We folded in silence for a few minutes. "They told us in nursing school," she said after a while. "… not to get emotionally attached to our patients; to keep our personal life separate from our professional life." She sniffed and gave a sad chuckle. "They didn't know your Mama."

The lump in my throat prevented my reply.

"I'll never forget Eve Campbell," she whispered. "She was quite a lady."

"Yes," I choked out. "She sure was."

We went back to our folding and packing in compatible silence.

"Bonnie?"

She looked up, met my eyes.

"I just wanted to thank you. You were good to Mama and I know I couldn't have done it without you. I ... I think I'm going to sell this place. Not until after you find another position. You can stay here as long as you need to. It's ..." Tears welled up again, but I blinked them away. "... the least I could do. "

She drew a deep breath, then let it out. "Figured you might. I heard about what Raine is wanting to do."

"You did? How?"

"You think I live under a rock or something? I got ears. Everybody in town probably knows. Raine hasn't been exactly keeping her decision a secret."

"Yeah. I guess you're right." I sighed, before continuing. "It was bad enough having Pearl for a boss. I just can't face replacing her with Raine. Hello Rock"—I pantomimed a mock introduction—"meet Hard Place."

Bonnie laughed. "Exactly."

"Mama was the only reason I hadn't already left."

"I figured that."

"Not that I wouldn't love to stay if the circumstances were different. I mean ... I *love* Fernandina Beach. It's my home." I shook my head sadly. "But . . ."

Bonnie reached over and squeezed my hand. "It's okay," she assured me. "And I think your mama would understand, too."

"Thanks, Bonnie."

She folded the flaps down on her box, leaned forward and chucked me under my chin. "Just keeping it real, girl." Then got to her feet.

I listened to the slap of her flip-flops against the hallway floor and smiled.

***

After sealing the final box with a strip of tape, I stacked it neatly with the others on the floor at the foot of the bed, then hurried from the room without allowing myself to look at anything else. Packing clothes was one thing; packing knick-knacks and memorabilia, pieces of my mom's life, was something else. I knew I couldn't put it off forever, but there was plenty of other stuff I could start boxing up. I'd save all that for later.

I halted in the dining room doorway. My dad's gaudy seascape—the only one still on display—hung on the wall above the buffet, just like it had for years. The others—all variations of the same thick, over-mixed, muddy colors—were crammed in the back closet. I usually tried to ignore it, because looking at it only made me miss Granddad's beautiful work more, but this one's ugliness seemed to act as a magnet, drawing my eyes, reminding me of another canvas I'd recently seen, heavy with paint—

No! My brain slammed the door on the thought.

I hurried closer, actually *looking* at it, this time. In the past, I'd avoided it, simply because I'd had to hide my feelings so Mama couldn't see how I felt. Now I could make all the ugly faces I wanted without having to worry about Mama seeing them, and I did. The thing was hideous. I hated it, while at the same time, I felt guilty for feeling that way.

I swallowed hard, trying to squelch the guilt. I was moving—simple as that—and I wasn't about to take these ugly things with me. It was time for them to go.

Within minutes, I'd retrieved the collection of canvases from the closet and had them leaning in stacks against the dining room wall. Ugh! They were even uglier than I remembered. Worse than any I'd ever seen in a "starving artist" sale.

What could I do with them? Tossing them in a dumpster was the most obvious answer. I was sure no businesses would want them. They'd scare off clientele. The only possible place they might work would be a nightclub, someplace too dark, and the people too drunk to actually see them.

No matter. I'd worry about where they'd end up later. Right now, I just wanted them out of the house. I couldn't concentrate on packing until that task was done.

I tried lifting it off the wall, but I couldn't get it high enough to get it off its hook. It was too heavy and the angle was wrong. I needed a chair.

I'd just dragged one over, and was standing on its seat, lifting the large painting from the wall.

Knock, knock, knock-knock, knock.

I'd heard that particular sound before and my mouth went dry.

Ford.

I half-turned, the canvas in mid-air. I couldn't move. Black dots began dancing at the outer edges of my vision.

Knock, knock, knock-knock, knock. The rapping was louder this time. My arms—still holding the painting—started trembling from exertion. I still couldn't move.

Bonnie's flip-flops slapped down the hallway to the front door. The door creaked open, and I heard the low rumble of his voice, dark and slow-simmered, saying, "I need to speak to Lacey." Then two quick footsteps, and there he stood in the doorway. Our gazes met for an electric moment. Heavy lashes shadowed the depths of his sea green eyes.

My arms gave out and the painting crashed to the floor. The black dots must've invited all their friends to join them, because they weren't dancing anymore. They were crowding together, narrowing my vision to a tunnel that seemed to grow smaller and smaller. It was through that shrinking tunnel that I saw Ford dash toward me. I felt myself falling.

Then nothing.

***

Warm fingers combed my hair back out of my face. My scalp tingled at the touch. I turned my face to more warmth, and breathed deeply. Mmm, delicious ... the scent familiar, intoxicating. I felt my lips curve in a smile.

I opened my eyes to find myself cradled in Ford's lap, my nose pressed against the shirt stretched tautly over his chest. I gasped, and scalding color flamed across my cheeks. I scrambled unsteadily to my feet, almost falling into the floor in my haste. I retreated to what I considered a safe distance away from him, behind the chair from which I'd fallen, then cast a desperate glance around the room, looking for something … *anything* … to help me.

My dad's painting lay in the floor where it had fallen, frame splintered, canvas crumpled.

Wait! I took a step closer to it. Something was *off*. There were too many colors. The drab and muddy ones my father favored were jumbled together with vibrant, jewel tones that didn't belong.

Another step closer. Were there … *two* canvases?

I dropped to my knees, reached for the broken painting.

There *were* two canvases!

Grabbing the edges, careful not to fray them by pulling too hard, I tugged the top material away from the one hidden behind it, and gasped.

Granddad's painting!

My hands were shaking now. I plucked away the splinters of broken frame, extracting staples, pulling and separating, slowly revealing the masterpiece underneath.

Stunned, I looked up at Ford. I knew my mouth was hanging open, but I didn't seem to remember how to close it. My breaths were coming in shallow, little gasps, my heart hammered, and my brain was having trouble putting all the pieces together.

Not so Ford.

He rushed over to the nearest stack of paintings and grabbed one, flipping it over to the back. After picking at one of the edges until he could lift it up, he looked at me with an excited grin. "There's another one under here."

His words had me scrambling to my feet, heart pounding harder. I snatched up another painting. It only took a few seconds. "Another one!" I squealed.

We systematically went through the entire lot of paintings. By the end of the search, we'd discovered twenty-seven of my grandfather's missing paintings, plus a couple more that I didn't remember ever seeing.

I leaned back against the buffet, limp with disbelief, staring in amazement at the gold mine that lay around me, not quite able to grasp what it meant. I lifted my dazed eyes, watching Ford slowly straighten from bending over the last of the paintings. Our eyes met and awareness crackled between us.

"Why were you upset when you thought I'd been on a date with Raine?" he asked in voice that vibrated low.

"What?" I asked, struggling with the huge jump from Granddad's paintings to my jealousy over him and Raine. "Are we playing twenty questions, now? Because I have a few of my own."

He didn't speak again ... not vocally, anyway, although his eyes had plenty to say. I stared, heart hammering, unable to look away. I felt a flush creep slowly up my neck as I let out a shaky breath. One corner of his mouth tilted up and he took a deliberate step toward me.

A hectic pulse started hammering at the base of my throat, growing more frantic with every step he took. Then he was directly in front of me, reaching down, grasping my limp hands, pulling me up. My legs threatened to collapse under me. Stupid, traitorous things had all the strength of overcooked spaghetti.

His eyes devoured me like I was all of his favorite things to eat wrapped up in one. He took my face in hands that weren't quite steady, and I struggled to drag enough air into my lungs. My cheeks—my whole body—felt fever-colored, and when he stepped closer, closing the sliver of space between us, my pulse skyrocketed. Everywhere we touched caused a throbbing awareness that lingered just under my skin.

His lips brushed along my jaw and I blindly turned my face, my lips searching for his. A low laugh rumbled in his throat and his arms gathered me closer. I molded to him like a second skin, marveling at the way we fit together.

He drew his head back, just enough to look deeply into my eyes. "I have no idea how you went from being 'that crazy Campbell girl' to the woman I'm holding in my arms, but what I do know is that I love you, Lacey." Then his lips returned to mine, and time ceased to matter.

"Ahem."

I heard the sound, and knew it was Bonnie, but chose to ignore her, pulling impossibly closer to Ford's warmth.

"A-HEM." It was louder this time, more strident. Our lips broke apart and I gave Ford a tender smile, my hand against the side of his face. The look he gave me should've singed my hair.

I turned with a sigh to face the nurse. "Yes?"

She held one of the boxes we'd just packed. "I was going to take some of these things to Goodwill, but I heard a crash and wanted to make sure you were okay." Her dark eyes sparkled with suppressed mirth. "But I can see now that I didn't have to worry."

My cheeks heated and I laughed. "Nope. Sure don't."

"What's all this?" She indicated the pictures scattered over the dining room floor. "You doing a little house cleaning?"

"Something like that," I said, giving her a mischievous smile.

"Hmph," she answered, then added. "'Bout time. I always hated that painting."

Bonnie's eyes went to Ford. "Those muscles work?" she asked, giving him the once-over, chuckling at his blank expression. "C'mon, give an old woman a hand with some boxes."

"Yes, ma'am."

I laughed as Ford scurried to do her bidding. Returning to the dining room, I started gathering the paintings into neat stacks.

It was then that the memory of my sous-chef's voice echoed in my head, sounding as clear as if she was standing in the room with me. "You should buy this place …"

I stilled. Deer in the headlights. Mia's voice continued, "… You'd do a better job of running it than Pearl ever thought about doing."

I remembered pooh-poohing her suggestion at the time, citing no money as my reason for refusal. I stared at the paintings and my heart began thumping.

The lack of money wasn't an issue now. I could outbid Raine. Buy it right out from under her. Black Pearl Bistro could be *my* restaurant. *I'd* be the boss … not Raine, and I wouldn't have to move. I could stay in Fernandina Beach if I wanted to.

But what about Ford?

Reality check.

Ford still worked for the SBI. He lived in Tallahassee. And now that this case was closed, he'd be on his way back to Tallahassee. Nothing had changed in that respect. What had changed was that I was free to move now. Nothing was really tying me here. Tallahassee had restaurants. People still had to eat. And if I didn't find one I really liked, I could always use the money I'd make on selling the paintings to open my own place.

The only problem I could see was whether Ford wanted me in Tallahassee or not. Yes, he'd said he loved me, but what exactly did that mean?

I heard his feet thumping back up the stairs and turned toward the door. Guess I was about to find out.

He was wearing a funny expression as he came in. "What's that look for?" I asked.

He shrugged. "Just remembering something I heard at the hospital when I went by there looking for you before coming here."

"You went to the hospital?"

"Yes ... but you'd already checked out."

He gave me another scorching look and I shivered as he drew near.

"W-what did you hear?" I couldn't keep my voice from quavering.

"Mmm ..." His finger tucked a strand of my hair behind my ear. "It had to do with something Raine said."

"Raine!" I shot him a squinty-eyed glare. Simply hearing him speak her name made me mad. "What did she say?"

"That she was looking forward to being your boss."

"Right!" I scoffed. "*So*, not happening. I—"

"What I was thinking"—he interrupted my rant—"is since you're about to become a *very* wealthy young woman." He made a sweeping gesture at the array of paintings leaning against the walls. "And you don't want Raine for a boss. What's stopping you from buying the restaurant? That way, *you'd* be the boss." He paused, looking puzzled; probably trying to figure out the look on my face. "Lacey? What is it?"

I threw my arms around his neck, and gave him a resounding kiss. "That's exactly what I was thinking. But what about you?"

"Oh, didn't I tell you?" he grinned. "You're looking at the new chief-of-police of Fernandina Beach."

"What?" I squealed. "You're kidding."

"Nope. Craig offered the job to me when I saw him at the hospital. It's mine if I want it."

"Do you?" I asked, sobering. "Do you want it? Really? Fernandina is a long way from Tallahassee, and I'm not just talking about distance, either. Working for the SBI? That's a law enforcement person's dream come true."

His face went serious too. "Well, they can have it. My dreams run more along the line of settling down in my home town with the woman I love … for as long as we both shall live."

I tilted my head, laughing. "Ford Jamison, if that was a proposal, it could use a little work."

He grinned. "I was going to wait until I had a ring, but if you insist …" He dropped to one knee, grasping my hand in both of his. "Lacey Campbell, please marry me. I don't think I can wait any longer to get started on our life together." He cocked his eyebrow. "Was that better?"

"A little," I beamed with happy tears stinging my eyes. "And … *yes!*"

THE END

Frutti Mare with Fettuccini
1 lb. prawns - shelled & deveined
¼ c. olive oil
1 T. shallots – chopped
1 T. garlic – minced
1/3 lb. scallops
1 c. ripe Roma tomatoes – finely chopped
1 c. chicken broth or clam broth
2 T. parsley – finely chopped
½ tsp. oregano
½ tsp. cayenne
10 small fresh basil leaves
3 T. brandy
8 steamer clams
¼ lb. calamari cut into rounds
8 mussels – well scrubbed
½ lb. Dungeness crabmeat
1 lb. fettuccini

- Cut the shrimp lengthwise in half. Set aside. Heat the oil in a skillet and add the shallots and garlic. Cook, stirring about one minute. Add the shrimp and scallops and cook, stirring about one minute. Add the tomatoes and broth and bring to a boil. Let simmer about one minute and add the parsley, basil, oregano, cayenne and brandy.

- Add the clams, calamari and mussels and cover tightly. Cook until the clams and mussels open, about one and a half minutes. Add the crabmeat, stir gently and remove from the heat.

- Bring 4 quarts of water to a boil and add fettuccini. Boil for 10-12 minutes until al dente.

- To serve, divide the fettuccini and add equal portions of the clams and mussels to the top and then pour over the remaining fish and sauce. Serves 4.

Yellowfin Tuna with Melon Salsa

¾ c. coarsely chopped honeydew melon (cantaloupe with substitute)
¼ c. chopped red onion
½ c. red bell pepper – diced
2 T. chopped fresh cilantro
4 tsp. olive oil (divided)
1 T. fresh lime juice
1 tsp. minced seeded jalapeno chili
2 5-6 oz. fresh yellowfin or albacore tuna steaks (about 1" thick)

- Prepare grill (med-high heat)

- Mix melon, onion, cilantro, 2 tsp. oil, lime juice and jalapeno chili in a small bowl.

- Season salsa to taste with salt and pepper. Let stand 15 minutes.

- Meanwhile, brush tuna steaks on both sides with remaining 2 tsp. olive oil and sprinkle with salt and pepper. Grill tuna until just opaque in center, about 3 minutes per side. Transfer tuna to plates. Spoon salsa alongside and serve.

Grilled Swordfish Kebabs

3 skinless swordfish filets (about 1 lb. each) cut into 1.5" cubes
8 oz. button mushrooms
2 zucchinis – cubed
juice of 1 large lemon
5 T. olive oil (divided)
salt and pepper to taste
2 med. tomatoes – unseeded and cubed
2 small red onions – chopped
1 med mango – cut into small cubes
2 T. champagne vinegar

Salsa: Toss tomatoes, onions, mango, 3 T. olive oil, vinegar and salt and pepper to taste. Refrigerate until ready to use.

- Brush grill with oil and heat to med/high.

- Cut the veggies into cubes, trying to get the sizes as similar to the swordfish as possible.

- Starting with the fish, thread fish, zucchini and mushrooms until the skewers are filled. Brush with remaining olive oil, season with salt and pepper and grill, turning 3-5 minutes on each side. Spray with lemon juice when done. Serve salsa on top of skewers.

For more on Leanna Sain and her novels, please visit:
https://www.amazon.com/Leanna-Sain/e/B001JOW6O4/

CPSIA information can be obtained
at www.ICGtesting.com
Printed in the USA
LVHW051119261119
638402LV00003B/73/P